By: Katie Blanchard

# Copyright

*For my mother,*
*who taught me that girls stick together.*

# Warning

This story does deal with domestic violence. Although, the moment of violence is never shown throughout the narrative, it is still spoken about. Sensitive audiences should heed caution in reading this tale.

# One

"You haven't been gone one day, and I already have a new stray."

I hear the cans in the pantry slam on the shelf as Ramona grumbles once again about my leaving. She's in her early sixties, bare minimum, though I'd wager she has a few more years behind that famous scowl of hers than I think. I have never asked. We've known each other for months, but I'm still terrified to bring out her bark. With Ramona, it's worse than her bite at times.

"See? You don't need me," I call over my shoulder. I'm met with a grumble echoing in the pantry as a response.

I look behind me to see her short auburn curls bouncing next to the door of the kitchen cabinet. The mask of hairspray on her head is no match for the sweat of helping me move, and the curls, fried from a cheap curling iron, are beginning to deflate. She turns her head out toward me, catching me spying on her. Her lipstick bleeds out onto her crepe skin, and when I stare at the crimson running into her frown line, it only gets deeper.

"Quit looking at me and get to work. We still have rooms to clean at the motel," she shouts, slamming her wrinkled hands down on her hips for an intimidation factor. I almost laugh because of her tiny stature, but I know better.

I look about the living room where I'm sitting on the floor, filling the bookshelf. There are two cardboard boxes in the middle of the floor. That's all I have to my name. All my possessions fit into two medium-sized boxes. We'll be done in an hour if that. I sigh. It's not much, but it's finally mine. It wasn't long ago that I was sitting in a mansion with thousands of things around me, but now my life has been reduced to two cardboard boxes, all thanks to Stewart and his whore.

"I can't believe you came to help me. Who's running the place?" Ramona owns a motel just outside of Pittsburgh. It's a cheap little place, with a few sketchy clients scattered about, but mostly it's a haven for women, the strays, that Ramona helps. Women like me, that got kicked out on their ass and have no place to call their home, and nowhere and nobody to run to for shelter. Now, I have that place— this apartment.

"Hannah. She's a stray from years back. I asked for a favor." Ramona never leaves the motel. I'm touched to know that under her hard exterior, I've wormed my way in enough for her to consider it.

"Oh." I tap on the trunk next to me. It's the only thing here in this apartment that I didn't acquire within the last couple of months. It's been with me since childhood. It was my mother's, and I wasn't about to let Stewart keep it even if it meant going to the house and facing his pregnant mistress to get it.

"Where's that boy of yours? Shouldn't he be helping us move all this shit?" Ramona dismounts from the two-step ladder in the kitchen to glare at me over the tiny island that completes the kitchen section of the ample open space.

"Billy? He's not my boy, and you know it." I glare. "Besides, he had to work. Something about an undercover job." I shrug. Billy, a part of my old life that transferred over into my new, was not the romantic hero that Ramona was begging for him to be, and her constant reference to Billy being more than what he is annoys me.

"He likes you. I can see it in his eyes, Jane." She waddles out of the kitchen, satisfied with the completion of her task, and rips open one of the cardboard boxes on the floor. I shuffle over from my spot to mirror her image with the other box, having completed my task at the bookshelf.

"I don't feel like arguing with you," I groan. There will be other days and other times that I can take up this argument with Ramona, but today isn't one of those times that I have the energy for it.

"Then don't," she cackles, and it immediately breaks out into a cough — too many cigarettes.

"Let's just finish this, huh?" I raise my eyebrow at her. "Before your lungs give out." She frowns at my own annoying tick— reminding her that the cigarettes will give her cancer.

"Looks like we'll make it back before lunchtime." She surveys the contents of the boxes and realizes her morning off wasn't worth it. I feel guilty that Ramona's first day off in as long as I've known her is for nothing.

"Yea," I whisper. "Thanks for coming, Ramona. I know it's not much to unpack." I hold my right elbow in the opposite arm, itching the back of it in embarrassment, suddenly aware of the little bit that I have to claim as my own.

"No problem, kid. Too bad they never found your stuff in that car." She pats my shoulder — *that car*. A shiver of ice runs down my spine and sends me clinging my arms around my body tightly for warmth — *that car.*

"Well, at least everything is fresh for your new life." She tosses a throw pillow onto my secondhand couch, unaware that I'm struggling to breathe in the encompassing feeling of that night flashing back into my mind.

"Yeah. My new life." I exhale, and the apartment comes back into view.

"Quit your moaning. It's better than it was. Now you have me." She digs her wrinkled hands into the box and gathers up a few more living room items that I bought to make the space feel homey. Useless purchases as Ramona called them, but they bring a certain level of peace to me. Those items represent that I'm not just surviving, living day to day only satisfying my means, but that I'm breathing in a life all my own and thriving. At least I hope to someday.

"That it is." I kick the other box into my bedroom because the only things inside are my clothes.

My life before coming to Ramona's motel may have looked glamorous on the outside, but inside I wore the marks of Stewart's frustration with my inability to fit in with his crowd. Still, I never left— believing the punishments would stop as soon as I mastered the skills that he desperately thought I lacked. I lived every day thinking that I would reach that level and suddenly my husband's hand would drop and never land on me again. That level, that day, never came. There is no such spot.

I start to hang my consignment store purchased clothing in my small closet. The entire apartment is smaller than my closet when I was married to Stewart. Still, I'm happier here than I was in that big old mansion. If only my new life came without the nagging feeling of being found by that maniac driver, the owner of *that car*.

"Well, I'm done with my box." Ramona plunks down on my bed and begins placing shirts in the box on hangers for me. She doesn't even need to be asked. We have become in sync the last couple of months, working like a well-oiled machine knowing the other one's actions and what needs to be done. We immediately jump in to help and get the job done without a single word being said

"Ramona, maybe this is stupid," I blurt. "It's safe at the motel with you." I grip the edge of the last shirt I've hung. This move, leaving that haven, could expose me. He could find me here. He never found me at the motel. I was hidden well there.

"Nonsense. Your boy toy told you this is the safest complex. He's a cop; he should know which places see the most crime." She hands me a group of shirts to hang and starts work getting my khakis on pants hangers, prompting me to continue working.

"You're right, but do I really need my own space?" I wish there were a concrete answer letting me know if this apartment is going to work out or not, there's too much at stake in the unknown.

"Kid," Ramona sighs, "this is a new step, and it's all your own. I know it feels scary, but you can do this."

"Okay."

"Besides, I don't want your ass living near me anymore." I chuckle.

"Ramona!"

"I'm serious. Your snoring can be heard through the walls." I know she's dramatic on purpose to ease the fear in my chest. She knows what people need, sensing their emotions, and hands it over. Even with her sarcastic mannerisms, she can't hide her empathetic golden heart. I see it.

"Thank you."

"Don't thank me for that. Thank me for not warning your neighbors." I hum in response.

What would I do without Ramona? One thing is for sure; I would have died that night if it weren't for her help.

# Two

"Ew. What is that?" I watch from behind Paige, the new "stray" Ramona has taken in, as she pokes at a lump of questionably wet white tissues on the tile bathroom floor with the handle of the mop. It doesn't move at least, so whatever it is it isn't alive. I shrug. It's not the worst I've seen cleaning rooms with Ramona.

She turns to me as I tie back the blond curls from my face. She wears a look of horror. I remember a similar expression on my face my first day here, so I let out a chuckle. She's going to be a fun one to break in. *Good luck, Ramona.*

"Am I expected to clean this?" She whispers to me, no doubt afraid of the small beast Ramona who is lurking in the bedroom area. She may have taken Paige in, but that doesn't mean she couldn't throw her out. At least, that's what Paige thinks. I know without a shadow of a doubt that Ramona would never kick a woman in need out of here. She's too kind. I would have shown half a dozen of them the door from her stories alone.

"I suggest you use gloves when you pick that up." I take two latex gloves from the bathroom caddy myself and nod for her to do the same. She obliges, and I walk past her and start to pull off the shower curtain. When I chance a look behind me, I note she's hanging her head out of the bathroom doorway watching Ramona, so I creep behind her.

"What are you looking at?" She jumps, and I immediately feel guilty. You shouldn't scare women who are running from their past. Ramona has told me several different stories that involved her tone changing to accommodate the woman she was helping and what she went through. "Sorry," I mutter to Paige, hoping I didn't cause Ramona's progress with her to backtrack.

Ramona is calmly throwing used condoms off the comforter and into her garbage bag. The gloves are her sense of protection, as they are now mine, but I remember being in Paige's shoes and longing to have the floor swallow me whole than touch and clean up such a disgusting mess. People are pigs when it isn't their space. They don't care about what they leave behind because they know nothing of the people responsible for cleaning it.

"You'll get used to it. Come on." I nudge her into the bathroom, and she stops dead before her current adversary, the lump on the floor. I watch her throat bob as she swallows hard preparing for the next step, or how she can get out of it. If she thinks I'm doing it, she has another thing coming. I've picked up my share of those questionable things, and now the time has come for her dose of reality. I got walloped with it my first day here, and it helped. Now it's time to pass on the knowledge.

"Disgusting." She gags into the crevice of her elbow. "Can't I leave a note for them to pick it up?" She's begging. It's clear that she's gotten her way with this technique before.

"No, princess, you can't leave a note for them to pick it up. Cleaning is part of the service a motel provides." Ramona's scratchy voice is laden heavily with sarcasm, cutting into the bubble Paige thought the bathroom provided. I watch her flinch at the brutality of Ramona's tone and words. The old lady wasn't one to sugarcoat things. She didn't feel it necessary to beat around the bush. No, she went in for the kill at times. Not exactly the tactic I would take myself considering half of the women she takes in are abused, but she hasn't had a bad turn out with the method.

"Besides, they checked out this morning. What are you going to do, hunt them down?" She cackles, and the laughter cracks into a cough as her lungs protest the action. I shake my head. I've told her time and time again to lay off the smokes. It's probably too late for her lungs anyway.

I hold the garbage bin for Paige and motion to the lump on the floor.

"Just pick it up and throw it in, then it's done with." I watch tears form in her eyes. This isn't the life she pictured having. It isn't the life most women envision. From the bit that I gathered from Ramona on the way over here, Paige was abused by her boyfriend, betrayed by someone she loves. The abuse got worse as his drug use did. Her life was a living nightmare every day, never knowing when it would be her last. Ramona was her escape. Hannah told her about the life she started here. It always sounds good until you are forced to do the work.

As she reaches down to grab the lump, I note the bruising around the bicep of her arm, shaped perfectly like a hand that demanded her attention. I turn my head as the memory floods me, causing my throat to tighten.

*"You will learn to listen. I have to teach you, Jane."*

I wore the same markings from Stewart when I arrived here. His power came from my weakness, as well. There were no drugs involved, only money, but Paige and I are the same. I woke up every day never knowing what my offending action was going to be that day.

I hear the lump hit the bottom of the canister, and I look back at her. Her cheeks are dry; the tears refused to fall. She's accepted that this life, albeit filthier, is not nearly as bad as the one she left behind. She'll make it. She's strong.

"Hurry up. We have ten more rooms today, not including your own, which you'll do yourself, and I have three rooms checking in at three." I watch Paige's shoulders slump at Ramona's words. She'd better toughen up against the old bird if she's going to find her voice in these walls. There's always someone on the outside, screaming and carrying on, if you don't build up what's within, you'll never find the confidence to face what's out there.

"You did well. Now, clean the toilet while I wipe down the shower and the vanity." I set the garbage pail down in the middle of the floor to remind myself that it needs to be emptied before I leave this area. Paige nods, and heads for the toilet, pushing her shoulders behind her. My manner of speaking works better than Ramona's with Paige. I tell myself to butt out. I don't need to take on responsibility, as Ramona does.

The second she opens the lid, I'm sure that she's going to throw up. I back up into the shower space and away from the toilet out of instinct. Someone kindly left the insides of their stomach on display, not bothering to flush the trophy down.

Well, we found the source of the smell in here, but there's no prize waiting for us at the end of the challenge.

"Oh, sweet Jesus." Paige steps back, clutching her hands around her nose, gagging. Then she uses her foot to depress the handle and flush the offending show down the drain.

"You break that fucking toilet, and it's coming out of your pay." Ramona fills the doorway of the bathroom, a feat I didn't think possible with her small stature. The smell hits her face, and she almost falters. Almost. She wouldn't dare give Paige the satisfaction of agreeing with her that the bathroom is disgusting beyond words. She will not baby her.

Paige points at the toilet. "But —"

"I don't care. I've seen worse, and I don't have the patience to listen to your whining today. Just scrub the damn toilet and move on." The dry curls bounce on top of her head as she shakes her finger at Paige. The color of her face almost matches the redness in her hair.

I watch from behind as Paige's shoulders square up, and I think it will be her moment, but as quickly as they rose, they fall just as fast.

"Yes, ma'am." Her reaction annoys Ramona, so she slams her hand against the bathroom doorway in frustration before heading out to strip the bed.

I want to tell Paige to stand up for herself, and that Ramona is only testing her until she finally does, but I know it will ruin the process. Everyone learns in their own time how to find their voice. I give Paige a closed-lip smile and move around her, tossing the shower curtain out of the room and into the hallway. I spray the mirror down and wipe it clear as she scrubs the toilet in resigned silence. The sight of my reflection draws me back to the first time I was forced to look at it honestly.

*"You were stupid. You signed the prenup papers without so much as a level head on your shoulders. You let a man take away the love you had for yourself because you believed he loved you more. You don't swap those things. Do you hear me? You never give away the love you have for yourself. It's not something that you bargain with or throw away. It's something that is supposed to remain. Don't be stupid again."* Ramona's face softens with her words.

*"I was in love. I didn't think,"* I mutter, scratching my elbow in an embarrassing gesture.

*"There. Right there. You didn't think. You were stupid. The first step is admitting it, kid."* She offers me a half-hearted smile to inform me that she isn't trying to be cruel, but the words need to be said. She doesn't possess the eloquence to sugarcoat things, and she doesn't chance me not grasping the meaning of her words by making them pretty.

*"I was stupid,"* I agree.

*"Love is for your soul. You get that straight in your head right now, kid. It's for your soul. There's nothing wrong with being in love. Love, however, does not bring you financial security. You do that yourself, and you don't throw that duty on anyone else. I don't care how they promise to take care of you. You make sure you can take care of yourself. You made the classic mistake of thinking he meant it. Fuck, you gave up your safety, believing it was the price to pay for it. Okay. Now, you move on and prove to yourself that you can make it alone and that you won't be stupid again. Fix the relationship you have with the person you spend every waking and sleeping minute with."*

*"Yes, ma'am." I nod.*

*"No. No." She takes my arm— it's the gentlest touch I've felt in a long time—and directs my body toward the mirror, tapping on my reflection. "Look at yourself in the mirror and promise those words. I'm not the one who needs to hear them."*

My eyes wander over toward Paige. She'll learn in time, as I had to, that her past needs to die for her to live.

# Three

I've picked the phone up and set it back down five times before deciding to go through with the call. I don't care for Paige, or long to stick my neck out for her situation, but Ramona is the reason why I'm alive today. She's the sole reason I keep picking the damn phone up. I want to help her. I want to ease the stress of taking on a stray.

"Hey, I forgot to ask you if you needed anything at the store," I say into the receiver when Ramona picks up on the third ring.

"No, you didn't." I roll my eyes at her, and I am glad she can't see the display of defiance as I open my car's door to head into the store. The vehicle is preowned, and the radio doesn't work all the time, but it's mine — something for me that I secured myself, not Stewart.

"Dammit, old woman, are you going to make me say it?" I groan as I slam the door behind me then immediately touch the latch to apologize to my car for such abuse. It doesn't matter if it's a cheap clunker, it's mine, and it deserves maintenance and care.

"Yup," she draws out.

"Is she in the room with you?" I whisper, annoyed that Ramona has caught on to what I'm trying to do.

"No." I hear the click of the lighter on the other end.

"You should stop smoking." I admonish.

"Just get to why you called." She exhales her first drag.

"Does Paige need anything? Is there something that I can get at the store that will help you out?"

"Softy," she teases. "Big old squishy softy."

"Is that a yes?" I throw my hands up, and a man walking by in the parking lot eyes me curiously. *Step away, sir, because I'm about to rip an old lady a new asshole.*

"Probably needs what you needed when you first came here." I can hear her inhaling on her cancer stick.

"Everything," I scoff.

"No. No. Don't go spoiling her now." She warns me.

"I wasn't. I was trying to help you." It's the truth. Paige means nothing to me. I'll cheer and champion for her success, but I don't long to be a part of it. Ramona, however, did everything for me when I first arrived with nothing, and I know the expense it must have cost her to clothe and feed another human being. It's been running through my mind the whole drive over here.

"You know, Jane, I was just thinking..." After a near minute of silence, I give in.

"You were thinking about what?" I grab a shopping cart, shoving the seat open on it with great force.

"The freezer here might start getting low on meals again, and I'll have to take out a few toiletries from the motel's stock. Can you note that in the inventory? I'm not feeling up to it tonight, but I should be able to get those tomorrow."

"Got it. You know you could just come right out and ask me to pick those things up. It's not like I don't owe it to you."

"You owe me nothing. It was just a thought I was having. I'm sure I'll hit up the grocery store tomorrow and make sure the freezer is full. I just haven't gotten a chance to do it." Conversations with Ramona can leave you wondering if she's even aware she's talking to you or just muttering her thoughts out loud.

"Got it. See you tomorrow, Ramona."

"See you tomorrow, kid." She hangs up.

"Lord, she gives me a headache," I whisper to aisle one. I head to the frozen section at the back of the store, and throw in a handful of the meals I know Ramona keeps on hand. I don't want to buy anything fancier, lest she calls me a show-off, and I don't wish to have Paige knowing it was me. I don't plan on starting a friendship with her like Ramona. I'm not that patient, and my past has left me scarred, I want to watch out for myself and not be responsible for others, but I owe Ramona even if she says I don't.

I head up and down the aisles, grabbing two bottles of the body wash that's on sale, one for me and one for Paige. I get her a toothbrush, toothpaste, and a thing of deodorant. I tell myself that I'm not overly kind, I'm just making sure that my work environment doesn't stink. I'm not about to start taking strays in like Ramona does.

I head over to the fruit section again, not ready to leave the store and head back to the apartment yet. I'm proud of being able to obtain my own space, but it's going to be weird not sleeping at the motel anymore. It's going to be lonely. I've gotten used to Ramona being a wall away, now on the other side of my walls are strangers.

I browse the fresh watermelons in the center of the store, and it reminds me that I don't have any knives in the apartment, especially one big enough to cut a watermelon. Better remember that. I take my phone out of my purse and use the notes app to type in "watermelon knife." I've been storing things I need inside my phone whenever I think of them since securing the lease. I browse through them and see if there's anything I can pick up while I'm here. It's incredible how you overlook so many things when you first move into a place.

"Hand soap," I mumble, reading my list. I turn the cart toward the aisle that holds the soap.

"Jane?" I look up from my phone and stop dead. In front of me, wearing a maxi dress with her hair in a chic bun on top of her head is Shana. Behind her in the shopping cart is an infant's car seat. I flick my eyes away from it before I gaze on the child.

*"You are a useless woman, Jane. You can't even produce a child."*

"Shana," I regard and try to walk past her casually. I don't want to think about her, or the baby, or Stewart. I'm in my new life. My new life where they weren't supposed to enter. Why is she shopping here, anyway? Billy said this was a safe space. I know he meant the maniac driver, but I should have specified that I didn't long to see the mistress of my ex either. I should have declared this half of town in the prenup. Dammit. Suddenly I can't wait to get out of the store and back to my apartment where it's safe.

"Jane, wait," she calls, but I shift my shopping cart toward the checkout line and tell the cashier to please hurry. I don't care what Shana wants to say to me, and I don't want to look at that child. The child Stewart stole from me.

# Four

"Let me guess, two bear claws and two coffees?" The girl behind the counter that I've come to know as Melinda cracks a smile at me. I've been meeting Billy at this coffee shop for months now, and I've made it a mission to break the tough exterior of the brunette behind the counter. She doesn't wear a nametag like everyone else, and finding her name out took at least a month and a half.

"You bet," I smile back. She shakes her head at me.

"What's your name, babe?" She asks, unable to resist anymore.

"Jane." I work hard not to smile.

"Melinda. But you already know that don't you?" She writes my name on the cups and places them to the right for the girl next to her to fill them up.

"It took great detective work." I hand over a ten-dollar bill. "You don't smile like everyone else. You got a mean scowl." My mind drifts to Ramona, and how she's quickly become my favorite person in this world, maybe that's why I feel so drawn to Melinda's character. It's honest. She doesn't plaster an emotion on her face for the sake of it; it's only there if she feels it. I haven't decided if I want to adopt that personality trait or not.

"Usually, that keeps people away." She hands me my change, and I dump it in the tip jar as usual.

"People who don't understand that kind of face." I take the bag of bear claws from her and head over to the pick-up counter. She follows down the line.

"Maybe I just didn't want to talk to your mean scowl," she quips.

"Even so." I grab the cups. "You did."

"Well, I figured if you were so hellbent on finding out my name, I should talk to you."

I laugh. "Every regular customer wants to know your name. They're all too scared to ask."

She shrugs. "Have a nice day, Jane."

"See you tomorrow, Melinda." I counter as I head over to the table in the back.

It's become my unofficial spot when I meet Billy up here. It's behind the half wall of the café dining room and out of sight from most of the customers and the picture window of the street. It's quiet in the middle of chaos. In this space, the world melts away, and it's just Billy and me enjoying our coffee and conversation.

I set down Billy's cup and place a napkin on the table before I put his bear claw down. I let the hot liquid from my Styrofoam cup hit the back of my throat and roll down, warming my insides as I stand next to the table, looking around at the patrons. There's the crowd that I'm used to seeing and a few worn-out looking faces tapping feverishly on their laptops. I wonder if they're writing the next great novel or an essay that's due tomorrow. There are only two newbies relaxing at the tables today. A young college-aged girl staring out the window, and an older lady rubbing her knee relishing in a break from walking.

The typical mocha-colored walls hide behind ridiculous amounts of metal paraphernalia, proclaiming the love and dedication to coffee. The décor is nothing out of the usual by coffee shop standards, but somehow the building feels warmer and more inviting than other cafes I've been inside. Perhaps, because of the connection to the man pulling the entrance door open, and the sense of security he brings with him. I wave Billy over before sitting down.

"You beat me again," he laughs. He looks down at his watch. "I'm even five minutes early."

"You need to be at least eight to beat me." I wink back. "Sit." He shakes his head and takes the chair out from underneath the table before plopping down in the seat.

"I'll have to pre-order and pay for next meetings bear claws," he teases.

"You helped me in so many ways, pastries and coffee are the least I can do." I grip his hand over the table before letting go.

Billy's impeccable posture puts his dark brown hair in line with the sun coming through the window, and it creates a glow on top. It's a little thinner these days, wrought from the stress of keeping me hidden from my attacker, but it still bounces with the movement of his head. It's a full-time job of Billy's teaching me to lay low and failing most of the time.

"So, how's work?" I try to change the mood to something lighter. Billy doesn't like it when I remind him about how we came back into each other's lives. I'm not entirely fond of the memory myself, but I am grateful to be sitting across from him knowing without his presence, I would have perished that night at the hands of a lunatic.

"Good. Same. Same." Always the silent type when it comes to his job. Perhaps it's because he's a cop and would like to keep the things he sees separate from the rest of his life. I can't blame him for that. I'm not sure I could handle a job such as his.

"What's new with you?" He asks between bites.

"I'm all moved into the apartment." I perk up. I can't wait for Billy to see it, for him to gaze upon something he helped me achieve.

"That's good." He smiles. "I'm sorry that I couldn't be there to help you move. Did you end up doing it all yourself?"

"No." I hold my finger in front of my mouth, signaling that I need to chew what's in there before I talk any further.

"You didn't hire a moving company, did you? I told you they only rip you off," he scolds. The line in his forehead deepens as he hurries me to chew and answer his question.

"No, no." I swallow. "Ramona helped me."

"Oh." He settles back down in his seat.

"Besides, what would I hire a moving company to move? I had two boxes to my name. That would be a waste of money. You and I moved the couch and bed in already. There wasn't much but knick-knacks and clothes after that."

"True." He slurps down some of his coffee.

"And after that night," I shudder, "I don't want anyone knowing my address."

"That's smart, Jane." He stares down at the last half of his morning treat, quiet, the memories flooding him. "At least you have a great last name now." He laughs.

I chuckle in agreeance. My identification was lost to the car as the maniac ran away. Billy helped me acquire a new one and a different last name— his. He told me to pretend that I was a cousin of his if I was in trouble and that they would immediately call him. I didn't mind borrowing his last name. It was better than being branded with Stewart's.

"Hey, I think I'm making Melinda my friend." I switch topics on him.

"Really?" He laughs, thankful that I was done talking about that night. He hates the conversation, usually leaving shortly after I bring it up.

"She finally talked to me. I'm wearing her down." I peek my head around the greenery perched on the half-wall next to the table. Sure enough, Melinda is glaring at the next customer in line.

"She's a tough cookie to crumble." He laughs, gulping too much of his coffee and burning his tongue. I have to suppress a giggle in my throat at his misfortune. That's what he gets for saying such a terrible pun.

"Yeah, kind of like Ramona, who, by the way, has taken in a new girl. A stray, as she calls us."

"Oh, yeah?" He mumbles between bites.

"Her name is Paige. She got pretty banged up by her boyfriend and ended up at the motel door courtesy of Hannah, her friend, and also another woman Ramona helped. She's young. I would venture that she's not even legal to drink yet."

"I hope Ramona can help her," he says.

"Me too. She wears the same kind of marks on her arm that I did when I came there. At least she didn't have the ride from hell before getting there," I sigh. "I'm sorry, I hate bringing it up so much like this. I know neither of us wants to revisit it, but it has been playing in my mind since she arrived. I keep thinking about when I first met Ramona and how I got there that night."

"It's fine." It doesn't seem like it is, but I'm going to take his word for it because there's something I have to know that only he can answer.

"Did they ever find him?" Billy's eyes rush to the table, and I have my answer before he shakes his head.

"No," He grunts out.

I scrub down my face and rest my chin in my hand. There's only so much security I can feel when that madman is still out there, with my license in his damn car. Irritation runs hot on my face at the thought of this animal not being captured yet. He worked for a damn driving app; how hard could it be to find him?

"Didn't any of the driving app's records show who he was?" I push to keep the agitation out of my voice. I don't want to tell Billy how to do his job, but I feel like this should have been closed by now.

"No."

"I mean, I know he isn't your favorite person, and he certainly isn't mine either, but couldn't you ask Stewart about it? He paid for the damn ride." My ex-husband's parting gift, after kicking me out of the household we shared for five years of marriage, was a dingy car with a toddler behind the wheel to drive me to a hotel. He found the shitty scum through a driving app, too done with me to offer one of his usual drivers or drive me himself. He didn't want the gossip going on with his employees, as if a younger version of myself popping in, bursting with child wasn't going to set off the chain of chatter.

"That turned up empty. The guy lied about his car and name to the app." His eyes challenge me. "I already sent an officer to talk to Stewart about it. I didn't feel like revisiting the past with him."

"I understand," I sigh, ashamed that I would dare believe Billy wasn't doing everything to find this man. "Sorry, I want this guy caught so that I can breathe easier. I mean, he fucking tried to kill me."

"I know."

"If you hadn't been there..." I swallow the lump in my throat.

"I know." His hand encompasses mine and gives a reassuring squeeze.

"How many times have I thanked you for that?" I whisper.

"Plenty." I squeeze his hand back before he lets go.

"Speaking of the past, you will never guess who I saw at the grocery store last night?" I pick up my pastry and shove the last bite in my mouth.

"Not Stewart." He nervously laughs. "He would never do the grocery shopping."

I laugh before taking on a more somber tone. "No. His wife and child."

"Oh." His coffee cup stays poised in the air, frozen in time. "I don't know what to say, Jane."

"Do you think he hits her?" I ask the table and myself more than I ask my breakfast partner. "He said he never had to hit Leona."

"He didn't *have* to hit you," Billy sneers.

"Yeah," I mumble. "Poor Leona. Did they ever find out who did that to her?" Billy gulps his coffee down, finishing off the cup.

"Not that I'm aware. I think it's still a cold case."

"She was a nice woman." He shuffles his napkin into his now empty pastry bag. "She didn't deserve that fate. After I catch your attacker, I should look in on it."

"That's sweet of you." I smile.

He stands and touches my shoulder. "Sorry to cut this short, but I have to go back to work." Like clockwork, when I bring up the driver, Billy disappears. Off to obsess over the case again.

"Oh. Okay." This was shorter than our regular coffee dates. "It was nice seeing you." I push a smile to my face, my mind still on the past. I watch as Billy turns to leave, but he only gets a few steps away before something draws him back.

"Hey, uh, stay low for a while until I tell you otherwise." Panic rises in my chest as his words invade my ear canals.

"What do you mean?" I stutter. I am glancing around at the people in the coffee shop with suspicion instead of light curiosity now.

"Don't do your running outside. Stick to the motel and the apartment."

"Why, Billy? You're scaring me." My hands begin to shake, so I shove them under the table to keep them out of sight of Billy. No one has noticed our conversation.

"We had another incident similar to yours. I'm not sure it's the same guy or what have you, but your info *was* left in the car, so I want you to be cautious. He could be looking for you. The woman had your built and hair color. Guys like that don't like unfinished business."

"Of course." I already am cautious. I stare at every guest of the motel as if they were sent by the driver to finish me off. How much more sheltered can I make myself?

"Here." He squats down next to me so that no one can see what he's handing me. "Take this." I watch as Billy produces a small gun out of his pocket.

"What?" I squeak. "Billy, I don't need that."

"You do, Jane. Take it." It feels strange in my hand, but I do as I'm told.

# Five

"What the hell is your problem?"

"Huh?" I look up from my seat behind the front desk area. Ramona has her shriveled hands on her hips and a pissed off look on her face, announcing that I didn't hear a single word she said.

"Sorry, Ramona. I was thinking. What did you say?" I sit up in my seat and look around the desk for a clue. It's better if I come to it myself, but I'm afraid this time I won't be able to pull it off.

"I asked if you cleaned rooms two and three." She stomps over to her computer chair and flops her body down, making the whole thing skate a little across the floor. She yanks on the desktop to pull herself back into place. I long to laugh at how awkward her short legs look, but I know she's feeling too pissy to banter.

"No, I asked Paige to do it." I start shuffling papers on the desk, cleaning up the space. I hate clutter.

"She's not yours to boss around." Her eyebrows furrow.

"Well, I was doing inventory and ordering so that you didn't have to." I roll my head toward her. "So, I figured I would keep her busy instead of hovering over her while she did it. Let her feel a little more in control of something."

"Oh." She nods. "Good job, kid."

I push my finger into my ear, jiggling it around a bit. "I'm sorry, what was that? I didn't quite hear you?"

"I said you're a spoiled once rich bitch who can't take a compliment with grace." I roll my head back against the chair as a deep belly laugh vibrates my body.

"Sounds about right." I click the mouse on the pad and wait for the computer screen to come back to life. "Although I am not rich anymore, am I? I have bills that I have to worry about paying myself."

"Oh, quit your whining." She sets her feet up on the desk and lounges back. The more of the motel that I've learned, the more she's slacked off. Well, I guess she's earned it. She did save my life and the lives of all those other women. I like running the motel, so I don't mind the extra responsibility. I enjoy it.

"Hey, Ramona," I ask after a couple of minutes of her sitting beside me with her eyes closed.

"Hey, kid." I shake my head at her.

"How many women do you think you've taken in over the years?" I click to print out tomorrow's guests checking out.

"Since I owned the motel, or since forever?" She opens her eyes and stares up at the ceiling, mentally counting in her head, but I'm already sure the number is astronomically high.

"What makes you take them in?" I ask, instead.

"Boy, you are nosey." She sits up, her possible nap forgotten. "Well, my parents always had a spare room because I was an only child. I guess word got around because Mama always tried to fill it with somebody passing by. Sometimes to make a little side cash, sometimes just for the company, I suppose. Then came the first woman who needed more than just shelter. Well, my mother never turned anyone away. Then that woman told her friend, and she told another, and so on and so on. The bed was always filled with someone needing out of a bad situation after that. They'd find their feet and leave, and then the next person would be knocking before we could wash the sheets."

"I don't think I could do it," I mutter toward the computer screen.

"Do what?"

"Save someone."

"I don't save people, kid. They save themselves. I provide food, water, shelter, and a job while they do it." I didn't feel like arguing with her or even worse exposing that she was the one I held responsible for saving me, so I drop it. Ramona would consider being called a saint a dirty sin.

"My mother always said, 'Girls stick together.' I guess it got stuck somewhere in this head of mine because I keep taking in you assholes." There was the bitter old woman exterior I knew and loved.

"No wonder you're so cranky." Just then, Paige came around the outside of the building and knocked on the door.

"Come on in, child." Ramona hollered.

"I'm done with the rooms. Is there anything else you need, Ramona?" I notice Paige is still staring at the floor or the wall when she speaks, but her shoulders seemed a little straighter today. Ramona was already working her magic, giving another woman a way to find her voice.

"No, no. You go on and relax in your room. I think there's a tv dinner in the freezer of the breakroom that's going out of date soon. Why don't you grab it and have yourself some lunch?" I almost break into a laugh at the same lie I heard pass her lips so many times when I started here. I turn my head away from Paige and back to the computer.

"Really? Are you sure?" There's hope in her voice. She's starving, and not used to food being offered. My cold heart beats hard in my chest with pity.

"Yeah. I can't eat them all before then. You'd do me a favor because I hate seeing food go to waste." It's incredible how straight she can hold her poker face.

"Thank you, Ramona." I can hear the smile in her voice, and I wait until I hear the door shuts behind her before turning back around to face Ramona.

"Liar," I tease.

"I don't want her feeling like I'm giving her handouts."

"When she checks the date, she's going to know." I start stapling papers together for Ramona and complete my small duties to close out my shift. Tonight, I am off early, and Ramona is taking the night watch.

She shrugs.

"Do you think she'll be all right?" I ask her.

"If she stops whining over cleaning the rooms, maybe." She swaps me seats and takes over the desk.

"Cut her some slack. People are nasty when they stay at a motel. It's a lot to take in when you first get here." I purse my lips in disgust at the memory of my first day working at the motel. On that day, I was handed a crash course in just how vile humans were when they weren't responsible for the mess that needed to be cleaned up.

"Oh, come on," she groans.

"No, I'm serious." I slide my jacket around my shoulders and rest my hands on my hips.

"You say that because you were rich."

"I wasn't always rich, Ramona, and besides Stewart was the one with the money, not me. The divorce made that evident." I shake my head. "Paige, however, just got beat up from her boyfriend who chose drugs over her, and now she's the low man on the totem pole scrubbing toilets. We keep telling her it's a better life, but come on; it's still shitty. She'll come around. I truly think so."

"I don't know. She has Bambi eyes." She stares out to the spot Paige vacated.

"What the hell does that mean?" I place both of my hands on either arm of my chair.

"I had a girl here once, with the same kind of doe-eyed expression that Paige wears. She didn't make it." I want to ask her more, but I've never seen Ramona look so lost. I'm terrified.

"Hey, do you need anything from the store? I'm going to run out before heading home."

"Yeah. I could use a pack of smokes." I glare over at her, but from the sadness in her eyes, I don't fight her addiction today.

# Six

Billy saved my life from that maniac driver, and I know he beats himself up daily that he never caught him that night. He works tirelessly on the case, following leads daily. He's done everything and lost sleep over my safety. Still, I've been known to defy orders to lay low and stick to the places that we both know are safe for me. The itch to find myself in other areas and break out of routine gets strong, and I can't fight it. The action is usually followed by a verbal scolding from Billy for jeopardizing my safety. I can't wait until he catches the creep so that I may enjoy the light of day without looking around every corner, waiting for a madman to jump out and grab me.

I turn out of the mall parking lot. Although it's where I want to wander, the grocery store will have to do this evening. Billy deemed the grocery store three streets over from my apartment, a safe space, and one of the few that I'm allowed to be. Now, being stripped of jogging outside, I need to relieve some tension — Ramona's heavy words at work float through my mind. I need to exhaust my body in some way so that Paige's impending doom over the shape of her eyes is no longer the thought consuming me, and wandering a store for hours might help.

Ramona doesn't talk like that. I didn't think she ever failed at what she does with women. Whatever happened with that girl was terrible enough to make her believe that Paige didn't stand much of a chance. I've never seen Ramona look that way in the past couple of months that I've gotten to know her. She's never once looked vulnerable.

I wonder if she saw Bambi's eyes when she looked at me for the first time. Maybe her theory is flawed. I can see how I could easily be cast as a woman who wouldn't make it. I had nobody in my life, no parents, no family, and no friends. Stewart was the only person I was connected to, and he kicked me out on my ass, trading me in for a prettier younger model. I could have easily given up.

Did Ramona see that when she looked at me that day? Or did her years of dealing with women coming through the door seeking help give her a sort of insight into their personalities?

I pull into the familiar parking lot. Familiarity is supposed to offer a sense of security, but I'm tired of the feeling. It bores me now being in a routine and a habit. Loitering for a few hours does cause a small thrill. It is against orders. I'm not supposed to lollygag as Billy calls it. That puts me in the area too long, and that man is still looking for me. He wants to end what he started.

He's attacked three other women since me, all my same height and build. Blond and slender, around five foot nine inches. He's looking for me, and there's only so much time before he finds me, or Billy gets to him first.

I touch the shelves of the store, staring at every item the place has to offer. I don't need anything, aside from something different inside my head for the time being.

"Jane?" I look up and see the same face I saw last time at this grocery store. I need to find a new place to shop. Is she staking her claim on this place by coming again and confronting me? Shit, she can have it for all I care. I don't want to touch anything that involves her or Stewart.

"Shana." Her sour name rolls off my tongue, and my words spit it to the ground. The unwashed dirty blond hair that dangled in strings around her natural face is gone, replaced by a more polished uniformed brunette color and a layer of makeup that doesn't allow the freckles underneath to poke through.

Gone is the yoga instructor I hired to help my husband de-stress because I was worried about his heart and newly diagnosed condition of coronary artery disease. I'm surprised now that his heart could even catch something like that, considering he didn't have one. But, something inside that old chest of his pumped wildly for Shana, enough to toss me to the side without warning. And I'm the dumbass who turned matchmaker for them.

I walk away from her once again, longing for the dull quiet walls of my apartment.

"Jane, please wait." She shoves her cart, with the infant car seat residing inside again, toward me.

"What do you need, Shana?" I bite out as I spin my body around in her direction. "I don't have any more husbands for you to get knocked up by and steal. I don't have any more mansions for you to take over and redecorate for your child blessed out of wedlock." I laugh, but it's cruel. "Well, I shouldn't say out of wedlock, Stewart was married at the time, just not to you." She winces as my words hit her.

"I'm sorry, Jane. I truly am." Shana tucks her chin to her chest like a guilty toddler.

"Do you cry into your hundred-dollar bills at night over it?" Her eyes find her child, and I feel like a bitch for the words making me feel any pleasure. I'm not this low. Stewart and Shana are, but not me.

"I'm sorry, that was rude." My eyes fall from her face and land on the purple circle on her arm, poking out of the cap sleeve of her designer dress. My head jerks back to her face, and she catches my line of sight.

"Does he?" I can't even get the words out. No, this is not my problem. I warned her. I fucking warned her.

"Jane, what do I do?" The desperation in her voice hits my heart without warning before I can put a good defense in place. I will not take pity on her.

"Pray that his heart gives out soon," I hiss. I turn on my heels and walk out of the store, Ramona's cigarettes forgotten. The tears falling down Shana's face are worthless. I fucking warned her.

# Seven

Billy would kill me if he knew what I was doing. He would launch himself into a conference-style rant about how stupid I was being, about the dangers that I was putting myself in, but I don't care. My body has vibrated about my apartment long enough with no relief, and I need to get out — the idea of me laying low forgotten. I can't walk the floors inside anymore, hoping that my body will exhaust the information inside of me. I need to run.

My feet hit the sidewalk in a cadence as I try to control my breathing to ward off a cramp. I don't belong to a gym, and a treadmill would do no good for the shit I need to get out of my head. A run outside is what I need — just a short run. I know I need to be cautious, so I won't be long. I pick up pace as I repeat the sentiment to myself. It won't be long. I need fresh air. I breathe it in, but all I can smell is the new paint of a nursery.

*"Oh, this is the baby's room. We just painted it. The nursery furniture comes tomorrow."*

I hit my feet harder against the concrete, hitting my stride, as Shana's words roar inside my head. I remember the day I went to get my mother's chest from the house so clearly. My ass had hit the driveway the day before, and the house stood mocking me, much like the new mistress inside. She followed me to the top of the stairs and delighted in my pain as I gazed on the room that was to hold the one thing I could never have.

A child.

Stewart took that away from me. I wipe an unbidden tear from my eye. His abuse, his hands, stole that from my future. There Shana was that day, flaunting it in my face. She didn't understand the suffering I went through only to end up with zilch. She didn't know what would be ahead in her future. She merely stood there, rubbing her growing belly, smirking at me for my misery.

I remember throwing up when I thought about what was to come for her.

*"I hope you aren't sick. I can't afford to be sick."*

My feet don't slow as I take the corner at the end of the street. Shana didn't know the true meaning of sick. Now she does, as she wakes up every morning to a certain kind of sickness that would make the devil flinch. Sweat rolls down my forehead as I recall staring into the medicine cabinet. I should have switched his fucking pills. They look like over-the-counter pain medicine. A month and the stress could have sent him over the edge. I can still feel the weight of them resting in my hands as I made the decision.

*If I switch them, he might die, and then he can't hurt another human the way he did me. Maybe a month of not having his prescription will be all that he needs.*

My heart pounds against my chest as I recall the pounding on the door from Shana.

*"Are you done?"*

I threw the pills back in their respective bottles and walked out of that house. Now, I need to do it again, metaphorically. I am done. Shana is not my problem. Her child is not my problem. I warned her. I picked up that fucking chest and made sure the corner lifted my shirt to show her the bruises. She saw them. I heard her breath kick at the sight of them. She knew. She knew and did nothing with a child of a monster growing inside of her.

My body doubles over as I gulp for air, bracing my hands on my knees. I did my best. I did more than anyone in my shoes could be expected to do. I warned her. I didn't have to tell her what she was getting herself into being with Stewart. She stole everything from me, and she didn't deserve my kindness. I didn't have to expose that to her, giving her a chance to flee. I could have let her have her karma served cold without it. Now, she has a child — a baby. Now, that baby is in danger.

"Ugh." My body pushes upward and releases the anger from within to the air — a man walking past jumps and nearly hits into a parked car.

"Sorry. Sorry. Rough day," I pant out, but he doesn't much care to stick around and find out how rough. Not that I would tell him anyway. How do you start that conversation? I shake my head and gaze around. I'm much further than where I told myself I would run. I need to head back to the apartment. I turn my body around and freeze as my eyes lock onto his face.

There's a blue car parked at the end of the sidewalk, and the man inside is staring at me. A chill runs down my overheating body, and suddenly I'm aware of how vulnerable running outside makes me. He's too far away to make out if it's the driver from before, but he's looking right at me, and something in his stare tells me that I must look familiar. Could it be him? It was a red car he was driving that night, but maybe he got a new one to evade the police.

*"I've always wanted to kill a woman. You'll be my first."*

I spin around, taking off in a sprint down the sidewalk. Maybe it's my imagination. I'm seeing ghosts because of the past is on my mind, that's all. A slender blond running could catch the sight of any man. It wouldn't be the first time I got catcalled while running outside. I yank at the bottom of my sports bra, wishing I would have thought to put on more clothes.

I turn the corner and head down the street, glancing over my shoulders as the blue car slowly makes the turn behind me. Shit. Panic vibrates my legs and pushes them faster down the sidewalk. Dammit. I touch the waistband of my leggings. I didn't bring the gun with me. Billy would kill me double if he knew that I left that piece of protection at home instead of bringing it with me. I'm supposed to be acting smart.

I take the next right, running in a circle to test if the man is following me or if I'm scaring myself for nothing. I loop around back to the spot where I scared the man with my scream, and sure enough, the blue car flicks on his turn signal to follow. He's tracking me. It's him. He's found me.

I dart down to the left now, frantic to lose him. My mind rapid fires looking for an escape route. I can't go back to the apartment. He can't know where I live. I could take him to the police station, but it's too far of a run, and it's through a less busy part of town. That would be stupid to leave a chance of people not being around to witness him should he jump out or hit me. I look back again, and he's almost right behind me, revving the engine to pick up speed.

The streets blur around me, and my stomach starts to ache with a side cramp. This was an idiotic idea coming out here today. *Think, Jane, think.* I see a store nearby that I could run inside, but then I'll be a sitting duck while I wait for the pain to subside. Wait.

I take note of the street nearby. Yes, this is it. I was stopped around here in construction the other day. I pick up speed, content with my plan. Cars have to stop, but runners don't at the construction zone. There's only one problem with the idea.

I turn down a quiet residential street where there is only one other car, and they're at the end, waiting at the stop sign. I can see the traffic ahead of me, and everyone stopped by the flagger working the construction zone. I hear the blue car pull down behind me and pick up speed when he notes the obstacle ahead of him. He knows this is the place where he can make his move. There's no one around here, and it's the last chance.

Against the cramp paining my side, I run for my life. It's downhill, so my body has a little advantage, but so does the car. I can hear the engine on my heels, but I don't turn around, fear of looking on that face again and becoming paralyzed. I keep my eyes on that stop sign until it finally comes into view, and I smack it with my hand. I wave to the car, still stopped there, and turn right. I can hear the screech of the blue car's brakes as he wills the vehicle to stop before causing an accident.

I keep up the pace, turning around to see that him stuck behind the car. I'm safe for now. I push down a few more streets before darting along a side road into a little mom and pop bakery. There's a kind older woman behind the counter.

"Are you all right, dear?" She asks as I throw myself down on my butt on the tile floor before her, grasping the wall to shield me. My chest rises and falls in quick succession. I glance out the window, left and right. There's no one, but I push back to the far end of the store.

"I'm fine." I smile as relief etches my face. "Hell of a run this morning."

# Eight

"Why is your hair black?" I yank down the tresses under Ramona's judgmental eyes. "And why is it short? What happened to you?"

"I needed a change," I offer her with a tight lip smile. "Don't you like it?"

"I love it. It's very Cleopatra," Paige chimes in, and I note she's eating a freezer breakfast meal I stuck in the breakroom the other day. There's color on her face this morning, and I catch a glimpse of her eyes when she speaks to me.

"Thank you, Paige." I show a toothy smile to her and leave my glare to Ramona.

"Yeah, Queen of Denial," Ramona jests. "Seriously, what is this?" She grabs the ends of my hair, inspecting it with rough hands.

"It's not a wig, so quit yanking on it like that." I pull my head to the side, sliding my tresses free from her grip. "I got my hair cut and dyed it, that's all." I throw my hands up to motion that this is no big deal.

"How'd you get to black so fast? It was god damn almost platinum before." She's back to yanking my hair, fanning it out in her greedy hand, hoping to find a spot of the old me.

"A lot of hair dye." I push past her to the front desk and drop my purse in the safe drawer and lock it.

"Are you going through a mid-life crisis?" Ramona asks, lifting an over-plucked brow at me.

"Jesus, that would mean I'm going to die at seventy-eight, Ramona. I'm only thirty-nine," I screech.

"Well, the hair makes you look older."

"Well, they were out of your ancient auburn, so I had to go with this," I quip as I take my seat in front of the computer, clicking the keyboard with more force than necessary.

"I don't think it makes you look older," Paige mumbles with food in her mouth.

"Don't be a kiss ass, Paige," Ramona barks, and I watch Paige flinch a little, but it's less than at the beginning. She's doing much better than I thought. I don't believe Ramona knows what she's talking about with her Bambi eyes theory. I don't think Paige even has what you would call Bambi's eyes. Hers look more like an almond-shaped green-pear color.

"Can we get to work, please?" I shout, throwing my hands to my face, pressing the knuckles of my thumbs into the bridge of my nose. I stay like that for a second before scratching my forehead and hitting the keyboard again to log-in.

"You in something bad?" Ramona won't drop it. She slides up close to me, leaning over the desk, invading my nasal passages with her morning cigarette and coffee smell.

"Nope." I click the mouse in irritation.

"Don't bring it around here," She points to Paige, who is obliviously eating now and staring at the television screen. Ramona doesn't want me to fuck up the new girl with my problems, and I understand her position.

"Nothing bad is going on, Ramona." I lean in toward her with a softer tone. "I was thinking about the past the other day after I ran into Shana at the grocery store. I started to think about how I was glad that I left that life behind me, and that I get to be my own person now, but I looked in the mirror and remembered that Stewart picked the blond hairstyle. I didn't. So, I decided that I would change it to something I want. I went to the drugstore and got a whole bunch of black hair dye boxes and got rid of him."

"And then you cut it yourself?"

"I went to that little place on the corner and told her to give me a bob. Figured it would be easy to maintain." I glare over. "Wait, are you saying that it looks like I did this myself?" I point at my head.

"No."

"Are you saying it looks bad?"

"No."

"Are you saying it looks good?" Before she can answer, I hold my hand up to stop her. "Never you mind, I don't want to know your thoughts on that question."

"So, this is a 'too many hormones bouncing around' thing?" She slides down into her chair, perching her hands into her lap.

"Sure." I shrug.

"I still don't believe you."

"We have three guests checking in today and two checking out. Rooms five and six will need to be cleaned, and I will need you to check on rooms one, three, and ten to make sure they are ready for our guests." I direct my words at Paige, and much to her credit, she hears me over the television that's sucking her brain out.

"Yes, Jane. I can do it," she answers, slurping her last bit of energy drink. How anyone can suck one of those down in the morning is beyond me. She hates coffee.

"Our inventory order should be here tomorrow." I look at Ramona, who is still trying to figure my hair out. "Did you hear me?"

"Yes, boss." She salutes.

"Ugh. I need coffee." I scrub down my face and push my chair back.

"You mean you didn't stop at your fancy place this morning?" Ramona's eyebrows disappear beneath the curl of her bangs this time.

"No. I woke up late," I lie.

"So? You could have come in late." She's pushing for information better than a cadaver dog searching for a body.

"I'll remember that for next time." I smile at her, challenging any more questions. She holds her hands up in surrender, and I pour my coffee. When Ramona looks away, I tug at my hair. I feel naked with my neck exposed like this.

I'll have to get used to it. Someone out there thinks that they're hunting down a woman with long blond hair. I can't believe we didn't think about changing my hair when the incident first happened, or when he started targeting other women with the same hairstyle as me. We were too focused on catching him.

I won't be stopping at the coffee shop until Billy says it's okay. I'm going to listen to him this time. I guess I'm going to have to stop and grab a coffee pot for the apartment on my way home today. Ramona is going to think something's up if I keep drinking coffee here in the morning.

"Oh, Billy called." I burn my tongue on the coffee in surprise at Ramona's words.

"Oh?" I cough. "What did he want?" I pretend to put my hand on the front of my jeans in a casual way, but it's so that I can check the metal in my waistband. I won't dare leave without this gun again.

"I think he said he wanted to take you to lunch today, or was it that he wanted to meet you for lunch?" She looks around the desk.

"Paige, where the hell did I put that note?" Ramona shouts.

Paige stands, laughs at something on the television screen as she drops her paper plate into the garbage can. She makes her way over to the desk without a word and produces a post-it note from the corner, bringing it to rest in front of Ramona.

"Thanks, child," I note that Ramona doesn't giveaway my nickname of 'kid' to Paige. It makes me feel a little special.

"I'm off to clean the rooms now." Paige smiles. She's taking the duty of scrubbing toilets better now. Ramona nods at her and starts to write something down at the desk.

"Your hair looks great," Paige whispers as she passes me. I tug on it one more time.

I hope it's enough.

# Nine

"Jane? Is that you?" I look up from the book I'm reading at the front desk and spy Billy standing at the partition window. He's staring at my hair, squinting his eyes in question. Shit.

"Hey." I smile.

"What? Uh," he stutters. "You look nice."

"Her hair is different, you moron," Ramona screams from her spot on the little couch in front of the TV. An avid soap opera viewer, Ramona hates her time to be disturbed by any sort of noise. She says that you have to watch the shows with all of your senses, so there can't be any disturbance. I think it's her ploy to get some downtime and soak in some other drama than whatever she's dealing with here.

"Oh. Soaps," Billy whispers. He's been around long enough to know about Ramona and her television time. He found out the hard way that her aim is accurate, and her shoes become a weapon when you talk too much during her favorite television show.

"Yeah." I look over her direction and chuckle. Then I swirl back around to catch him staring at my hair once again.

"Do you like it?" I whisper, deflecting all the questions that I know are racing inside his head. If Ramona was still feeling a certain way about the change, I could only imagine the theories running through the mind of Billy, the cop.

There's no way I'm getting out of lunch without an interrogation, although I plan on telling him about the man in the blue car anyway.

"Yeah. Yeah. It looks great on you." A genuine smile lights up his face, and I dare to breathe a sigh of relief.

"Get out of here," Ramona hollers. "I can't hear my show." She's holding a shoe up in her right hand, and Billy holds his hands up in surrender. It's funny to think anything can make it over to her with the volume of the little set blaring full blast.

"Ready for lunch?" He taps on the ledge of the small window.

"Yeah, let me clock out, and I'll meet you in the parking lot." He walks away, leaving Ramona and me alone.

"You're going to have to tell him," she mutters.

"What?" I log off the computer and spin the chair around. She's still groaning about my hair and how she doesn't buy my story.

"That you like him." I quirk an eyebrow up in her direction, but she doesn't turn to look at me. She's glued to the drama of someone's husband coming back from the dead for the fifth time.

"Tell me why you watch these again." My lip curls in disgust at the TV.

"Don't say you hate them again, or I'll make you say three Hail Marys," she scolds.

"Going to lunch. Hold down the fort, will you?" I tease and push her shoulder as I walk out.

Billy is waiting for me in the parking lot next to the passenger side of his truck. He's got on street clothes today instead of his uniform. This must be one of his rare days off. I don't know if he is forced to work as much as he does or if he picks up the hours because he likes it and doesn't want to be at home. He once admitted to me that he was lonely there. Now, with my own space, I understand the feeling. I miss being near Ramona.

He opens the passenger side for me so that I can hop inside.

"Thank you," I sing.

"No problem." He smiles at me and holds my eyes for a few more seconds longer before closing the door behind me. Billy had always had a crush on me since the times when he was friends with Stewart, but he never made a move about it. Even now, with Stewart cleansed from my life and his, he doesn't come forward with his feelings. Part of me wants him to get on with it already, and the other half still doesn't know if dating a man connected to Stewart's path is smart. I wouldn't kick Billy out of my life, considering he's the one looking for the lunatic driver, but that doesn't make me warm to the idea of jumping into a romantic relationship. No matter how much Ramona tells me he likes me.

"Where are we going to eat?" I ask once he gets behind the wheel and shuts the door.

"Why did you change your hair?" Damn, already with the questions.

I look down at my lap, fiddling my fingers together. "I don't want to be recognized."

"Is this a personal thing or...?" He lets the rest of the question hang in the air.

"A safety thing." I look out the window on my side. I find the courage to start the conversation when I'm not looking at him. "I went running yesterday. I know. I know," I sigh and stare down at my trembling fingers knotted with each other. "I know you told me not to, and I understand why now. Some guy in a blue car started to follow me, and I'm sure of it because I even ran in a circle to see if he was or if I was just scaring myself."

"What happened?" Billy's tone is low; he's holding judgment until he has all the facts.

"I outran him. Well, that's not true. I ran him into the construction zone and ducked into a little shop off a side road for a few hours before I called Ramona to come pick me up. I lied and told her I had too bad of a cramp to make it home on foot."

"I see."

"No one was around when I left the shop, and she drove me straight to the apartment. I got some hair dye from the drugstore near the apartment, and I dyed my hair, then I went to the little hair salon and made the lady cut it short." I look up at his face, and he's staring out the front windshield right now. "I'm sorry, Billy. I know I went against your rules—"

"My rules? Jane, they aren't rules."

"I thought—"

"I'm trying to keep you safe, yes, but I don't want you to feel like I'm controlling your life. I'm not Stewart."

"I would never compare you to him." I shake my head vehemently. "Never."

"Do I want you to follow what I say? Yes, but that's because I want to keep you safe. Jane, you're my best friend. I don't want you attacked, hurt, or God-forbid killed. I advise you on what's the best way to keep that from not happening, but obviously I want you to use your common sense when those don't work."

"They do work."

"Well, if you would have followed them, then you wouldn't have gone to the drugstore or salon and changed your hair, and that was a smart decision."

"If I would have followed them, then I wouldn't have been running outside and been followed." I scrub my forehead.

"Yeah." He sighs. He can't deny the truth in that. If I wouldn't have gone out yesterday, then I wouldn't have needed to change my hair. Well, it's probably for the best I did. If that man is targeting blond women, then I need to be the opposite.

"But at least you know what car the man was driving," I squeak.

"Yeah, that's true." He looks at me and smiles. "I'm glad you're safe. That was smart thinking, Jane." He reaches up and runs his hand through the left side of my hair. "I hardly recognized you when I first saw you. We should have changed your hair before. I can't believe I didn't think of it."

"Well, it is a touchy subject telling a woman to change her appearance." I give a small chuckle.

"But," he puts the key in the ignition and turns the truck over, "about the running."

"I know, I'm sorry. That was stupid of me. I needed to clear my head, and it's my fall back to run. I tried walking the apartment, but I couldn't get any relief from my stress. I have to run, Billy. I have to be able to move. This is killing me."

"You can use my gym pass. I'll put you on the membership." He pulls out of the parking lot. "Your name will be under Jane Voss. My last name, as always." He gives me a tight-lipped smile. I know he's upset that the man found me yesterday but proud that I lost him. Hopefully, this will be a break in Billy's case. There has to be some good that comes out of yesterday's incident.

I reach up and run my hand through my hair again. My hand doesn't feel as good as Billy's did, but it gives me an idea. If Billy didn't recognize me, someone else wouldn't either.

"Naples? Are you feeling like Italian for lunch?" He cuts into my thoughts.

"Italian sounds just fine."

# Ten

When you don't want the devil to appear, she's right on your shoulder, but when you're stalking to find her, she's nowhere. It's been three days of coming to the grocery store at the same time I was here last, but there has been no sign of Shana. I loop around the aisles once again, searching for her brunette hair. I wonder why Stewart chose for her to darken her hair when he told me to lighten mine.

I pick up a cereal box and bonk myself on the head with it. I shouldn't be here, not with a murderer looking for me. I was lucky to escape him twice now. I might not be so fortunate next time. Third time is a charm and all.

I can't leave yet, though, not until I'm sure Shana isn't coming to the store today. I must clear my conscience of this mess once and for all before I can drop it, and finally give up the guilt on my heart. I'm the one who invited her into the house. She was there because I called her. Stewart gave me a list of yoga instructors on the internet that he would approve of coming to the house, and I chose her. I'm the reason they met. I picked her.

I'm about to give up the chase when I see her breezing in the entrance with a wrap contraption around her body. I'm not an idiot, and it doesn't take me long to deduce that she's carrying her baby in that fabric thing. It looks complicated. I'll never have to worry about figuring one out at least. The truth hurts, but when you cover it with humor, it's supposed to hurt less. It doesn't. It still fucking stings like the pain in my ovary as the cyst burst from Stewart's blows. They took it. Money buys things that it shouldn't be able to — silence when there should be screaming. No one glanced my way after he flashed green stacks in front of them.

I watch as Shana grabs a shopping cart and pushes the seat portion open. Up until now, she's had the infant car seat in the main hold. I wonder if she'll be doing a lot of shopping today so that I might be able to observe her for longer. I bite my lip at the prospect of getting to know her without her knowing I'm here. People show their true colors when those they want to impress aren't around. Shana loves to impress me. She's the one with the money now. She won Stewart.

*"Did Stewart tell you that he had to order my ring from Italy, Jane? Isn't it stunning?"*

Her chubby hand thrust toward me, begging for attention, while my new-to-me clothing stuck to my body in uncomfortable ways. She was happy to show me about my own house that day as if I didn't occupy it the night before.

I follow far enough behind her that she doesn't catch on. I'm just another shopper on a similar route. I notice that she turns and looks around at the people passing her by as if searching for a familiar face. She's expecting to meet someone here, perhaps. Maybe a mom friend. What's Shana like with other people she dares to call friends. Three aisles in, and she hasn't grabbed a damn thing off the shelves. Her shopping cart is empty.

I go ahead of her in the next aisle when her rubbernecking gets to be too much. I don't want her to notice my face. However, the next aisle is the fucking baby aisle. The blaring reminder that I can't have children is all around me. I stare down at the happy infant on the package of diapers, and it melts a little of the cynic inside of me. Kids are great, but I didn't have a reliable partner to parent alongside. I would have turned out like Shana. Perhaps everything does happen for a reason, although the brutality of it didn't need to happen.

I stick my tongue out at the baby on the box and watch as Shana turns the corner of the aisle looking depressed that she's not finding whoever it is she's looking for in the many faces here. Her "friendly" ways must have gotten the best of her again. I called her a friend once, and she stabbed me in the back in the worst possible way.

"Well, I guess while we're here, we will get you some more formula." She bounces the bundle strapped to her chest and rubs her hand down the front of the wrap. She takes a deep sigh, and I look on as tears fight to release from her body while she begs them to stay inside.

An older woman turns down the aisle behind Shana, and the sniffling coming from her starts to attract the stranger's attention. The older lady stops to stare at her, openly intruding on Shana's moment of weakness. There's an uncomfortable tightening in my chest as I take in the scene. I act before I realize it's my decision.

Grabbing a bottle of body wash from behind me, I walk over to Shana and her cart. She might not be my favorite person in the world, but she doesn't deserve to have her emotions gawked at in a public grocery store. No one does.

"Hey, don't worry. It's just the baby swings. I'm sure you'll find your grocery list," I fake. I look at the passerby. "Mom brain is nothing like pregnancy brain, am I right?"

"Oh, yes." She pats Shana's back. "All that is temporary, my darling, and worth it." She winks at me as if it's a secret we veteran moms share. My heart shatters a little inside that I'm not in that club.

The strange woman pushes past after grabbing a bottle of baby powder, satisfied that the drama was only a simple newborn sleep deprivation mood swing, nothing juicier.

"Thank you," Shana sniffles, and finally looks up at my face.

"Jane?"

"Yeah," I groan. I toss the baby wash into her cart. She can fucking buy it for my efforts.

"I thought you weren't here." I'm the one she wanted to find here, not some other mom, me.

"Do you need something, Shana?" I venture, trying to keep the frigidness out of my voice, considering the store is cold enough. But despite my best efforts, I turn bitter in aisle five.

"I need to talk to you, Jane. I need help." She pushes up the sleeve of her jacket to expose a fresh bruise.

"It sure looks that way," I deadpan. "If only someone would have told you and warned you ahead of time, you could not have married him."

"Stewart," she answers the question that I didn't ask. "He hits me."

"I know, Shana. That's his dirtiest little secret. The catch to landing the greatest catch in the city." I lean into her. "But you wanted him so bad."

She cowers in shame, and I enjoy her pain too much. I'm no better than Stewart, and I'm letting my past control my present. I exhale and groan, releasing my irritation having let him control any part of me still.

"Shana, you need out." I almost offer up Ramona's name, but I don't need to hear Ramona telling me how dumb I am for getting involved. I promised her I wouldn't be stupid again and telling your ex-husband's mistress, a woman who wronged you, that she could stay where you work sounds really fucking stupid.

"Yea. I know." She picks at the formula bottles on the shelf, pretending to be distracted until the bundle on her chest makes a noise, drawing our attention. I look upon the child's sleeping face. She's simply perfect. Her skin is pale with newness, and her eyes are a deep bark color. It reminds me of the shadows in the forest at dusk. Her hand is exposed against her mother's chest, and I'm amazed by the tiny size of it.

"How old is she?" I ask, ignoring the pain inside my chest and the way my body aches to hold this child. I wish I could hold my own child. I wish I had the chance to carry a baby inside of me.

"Two months."

I sigh at the sound of her sweet age. Two months old, and her father is already letting her down. It was an idiotic thought to believe that her presence could stop the monster inside of him, but I had hoped. I prayed every night that having a child would take the anger away from Stewart's heart and replace it with something wholesome. Yet, here her mother stands in a grocery store crying because he didn't change.

"I want out, Jane." I hear the determination in Shana's voice. She's sure.

I nod, never letting my eyes leave the baby's face.

"Delilah and I need out."

I continue nodding. Happy to hear that she has some sense in her. My conscience can be clear. She's going to leave Stewart and save this beautiful child from a life of terror. He'll be exposed for his sins.

"Get me out, Jane." Desperation replaces the confidence of Shana's voice.

I flick my head toward her. "Me. Why me?"

"He won't let me out."

# Eleven

**"I** don't understand how I can help." I push my hair back away from my face, exposing the near makeup-free skin beneath. Shana looks on in jealousy, her makeup heavier than she wants to apply it. I remember the freckles dancing on her sun-kissed skin the day I met her. Stewart has strict rules about appearance. You must appear perfect in every way when you are Mrs. Miller. No hair out of place, and no less than a full face of makeup.

"Jane." Shana leans in closer, looking around us for any more nosey shoppers eavesdropping on our conversation. "You know what he's like and how controlling he acts. You got out."

"I was thrown out," I hiss. I can't believe she needs to be reminded of that fact. It's as if her part in my downfall slipped her memory. She had me dismissed so that she could lay in her bed of sin with my husband. I suppose I would forget that piece of information, too, to better sleep at night if I were her.

"I know." She bows her head in shame, and I'm half-tempted to believe she feels the emotion, but Shana's screwed me over once before. How does she expect me to trust her now? The monster inside of Stewart could be cunning as well.

*"Jane, I love you more than I've ever loved anyone. I want to be good for you. I can change. I swear, I can."*

Those words were usually said with a bruise on my body and fistful of flowers in his hand. I trusted in each syllable every single time. After all, people make mistakes, and he was trying to change his. He was stressed at work. Everything was going to change after his big case was over, and he could breathe for a second. After it was done, Stewart got the diagnosis of coronary artery disease. I thought I could handle it, that I could find him a way to relax and everything would calm down. I was wrong.

"Shana," I sigh and lean my body against the shelf nearby. The stillness of her body does nothing to soothe the small person strapped against her, so she starts to bounce from side to side, calming the fussy child almost immediately.

"We need help. Delilah," she directs her attention to the bundle across her chest, "she and I need your help." I didn't need to know her name. This all would have been better without the baby having a damn name.

"Isn't there someone else? Anyone else?"

"Jane, listen to me. That's all I ask. I'm not asking you to ride in on a white horse and scoop us up. I know I need out, and I am trying to come up with something, but I need another person to help me figure it out. I need a fresh pair of eyes."

"Do you realize who I am?" I fan down my body for emphasis. *Take a look at me, Shana. I'm the one he married before you.* "You need to find someone else. A police officer or something."

Shana laughs. "What are they going to do?" She sounds bitter.

"There's no one else. You know Stewart. You've been in a relationship with him. I can't talk to someone else. I—"

"Can't let him find out." She nods. "Who better to talk to than the ex-wife who doesn't ever want to speak to him again?"

"Yeah." She continues bouncing, half out of instinct to quiet the baby and half impatience waiting for my answer. I want to run the other way and tell her to figure it out for her damn self. This isn't my fight. I turn away from her as a sob breaks inside her throat. It stops me.

*Girls stick together.*

Ramona's words haunt me here in aisle five. Is there a clause in that contract? Maybe a part that says unless she screwed your husband and got you tossed out on your ass while she knew it was going to happen. However, I escaped a bad marriage with an abusive man, so who lost in that situation?

"There's a coffee shop ten blocks from here called Mitz. Walk around the store and think about what you're asking of me. If in twenty minutes you still think it's your best idea, then meet me there. If you don't show in an hour, I'll leave, and I don't want you to contact me ever again."

"Okay, I'll be there." There's something horrible inside her voice. It's hope. I turn around and advance on her.

"Listen, Shana. I'm not your friend. I'm not anywhere close to that. I'm doing this only because my conscience won't sit well if I leave a child in the grasp of Stewart's claws. I couldn't care less about you. Know that. Let it sink in. You are asking help from someone who hates you," I seethe. My words hit her hard, like a punch from her husband, but she doesn't falter.

"I understand." She tucks her head in submission. The same position I had to take every time my ex-husband told me that I was worth less than the dirt on the bottom of his shoe. I knew to bow and take it. My stomach churns at the thought of being anything close to that evil.

"Twenty minutes. Wait twenty minutes. Mitz." I say it softer. I don't know what I'm getting myself into, but I know out of all the people in the world I'd rather be like Ramona than Stewart.

# Twelve

"Whoa. I like the new do." It takes a minute for Melinda to recognize me as I'm ordering coffee.

"Thanks," I rush, my mission to make the mean girl at the coffee shop smile forgotten. It's no longer a fun challenge. The challenge now is to have the tile floor open up and swallow me whole so that I don't have to sit across from my ex-husband's mistress-turned-wife. The last time I sat across from her was when I was hiring her to teach Stewart yoga, and I thought it would help him relax. It helped him move on to his new wife. That meeting changed the course of my life.

"Bear claws?" Melinda draws me out of my memory, and I look upon her confused face.

"No, he's not coming today." I flick the ten-dollar bill in my hand. "I mean, yes. She's probably going to be hungry. New baby and all, right?" Melinda doesn't have the answer for me because she doesn't even know what I'm talking about right now.

"What?" Her finger hovers above the cash register button, and her mouth is agape.

"Aren't new moms always hungry?"

"That's the rumor, but I wouldn't know. I don't have kids." She drops her hand to the counter, aware that the decision to purchase bear claws or not is going to take a little longer than expected.

"Neither did I, not for lack of wanting kids. No, my husband had to end that idea." I roll my eyes at the sacrifice I gave.

"I didn't know you were married. That cop?" She inquires.

"No, that's Billy." I wave my hand.

"Oh?" She tries her best not to screw her face up in judgment, but I see it anyway.

"Not like that. I'm divorced. Billy is just a friend. No, I would never do something like that. My ex-husband did that to me. I could never be as heartless as him." I tap the counter. "I'm meeting some girl I hate here today, and I don't know if she'll want a pastry to eat or not. But, seeing as I've already ordered her coffee, I might as well get her something to shove in her fucking face," the words spew from me like verbal diarrhea all over the place. There, I poured on more information than a stranger ever needed to know about me, but some parts of it felt good.

"So, two coffees, two bear claws, and a Xanax for you?" She giggles and punches the buttons.

"If you sell them, throw it in." I rest my head on the counter, holding my cash above it for her to take.

She laughs and snatches my ten-dollar bill. I hear her pop the register drawer open and make change. I raise my head back up. When she hands it back to me, I instinctively dump it in the tip jar. Routine feels good to have at this moment.

"It suits you, you know?" She leans into the display case and grabs two bear claws with her silver tongs, tossing them into small bags.

"The insane ranting?" I take a deep breath. "Crazy looks that good on me?"

"Well," she closes the lid, "that's to be expected of someone like you. Marie tells me you work with Ramona at the motel, so that tells me that you haven't had the best lot in life." She glances my way for confirmation, and I nod. She folds each bag containing a pastry and pushes them across the counter. "But I was talking about the hair."

"Oh." I tug at the bottom of it, still getting used to feeling the air on my neck. Melinda laughs at the action and begins to pour coffee in Styrofoam cups for me. It's then that I notice she's the only one working the counter right now. This must be their slow time of day. I'm never in here around now.

"When you get done with your coffee and bear claw with the girl you hate, tell Ramona I said hi." I grab the cup and almost spill it all over.

"What? You know Ramona?" The only people who know Ramona are the ones who have needed her help. She doesn't make friends outside of that world. "Were you a...?

"Stray?"

"Yeah," I nod.

"Homeless," she shrugs and points to herself. "Or, at least I was once. She helped me. She has a big heart."

"Yeah, and a mouth that could rival ours." I laugh, and Melinda joins in. She waves me off, and I take the coffees and treats away, only to return.

"Shit," I mutter.

"What?" She stops swirling the rag on the counter, cleaning up a spill.

"Can new moms drink coffee?" I glance down at the second cup.

"If they can't, then that ends the idea of me ever wanting to reproduce." She laughs and turns around to the little fridge behind her, grabbing a water bottle. "Here."

"What do I owe you?" I set the coffees on the counter and start to dig in my pocket for more cash.

"Nothing."

"But—"

"You already over-tip, I'm sure you've earned a water." She winks and shoos me away.

I go straight for my habitual seat at the back, the one Billy picked out when we first came here. It's comforting knowing that the outside world cannot peer in and locate you from this location. That's the security I needed that day, meeting Billy sharing the nightmares of the driver. Shana will long for the feeling as well for this challenging conversation. I want it to be a private one, not only for Shana's sake but for my own. I don't want eavesdroppers knowing that I would dare meet with the mistress. It seems against the natural order of things.

I chomp into my bear claw, gnashing my top teeth against my bottom ones. Why did I come here? I should leave and forget this whole thing. I don't want to get involved with anything that concerns Shana. I feel guilty, though. It was my fault that she was even in my life. I was the one who set up a meeting with her, and invited her into my household.

Stewart had just been diagnosed with coronary artery disease, and I, the loving wife, thought it would be a good idea to find ways he could de-stress. I blamed his job for the growing abuse and the new disease. If I could find a way for him to relax, then it would all disappear. I looked at Shana as the way out of those beatings. Little did I know how true that was going to be. I thought she'd teach him yoga and do private lessons with him. Instead, she found herself a new lifestyle worthy of throwing that alternative one away.

Now, she was looking for me to get her out of it. She wants me to provide a new perspective on her situation, but I don't have any. I didn't get out of my marriage with Stewart because I wanted to, I got out because he tossed me aside like garbage. If Shana didn't come along, I'd be there still. I wouldn't have had the courage to leave or even entertain the idea. I never threatened my absence, even at the worst of it all. The money and roof over my head kept me in place. I sacrificed so much for something I never got. I have nothing to tell Shana, but to wait for him to find a mistress that he loves better than her. That's how Leona got out. That's how I got out. And now, that's what Shana needs to do to get out.

I stand up to leave, but just then, the door opens, and the bells overhead chimes alerting me that it's too late to make a clean break out of this situation. Shana is here. I watch as her eyes dart around the room looking for me, and I want to scream for her to stop putting so much faith in people, especially me. She locates my face, so I motion her over and watch as she awkwardly balances an infant car seat in the elbow of her arm.

"Hey, Jane."

"Shana." There's no sense in introductions as if it's a new day. I shake my head. "Sit." She glances down at the car seat as if something is glaringly apparent, and I'm not picking it up.

"Um, where are the highchairs?" She asks.

"She can sit already?" I'm amazed.

"No," she laughs, and it takes everything in me not to throat punch her, "you can turn them upside down, and it will hold the seat."

"Oh. Information that women who don't have children might not be privy to," I bite out. I watch as she ducks her head in embarrassment for not remembering. I point to the corner by the restrooms, and she waddles over that way, retrieving the coveted item.

"I, uh, I got you a coffee and water. I didn't know if you were allowed caffeine." I motion to the contents on the table and sit down in the chair up against the wall. "You know, with the baby and all." I awkwardly scratch the back of my head.

"Thank you. That was very thoughtful of you." She sets the car seat on the nearby table and a giant purse on the chair across from me. I watch as she flips the highchair over and sure as shit, the car seat fits snuggly inside just like she said.

"Well, I'll be damned," I mutter.

"Huh?"

"I got you a bear claw, too, I said." I push the uneaten pastry in its bag toward her. "They're good."

"Thank you, Jane." Her eyes capture mine, and it's the dumbest thing I have ever let happen because I can't ignore now that Shana is human. I can see it there in the way she looks at me and genuinely shows gratitude that I thought to buy her a stupid baked good. I soften against my will—against her mahogany eyes.

She opens the bag and stares at the bear claw. I can hear Shana counting the calories inside her head. I forgot how strenuous it was to be Stewart's wife for a second, but I'm sure he's on her back about losing the baby weight. I have gained a happy ten pounds since the split, blaming most of that on the delicious treats here at Mitz, but I know it was from the freedom to not fear food anymore. Shana adjusts in the seat and mistakes my face for confusion.

"Sorry. I still have to wear this giant pad, and it's uncomfortable," she whispers. She's embarrassed by the natural course her body is taking to heal itself from enduring giving life to another human being — stupid ass Stewart. I try not to put on my team colors for Shana yet, but the fucking shirt feels like it's in the shopping cart, and maybe a size too small as all of this feels uncomfortable.

"No, no, you're fine. Please don't apologize for stuff like that. Stuff that you can't control." I lift my eyebrow to let her know I'm not just talking about her uterus bleeding. She might not be my favorite person in the world, but no one deserves to live a life in fear because of the abuse of the person they love.

She bites into it and moans appreciation for the sweetness that bursts on her tongue.

"We don't have much time, Shana. Your groceries will get too warm, and then Stewart will suspect something. Give me the facts and tell me why you think that I can help you." I approach the situation as Ramona would, straight to the nit-ty-gritty, this being a potential stray for her motel and all.

She looks down at her lap and wipes some icing from the corner of her mouth. She's embarrassed by what she believes to be a lack of strength in herself, unaware of how brave it is telling someone that your loved one abuses you. "I told him the first time that he hit me that I was leaving. He seemed sorry, so I stayed. But—" Delilah makes a noise, and Shana's head shoots toward her.

"He did it again," I finish for her.

She pats the baby's thigh, and it quiets the infant. She nods to me. The confident woman I saw standing in the house when I picked up the trunk is gone. She's nervous about making any noise or having attention drawn to her, something she probably thrived on before Stewart came into her life.

"You signed the prenup?" I know the answer before she bothers to say it. Stewart would never marry without a prenup put in place. He wasn't a fool about love. Everything was business to him.

"Yes," she whispers.

"Oh, well. You go live with your parents until you're steady on your feet." It's as simple as that.

"He'll get joint custody of her." She talks to me but stares at Delilah.

It's *not* as simple as that. It was simple for me because I didn't have children with Stewart. It's the first time I feel a little gratefulness for my empty womb.

"Tell the police about the bruises. You have them on your body now. Take the pictures. Go to them now," I urge her. I push her food toward her. She needs the sweetness. I get to leave and go back to an apartment I made for myself with no Stewart in my life. Shana doesn't.

"I can't." Her voice cracks at the end of the small sentence. Those two words are shattering her insides.

"Why?" I make to rally, tell her to forget the money and leave.

She hesitates, and I watch her eyes get misty. I'm scared to ask. I look over at Delilah.

"Why, Shana?" I make sure to be soft.

"He said he'd hurt her if I do."

I feel the tear fall down my face as it mirrors the one hitting the table on Shana's side.

# Thirteen

"Do you ever think about Stewart?" I chug back my cheap malt beverage and look to my left as Billy hesitates, his lips on the bottle, before ultimately deciding to do the same, letting the liquid slide out of the bottle and into his mouth. He relinquishes the alcohol at the mentioning of my ex-husband's name.

"Is that why you called me out here?" He raises his eyebrow. I can tell it zings a little as he does his best to recover a neutral face. No one with a crush wants to hear about exes and old flames.

"No." I point back inside from my spot on the little balcony. "I wanted you to see the new place, and I like hanging out with you." I may be juggling a lot on my plate now, and I'm not sure a relationship with Billy at this point would be the most fabulous idea, but I can't deny that hearing you are desirable to hang around makes a person feel good, and Billy is a person who deserves to hear it.

"It looks great. You did well for yourself, Jane." He clinks his empty bottle against the full ones still inside the cardboard six-pack container as he places the empty one back into its original slot.

"Yeah," I glance back from the small balcony to the living room space, "I guess I did." I begin peeling the label on my Bahama Mama-flavored drink.

"I honestly thought you'd move in with Ramona for good. I've never seen her get along with someone so well." He chuckles over the idea of Ramona getting along with anyone. She's a feisty old lady with a heart of gold caged up inside, but most people don't understand that about her. She doesn't let them in or outwardly show good humor.

"No. She's got her own life and doesn't need me burdening her," I stuff the label inside the empty bottle and return it to the six-pack container. "Besides, I made room for another woman who needs her help. Paige will be able to use the room now."

"You always think about others." He cracks open another bottle. It doesn't sound like a compliment when it falls from his lips, and I want to press him further.

"Wha—"

"—So, what did you want to talk about, Stewart-wise?" He interrupts.

I look up from the label I'm peeling on the next bottle to discover my companion has downed the next bottle in one go. He's less thrilled about the prospect of this conversation than I am. Billy used to be friends with Stewart, and their falling out no doubt created problems for Billy. Stewart is a powerful man in town, and he could be your best pal or worst enemy if you crossed him.

"You knew he hit me, didn't you?" I watch him under close inspection. I see every emotion as it hits his face. The embarrassment that he's found out, the sadness that he didn't do more, and the fear that whatever friendship we have formed has ended here and now with his admission.

"I had a feeling that he did, and that night, the last dinner party I came to... well, I knew." I watch the bob of his Adam's apple as he swallows the words down hard. They must taste disgusting.

"Because of the bruise on my arm?"

"Yeah, I had seen enough of those bruises in my line of work to know how it got there." He looks down at the six-pack, but all the bottles are gone. I hand him mine, which he gladly accepts.

"You argued with him, didn't you? I heard you two when I was out in the hallway. That was brave."

He scoffs as the tip of the bottle touches his bottom lip. "Brave?" He takes a languid sip. "If I were brave, I would have gotten you out of that situation right then and there." He doesn't talk to me; he's in a conversation with himself, scolding the actions of a man he once accepted as his friend.

"It's the most anyone has done for me in that situation." That hurts to say out loud, but not nearly as bad as what I need to say. "I should have tried to do something more for myself. I should have told someone. I knew it was bad and getting out of control, but I would shove that reasoning down to the back of my mind and tell myself lies until I tricked myself into believing them."

Billy hands me back the bottle, and I take a swig, wishing for something stronger than a fucking Bahama Mama. It pains me now, being on the outside, still questioning if any action would have helped while I was in the marriage. It hurts knowing I'd still be accepting that kind of behavior because I didn't believe I deserved better. It's odd to think of this life, struggling to make sure my bills are paid on time and pinching pennies, is more prosperous than a life in a mansion. This is what living is supposed to feel like. Shana is stuck in the mansion that she unwittingly put herself in, believing that it would be a better life if she took my place.

"You got me out of the situation with the driver." He doesn't respond. "Stewart accused you of being infatuated with me." Perhaps the alcohol, albeit a small percentage, makes my lips braver.

"That he did," Billy teases, the mood lightening a hair. The fear that I'll be lost to him fades from his eyes. Only a trace remains.

"Were you?"

"I am."

"You are? Hmm." I try to hide my grin, but it's no use. I look over to see Billy smiling as well.

"So..."

"So."

"Good God, I feel like a dumbass teenager." I sip the bottle again.

"Are you infatuated with me, Jane?" There's vulnerability behind his eyes, and it's sweet and kind. All the things that my relationship with Stewart wasn't after our wedding day. The things that I had been tricked into believing they would be.

"Yes," I whisper, terrified to admit my own feelings aloud.

"So, are we dating?"

"What a lousy way to ask me, Billy." He just laughs in response. I reach out my hand, and he instinctively takes it. It's the first time we've held hands, and the feeling is natural and soothing. It's as if our fingers were meant to be conjoined like this from the dawning of time. We sit in the calm silence until the nagging feeling in my heart begs me to speak again.

"He's going to do it to her, too, Billy." I feel the tears well up in my eyes. I hate that this is weighing heavily on my mind. But, if Billy still carries the burden of what he didn't do three years later, then I know I won't forgive myself for not doing a damn thing for Shana, no matter what she did to me. It doesn't matter what someone does wrong to you; how you react is a reflection of your character, not theirs. I don't want to be someone who looked away.

"Yeah." His whisper is carried to my ears on the breeze of the evening.

"Can I do anything about the bruises he put on me?"

Billy stands suddenly, screeching the chair across the worn wood, dropping my hand. "No." He stands above me, pointing his finger down at me as if scolding a child. "No, Jane." I stare up, but the fight falls from him as quickly as it came. "I'm sorry, I didn't mean to yell." He scrubs his face and looks out over the small balcony. Silence falls over him.

A few trees give the back portion of the apartment complex a feeling of being near the countryside even though there are stores and bustle on the front side. I wanted to move farther away from the city, but it didn't make sense when the only thing I have is Ramona and the motel. I managed to move ten minutes away, at least. And the faux woodlands behind the building helps soothe the ache of lacking running space. Perhaps I could put a treadmill back here. I know for sure that I won't go running outside again, but maybe if I can trick myself the way the apartment complex tries to fool its occupants, I'll feel better.

"You can't." He rubs his forehead before resting that hand over his mouth and staring out at the view breaking the quiet. I follow his gaze, allowing him time to digest what I hadn't entirely swallowed today. We know Shana is in the hands of a monster, and we can't do a damn thing about it, but be thankful we are free from him.

"Jane," Billy calls my attention back to his face. He looks much older than thirty-three, six years younger than I am. He holds himself like a wise older man. The pain of everything he knows and has seen has caused the creases near his eyes to dig deeper under the skin and expose the shock to the naked eye. Hazards of the job, I suppose.

"Billy. He's going to hurt her. What if he hurts that baby?" A tear rolls down my cheek.

Billy puffs out a sigh and slams his body down in the chair, placing his head between his knees. I put my hand out to pat his back but draw it back. It wouldn't help Billy, and I'm not sure that my touch is what he needs at this moment when I seem to be the catalyst for his mood.

"You only see the good in people, Jane. I've never met anyone like you." He peers up at me, and I'm still not sure if that's a compliment, or if he's cursing me.

"There's no sense in always looking for the worst in people, Billy. You'll always find both, so why not look for the better of the two?"

He shrugs and leans back into the chair. "You shouldn't underestimate the evil that lurks beneath the surface of humans. Sometimes, it's much stronger than the good and harder to kill." Billy's job doesn't afford him an open-heart mindset. He sees too much of the cruelty that humans have for each other. "Why? Why, Jane? Why even try to get involved?"

"I didn't say I was getting involved. It's a thought I had today. A thought I've had every day since I bumped into her at the grocery store." I feel embarrassed. Standing up for others shouldn't be an annoyance, should it?

"Leave it alone, Jane. Do you hear me?"

I nod.

With that, and no alcohol left to drink, Billy stands to make his exit. "Do me a favor, please." His voice is pained and cuts through the night air. I look up at him, and I don't tell him, but there isn't much that I wouldn't do for Billy.

"What?" I whisper, terrified to find out what's causing the worry on his face.

"Don't go up against Stewart. You have enough on your plate, and you'll lose. Let Shana figure out if she wants to leave or not." He kisses my forehead before walking out of the apartment. I hear the slam of the front door.

"She said she does," I whisper to the night air.

# Fourteen

"**D**id you talk to your cop boyfriend?" Ramona's rasp is too much to handle before my morning coffee today. I skipped Mitz again to appease Billy. I can tell that last night, I might have gone too far asking about Stewart. Billy has yet to text me this morning. He always makes sure to check in when he wakes up.

I press the side of the phone, lighting up the screen. There's still nothing from here. I hadn't realized the loss of Stewart's friendship caused so much distress in Billy's life. No doubt, Stewart made Billy's life after breaking off association with him a living hell.

"Yeah, I talked to him last night." I pour coffee from the office machine into a small cup. Billy and I are sort of dating now, so I guess I can't yell at Ramona anymore about her nicknames, although my new boyfriend is ignoring me this morning.

I type out a quick good morning message and hit send. I'm not a child, so I can be the first one to break the silence.

"Did you tell him why you dyed your hair since you won't tell me?" Ramona cuts into my thoughts.

"I did tell you." I glare toward her before pulling my attention back to the phone— nothing.

"So, you told him the same lies?"

"Lord help me, Ramona, but you need to let a person drink some coffee before you start in on them." I tenderly put my lips to the brim of the cup to slurp the hot liquid. My phone lights up.

***Good morning. How are you today? Bahama Mamas are not my favorite. My stomach hurts today.***

I breathe a sigh of relief. He's not mad after all, just dealing with a stomachache. I set my phone aside and sip my coffee again.

"Slept in again today?" She eyes me up and down.

"Yup," I draw out.

"Liar."

I lounge back with my cup and shrug at her. I'm taking it black this morning without the usual amount of sugar I pour inside to sweeten the taste. Hopefully, it will seep straight into my bloodstream and kick me into gear. I didn't sleep well last night — Shana's words running over and over in my head.

"Wait? You didn't yell at me." Ramona screeches. I nearly spill the hot liquid all over my legs as I bolt upright.

"Yell at you about what?" I click the keyboard and glance over with a dead giveaway smile when I realize that she's talking about calling Billy my boyfriend.

"Well, I'll be damned. He finally made a move." She slaps her knee.

"Followed by storming out of my apartment," I sigh.

"What?"

"Ramona, have you ever taken in a woman that you hate?" I ignore her question. I don't want to rehash the disagreement with Billy if he's texting me normally this morning.

"I don't like a lot of people, Jane. You all eventually get on my nerves, especially when you lie." She wobbles over to the door and pushes it open, heading outside. I get up from the computer and follow as I have most mornings for months now. It's time to start the cleaning rounds.

"No, I mean a woman you hated that came to you for help."

"I've never known any of the women I've helped before they came to me. As I said, I don't like a lot of people." She crams the key into the maintenance closet and produces the cleaning cart. I set my coffee down on top and begin doing a quick inventory to make sure we have all the supplies we need for the day.

"Would you?"

"Depends," she sighs. "Why do I hate her?"

"She screwed you over in the past." I stare at the shelf on the cart with much more focus than necessary to avoid her hawk-like eyes attempting to read my thoughts. *Just answer the question, Ramona.*

"Well, that's on God to judge. Unless she killed a family member, I suppose I would help her." Ramona is lying. She'd help the murderer, too. So, that settles it. I will get involved with Shana and start collecting my own strays. Speaking of strays...

"Where's Paige?" I ask.

"Bambi said she had business to attend to today." Ramona air quotes the word business to enunciate that she doesn't buy the line one bit. It's hard to get anything past her suspicious thinking.

"Why are you hellbent on calling her that?" I grab a few extra rolls of toilet paper and stuff them in the cart, deeming the supplies sufficient for the day. Ramona shuts the door and locks it behind us.

"Because she is." She stands next to the cart designated for the bottom level rooms, but she refuses to push it when I'm much younger and able to do so without hurting my back. I learned that on day two.

"What the hell happened with the first girl that you called Bambi?" I give the cart a shove, and Ramona taps on the side for me to stop when we've come to our first room.

"Well, she's dead now." Ramona knocks on the first door.

"Housekeeping," I shout out before she slides the key into the lock.

"That's what I fear is going to happen to the baby," I mumble.

"The what?" Ramona yanks the cart into the doorway, propping the front door open with it.

"What?" I play dumb, but the eyebrow raise I receive tells me it was the wrong move.

"The baby?"

"Uh."

"That's it. Spill. You got new hair, and I know damn well it wasn't a change you made for style. Don't give me that shit again, kid. Give me the truth. If you're in some kind of trouble that could make its way here, you need to tell me." I pat the gun in the waistband of my khakis at the sound of her words.

"I was followed. I went running, and this car followed me. I lost him, but I kept thinking that it was the driver from the car the day I came here, so I dyed my hair when I got home and got it cut. Billy said that madman is still out there, trying to assault women that look like me. I'm terrified, Ramona, absolutely terrified." I shudder.

"That makes sense." She bobs her head. "I thought you were dealing with drugs or something, honestly." I glare at her in response.

"You don't know me, do you? I would never do such a thing."

"I do, but I've seen so many people change that I don't make the mistake of pretending to know anyone a hundred percent." She waves her hand for me to continue and perches on the edge of the bed in the room. "That explains your hair and your lie to me, but that doesn't explain the baby comment just now."

"Well, I bumped into Shana a while back at the grocery store. Remember, I told you?"

"Yes, the girl your ex-husband kicked you out for?" I nod.

"Well, she was pregnant with his kid. You remember?"

"Yeah. I'm old, not senile. Get on with it. I know all of this already." I watch her fingers tap her shirt pocket. She's longing for a cigarette right now.

"The baby was in the cart when I bumped into her at the store. Anyway, nothing happened because I darted out of there as fast as I could, but I bumped into her again there. I let her talk, and she admitted that Stewart hits her and then asked me what she should do."

"And you said?"

"I told her to pray that his heart gives out soon." I can't tell if Ramona is proud of my words or ashamed that I could sound so heartless.

"And?" She knows there's more.

"And, I sort of went back there after I dyed my hair to see if I could observe her without her knowing it was me."

"Stalk her," Ramona corrects.

"That's a bit heavy," I defend.

"How many days did you go before she showed up?" There's a hint of amusement on the old lady's face.

"Three," I whisper. "Okay, okay, I stalked her." A growl escapes the back of my throat.

"Don't lie, kid. I'll catch it every damn time."

"Yeah, I noticed." I grab the bathroom caddy from the cart and linger in front of her, wishing the conversation was over. "Anyway, Shana was looking for me."

"You think, or you know?"

"I know. She thinks I'm the only one who can help her get out. Stewart has threatened to hurt the baby if she leaves. I can't get it out of my head. What am I supposed to do?" I plead. Ramona always has the answers.

"That's a tough one, kid. I can see why your heart is pulled in that direction." She slaps her knee and begins to stand up and strip the bed without saying another word. I set the caddy back down on the cart.

"That's it?" I'm stunned. Out of all the people in the world, I thought Ramona would be the one to clear my head. I walk over the bed and match her actions on the other side.

"That's it," she confirms. Of all the words I imagined coming from Ramona, I didn't picture those. I figured she'd open her doors like she always has since she doesn't know Shana personally and have a history with her. At the very least, I figured that she'd want to gossip about it.

"She's in trouble, Ramona. Couldn't you hide them here? There's plenty of space." I stuff the old sheets into the laundry bag on the cart.

She shakes her head with vigor against the whole idea.

"You've done it before. You've helped me. I wouldn't ask for her if I didn't think she needed the help. You have no idea what Stewart is like when he's mad. I see it now that I'm on the other side." I want to give this problem away, away to someone who knows how to handle it better.

"No." She pushes past me to grab the bedding from the cart. Her stern tone signals that she'd like it to be the end of the discussion, but she nursed my ability to stand up for myself back to full health, and I'm not backing down any time soon.

"You told me about that woman from Dallas, who came up here and got married to Mr. Right only to find out that he had another wife. You housed her and her baby here while she went through a tough time, and her parents wouldn't let her come back."

"Good God. Why do you listen to me when I talk?" She fluffs a folded pillowcase out before taking a pillow under her chin and shimmying it inside the pink covering. She growls when she eyes my face, and she slams the pillow on her side of the bed.

"Am I not supposed to? In that case, it might help us both if you finally just shut the hell up, Ramona." I laugh as I fluff my side of the pillows into their place. Like a well-oiled machine, Ramona and I flip the comforter over the cushions and tuck hard with a karate chop motion underneath them.

"I don't tell you those things so that you'll hold them against me when they benefit you and not me." She checks the nightstand on her side for garbage, and I do the same.

"Ramona," I groan. "I'm not holding it against you."

"She can't stay here, Jane." She puffs at the floor and looks at me. "I know you want to do what's good, but it sounds like you're stupid, and I warned you against being stupid." So, she does have an opinion in this after all.

"How?" There was nothing stupid about trying to save the life of a child. Ramona is stubborn. She doesn't want to take on the task of two more mouths to feed, or training Shana, or dealing with a baby. What she doesn't see is that I will be there to help. Every step of the way, I will be here. This won't be a rehabilitation program that Ramona will have to see through by herself, but I need her guidance. I need her to take the lead.

"You have empty rooms. It's perfect." I beg.

"You just got out of that mess, and from what you're sharing with me now and what you looked like the day you arrived here, it was a pretty dangerous situation. Now, you want to jump back in." She wags her finger at me and moves closer.

"I was attacked that day. You can't say that all those bruises were from Stewart. Yes, he is a volatile man, but that's all reason enough to help her get out," I protest.

"You lucked out of that house, Jane. Men like that don't easily let someone go that they're used to controlling and having power over. You got so lucky. So many women in that position don't get as lucky. If you go back there in any shape or form, you're going to get yourself into trouble." She rips the sheets off the floor and stomps over to the cart before shoving them deep into the dirty laundry bag.

"I can't leave her, Ramona. I've tried to tell myself to do it, believe me, but I can't convince myself to drop it. I don't want to be helping my ex-husband's mistress-now-wife, but I can't tell myself to look away from it. So many people looked away from me when I was in that situation."

"I don't get it, Jane. She screwed your husband. She knew that he was planning on dumping you on your ass without your knowledge of the divorce papers, and she encouraged it. Matter of fact, she packed her fucking bags in that two-weeks' time that you were oblivious to it and had them ready to move into the mansion the same night that your ass hit the pavement. Then, she went straight to work, decorating her love child's room in your house. She didn't spend one second on her guilt. Why would you help a woman like that? How can you stand here and fight for her to be spared the life that she chose? She wanted it. She cultivated, manipulated, and worked her way into that life, a life that wasn't hers. She could quickly turn on you, looking out only for herself. Say she gets out, after a taste of that rich bitch life, what's to say she doesn't get tired of working for her money and blame the whole thing on you so she can go back? How do you see good in her? How can you trust her?"

I know the exhaustion behind Ramona's eyes. She wants me to see her side, see what is so blatantly clear. It's harder to see the good in people, even harder to trust and believe in that slim light, but I know one pure life.

"She has a baby, Ramona. A baby. An innocent life that he could flip his switch on. Kids mess up things, they break expensive shit, and they're loud. Those are all the things that Stewart hates. He's going to hurt her one day, I know it. I feel it in my bones." I grab onto her shoulders and force her to look up into my face. "I can't let that happen. I can't. If it all comes down on me, so be it, but I won't sleep another night in *my* life if I turn my back on that child."

"She's not strong enough, Jane. Shana is not strong enough." I let her shoulders go, and she paces about the room.

"We can make her strong, Ramona. We can teach her. You taught me. I know you can help her."

"No, kid." She advances on me until her small stature is taking over my personal space, and I feel intimidated. "That's where you're wrong. Dead wrong. Strength isn't something that lives inside of everyone the same. It has limitations. Every person has their limit before strength turns itself over and makes them sick in the mind. Strength is a weakness to some."

"What are you talking about? Strength is strength. Everyone can be strong."

Ramona's shoulders sag, and she turns away from me until her legs meet the chair in the corner of the room. She throws herself down, staring out the picture window for what feels like an eternity before allowing herself to speak again.

"I took in a girl before you. Bright little thing, but she had the fucking eyes of Bambi. Bambi. That's what she was, and I looked past it, figured I could make her strong. I believed like you that everyone had the same chance at achieving strength," she whispers, swallowing hard. "She had a man begging her to come back with him. He was an addict, and he sure liked to hit when he couldn't have his fix. She told him no. She found her strength and told him no. I was so damn proud of her."

"What happened?" I sit down on the bed.

"When she said no to him, something inside of her changed. It was anti-climactic for her to say no. It wasn't enough to say no to the person that took away her house, her car, her job, her money, her family life; she expected a better feeling than what she got. She thought that moment was going to be so huge you could feel it on Mars. Maybe she believed that it would bring her peace about all the things she lost and what she went through, but it didn't. She wanted revenge." She turns toward me. "Strength has its limitations. It's not the same in everyone. And let me tell you, I've only heard of Shana, and she sounds like she has Bambi's eyes."

"What did the woman do?" I ask. She waves me off.

"Ramona?" I call as she's walking out the door, pushing the cart to the storage room. "What did she do?" I scream.

That night as I left the motel, a newspaper article about a woman shooting six meth addicts before turning the gun on herself had found its way to my windshield. Shana isn't this woman, though, and I know she has the strength inside her to find peace being with Delilah. If Ramona doesn't take it on, I'll have to do it myself.

# Fifteen

I wait in the grocery store until I hear a baby's coo coming around the aisle. After our first talk, I left Shana at the coffee shop without so much as a goodbye. I got up and walked out. It was too much. Taking on two more lives was a lot when I barely have my shit put back together. I have a maniac out there wanting to finish off what he tried to do months ago. He's spending his days hunting me down, and yet, it feels small in comparison to the monster Shana is living with inside that mansion. So, I braved the light of day and came here to find her.

I turn into the aisle from my spot at the end cap, and Shana spots me almost immediately.

"Sha—"

"Jane. I didn't think I'd see you again," Shana smiles before realizing that our strange relationship is not a friendship.

I raise my chin in greeting and take up a silent pace beside her shopping cart, my confidence momentarily shattered. I don't long to be a fake person. There is no companionship amongst Shana, only the joint effort to fight a monster. She pushes along for the next three aisles without a word. I'm the first to break our silence beside the canned beans when I've sorted out my speech.

"I've tried to figure it out, Shana. It's a dead-end everywhere you turn—"

"Oh, that's okay, Jane. I came here today to tell you to forget about what I said." I note a sparkle to her smile, but she's still looking at me with dead eyes.

"What? How the fuck can a person forget that?" There's agitation inside of me. I came here today to tell her that I'm ready to help her, and she keeps interrupting me. "Shana. Listen. We will find a way out. I just haven't found it yet."

"It won't happen again. Stewart and I talked about it, and he said he's going to start therapy. Everything's fine." She runs her hand down the wrap around the front, soothing Delilah inside. Her toothy smile is full of hope and faith. It's convincing, but I'm not a damn idiot anymore.

"You believed that horse shit?" A woman down at the end of the aisle perks up from the can of peas she is holding. I shoot the woman a death stare before steering Shana into the next aisle where we can have a little privacy.

"Shana, that's a line of bullshit, and what's worse is you know it," I hiss under my breath. I want to shake her. How can she be the same woman who was standing before me just days ago asking for help to get out of her marriage? She sat across from me in the coffee shop so strong and sure of herself. Her mind was made up. I saw no hesitation when she admitted that she needed help. For God's sake, she hunted me down. Me, Stewart's ex-wife.

"It's not, Jane. He means it." To an untrained ear, her words persuasive and beautiful, but to the ex-wife of Stewart Miller, they sound like chocolate-coated horse manure being sold as Godiva, and I won't buy that shit.

"All right," I say, leaning against the shelf behind me, "I'll bite. Why does he mean it this time, Shana?" My words are laced with venom and irritation. I've lost sleep to aid my enemy, and now she stands before me expecting me to forget the effort.

"Not that it's any of your business or that I should expose the sensitive human side of my husband to you, but he cried, Jane. All right?" She flicks her head with emphasis. "He broke down when I brought up the abuse. He knows he needs to get help, and he's going to do just that. I don't think it's fair of me to cast him aside when he understands he's making a mistake, and he's willing to fix it," she snips.

Stewart Miller has cried more fake tears than any actor I've ever seen on the big screen, and I've heard the line about therapy more than a dozen times, yet I never saw a medical bill for it come in the mail. He bought himself some more time and more of Shana's loyalty with the same old song and dance I've seen performed too many times.

*"Jane, I'm so sorry for hurting you. I don't know what I was thinking. I get so mad sometimes, and I can't see past it — I blackout. I don't even know what I'm doing until it's done. I never meant to hurt you. This time I hurt you worse than I ever did before. Now, we can't have children, and it's all my fault. I'm sorry. Please don't leave me, Jane. I know I need help. I'm starting therapy tomorrow. I have an appointment, my love. I'm going to be the man that you deserve."*

I bought it. With roses in vases all over the house, and a fresh surgery scar on my lower abdomen, I ate every word up. He promised me change. He assured me that he knew it was all his fault that we couldn't have children. He even went so far as to tell me that we could adopt. Stewart Miller had finally hit the level where he was going to change. I had made it through the storm.

The next time he raised his hand at me, the real truth was laid out.

*"You're the reason I won't have a son to carry on my name. I gave up a good wife that I didn't have to hit for you, a worthless piece of shit."*

I turn toward the end of the aisle and start to walk away from Shana, away from the lies of Stewart that I can still hear to this day ringing inside my head. I can't leave the scar that he's placed on my body, but I sure can leave the new wife he's fooling.

"Jane," she calls.

"What? What, Shana? What do you want from me?" I step close, putting my face only inches away from her own.

"I want you to understand."

"Understand what? Why are you focusing your energy on my opinion of your life?"

"I don't know. I figured since I told you what happened that I should tell you not to worry about it." She shrugs.

"When you find out that the bottle you've been drinking is nothing but lies, remember that I told you so, Shana. Stewart Miller doesn't give a shit about you or that baby. He wants to hurt you and keep you under his thumb until he finds someone younger and dumber than you to fill your shoes. He'll grow bored of you. See, he doesn't care for obedience. Sure, you think that if you could just learn to do what he wants without him needing to yell that he'll stop raising his hand. You think if you master not pissing him off that you'll live harmoniously. Let me let you in on a little secret, Shana." I lean in close to her ear and watch the goose-pimples form on her shoulder. "There is no endpoint."

"Why do you root for him to fail?" The brainwashing from a master falls from her lips.

"I don't root for him to fail, Shana. I was rooting for you to get the fuck out and save the life of your daughter." She wraps both of her arms around the bundle on her chest as I back up from them. Her instinct to protect Delilah is strong. If only she would listen to that feeling when it comes to her husband.

"Forget it." I sigh. "Stay away from me, Shana."

"Jane, don't be like that just because he didn't get better for you. You should be happy that he's finally getting the help he needs."

"Yeah." I bite my tongue to keep from taking a sledgehammer to her pretty little dollhouse dreams.

"I'm sorry he didn't turn out to be the monster you wanted him to be in your story. He loves me. He loves Delilah. We are a family. We may not have come together in the best way, but it's love, Jane. It is true love."

"Are you convincing me, or yourself, Shana?" I raise my eyebrow in question as I turn on my heels to leave again.

"You'll see, Jane," she yells to my retreating back. "You'll see."

"Yeah, Shana, unfortunately, you will see," I mutter under my breath.

# Sixteen

"Two days. You disappear for two days, child, and you think you can pop back up without any explanation?" I walk into the office to overhear a tongue lashing being handed out by Ramona with Paige on the receiving end. Internally, I groan. This is not what I wanted to walk into this morning on only a few hours of sleep.

"I'm a grown adult," Paige yells back, and it stops me in my tracks. I've never heard her voice get over the decimal set for a mouse. I look over and see a different Paige than the one I'm used to seeing. Her hair is greasy, matted to the right side of her face. Her makeup is smeared and looks old as her eyeshadow runs down below her eyes. Wherever she was, she wasn't concerned about bathing.

"You sure are, and grown adults don't miss work without letting their bosses know. Jane had to pick up your slack." She motions to me, and I hold both of my hands up in surrender. Leave me out of this. I don't want any more drama with women. Helping others, even entertaining the thought, is not for me anymore.

I reach out to the coffee pot to fix a cup before removing my purse and getting to work. If this argument is any indication for the day ahead, I need to be caffeinated.

"I'm sorry, Jane," Paige spits out with anger.

"Whoa. Whoa." I place the carafe back on the warmer and lean against the wall for support. "I didn't start anything with you, so there is no need to get snippy with me." I stare at Paige.

"Sorry," she says softer. In the time she's been living at the motel, I've never taken to raising my voice toward her. "I'm very sorry, Janey." She's the only one I let slip with the nickname.

"No problem, Paige." I sit down in the computer chair and try to start the day, but Ramona isn't close to done.

"Just like that?" Ramona starts to pop her attitude with me, and Paige is thankful for the break in interrogation.

"She said she was sorry, Ramona, and I accept the apology. I'm not about to belittle or embarrass her by riding her ass any further. For what?" I lift my eyebrow at her.

"That's not what I'm doing here," Ramona yells.

"Isn't it?" Paige shouts, drawing attention back to her.

"Where were you?" Ramona slams her hands on her hips so hard that one of her acrylic nails pops off and lands on the floor near the desk. For the first time since I walked in on the argument, Paige tries to fix her hair and appearance, hoping to look a little bit more presentable in front of Ramona and me.

"You aren't my mother, Ramona. I was out. I had some stuff that needed to get done."

"What kind of stuff?" I can hear the air quotes without even looking at Ramona. I turn to the computer.

"What the hell? Did she give you this much shit when you started?" I know she directs the question at me, but I'm not turning around to acknowledge it. Paige wants a defender when she needs to stand for herself.

"Jane never ran off for two days when she started," Ramona scolds. She does sound like a mother, a worried one, but Paige doesn't see it as a kind thing. She considers Ramona as another person trying to control her.

"I had to take care of some business is all." Paige tries to rephrase her answer, but Ramona is well aware of that trick.

"Drug business?"

"No," the answer is low.

"Let me see your arm?" Ramona asks. I spin around in the chair.

"Ramona, let her be. She's trying. She came back." Paige looks at me like I'm her savior, the same way Shana dared to look at me when she asked for help. My heart lurches forward at her. Shana's request for assistance opened a portal in my soul, and now I can't push myself to walk away from someone in need.

"I can't help you if I don't know what you're using." Ramona doesn't look away from Paige.

"Show her," I encourage. I note that Paige is wearing a long sleeve shirt on a rather hot day. Even the office's air conditioning running doesn't stop the heat from getting inside. Ramona might be on to something.

"We can help you, Paige. We aren't going to call the cops or put you out on the streets. We want to help you so that you can get clean and get on to a better life, the same kind of life that you talked about having when you came here." I'm softer than Ramona, and Paige favors me. We are on the precipice of an intervention, and I'm terrified she'll run the other way if we make any sudden movements in the office.

"Okay," she whispers. She pulls her sleeve up to expose needle marks on her right arm. Shit. It's bad. She's taken her two days and gone on a binge, littering her arm with marks of drug use. It looks like she didn't spend a single hour free from sticking her arm with a syringe full of poison. Damn. She's in deep, and I'm not sure we can get her out without getting someone else involved.

"All right, child, all right." Ramona motions for her to push her sleeve down. "Do you want to kick this habit?"

"Yes, ma'am. I'm sorry." Tears hit the ground where Paige stands.

"Don't apologize to me, child. Apologize to yourself. Now, let's get you to your room and get you clean. I have a call to make." Ramona moves to wrap an arm around Paige's shoulder, but she draws away in panic.

"You said you weren't going to call the cops," she flings her body to the wall like an animal caught in a cage, trying to find a way out.

"We aren't," I repeat, not sure if that's Ramona's plan or not. All I know is that we need to get Paige calmed down.

"I know a lady that has training in withdrawal from the shit you're on. I don't want you going this cold turkey. It's too dangerous. She won't speak a word to anyone. She's a helper just like Jane and me." Ramona walks softly with her arms outstretched toward Paige. "It's going to be okay, child. We're going to get you help."

This eases Paige's mind and mine. She climbs down off the couch and allows Ramona to place her arm around her. I can tell it's the first tender touch that Paige has felt in a long time.

"It's okay, child. It's going to be okay." I hear Ramona whispering to her over and over again as they stand in an embrace, and it reminds me of my first week here, curled up on the couch crying over my lost life and the nightmares.

*"It's okay, kid. He can't hurt you anymore, and that driver won't be able to touch you here. You're safe. I promise you."*

It was the first time in my entire life that I felt secure. The nightmares lessened until her words took over, and I could finally breathe and look at the future with hope. Ramona doesn't stop until her promises are fulfilled. She'll get Paige clean and help her gain a new life without the drugs. She is a mother with no children of her own, but probably several dozen who love her like one.

"Jane," Ramona cuts into my thoughts, "call Greta, her number's in the top drawer, and tell her to come to Paige's room when she gets here."

"Yes, Ramona." I reach for the desk, set to help in any way.

"Can you clean the rooms for today?"

"I got it. Don't worry about it." We speak softly as Paige's sobs fill the space.

"Thanks, kid." She winks at me and takes Paige out of the office.

I push back in the chair, pulling my knees into my chest. Ramona didn't give up on Paige when she went back to the lifestyle that she had become accustomed to living. She didn't drop her and wash her hands clean. She held out with the patience of Job for Paige to come around. Perhaps, I shouldn't have been so eager to drop Shana. Stewart knows her to manipulate her. Fuck, he's had enough practice doing it to me.

I climb out of the chair and head toward the door to start cleaning the rooms. One thing is for sure; I'll be checking out Billy's gym after I get done with work.

# Seventeen

"Jane Voss." I give my name to the lady at the front desk. She wipes her glasses off again before reapplying the spectacles to her face and trying to find my name in the computer once again. "It's under the membership of Billy Voss, I do believe."

"Oh, okay, dear." She bites her lip and stares into the screen before her. "I'm new here, so I'm not quite sure how this whole thing works." She giggles at herself. I oblige her with a friendly smile, even though I want to scream for her to hurry up and call a coworker because I need to run. There's a crawling feeling inside my skin, begging to be worked out. I won't dare run outside again and risk the chance of being followed, but running inside is proving to be difficult as well.

"That's fine, take your time," I lie. It's not fine, and I would very much like her to admit defeat and call for help, but everyone deserves a chance.

"Perhaps if I search his name, I'll find it." She's not even talking to me, rather thinking out loud.

Oh, heaven help me! I turn my head around, pretending to take in my new gym when I'm actually trying to catch the eye of another worker to come and help this woman. There's no one in sight. It must be a skeleton crew hour here.

"Ah, there you are." She beams with pride. I smile back at her, instantly guilty for having given her a hard time in my mind. *Be like Ramona, Jane. Try some patience.*

"Oh, good. So, I can go on up to the treadmills, then?" I point to the faraway destination that I've been trying to reach for the last twenty minutes of standing here.

"Yes, dear, go on up." She clicks the mouse a few more times. "Oh wait, I need to give you a card." She pushes her glasses up as she tries to read the screen of the computer. "Now, how do I do that?"

"How about I go up, get a good run in while you do that?" I've had enough. "I hate making you feel pressure while I'm standing here. I'm sure it's easier without me hovering."

"Of course, dear, of course." She likes the sound of that better, no doubt feeling stressed from having my eyes burn into the side of her skull.

"Thank you so very much." I take off before she can call me back. I'm already dressed to run, so I take the stairs to the galley that holds the treadmills two at a time, no need to stop at a locker. All I need is my kind of therapy to clear my mind.

"Finally," I mutter as I reach the threshold.

I locate a treadmill far from other runners. I don't want a nosey neighbor trying to start up a conversation. Since the attack, I much prefer to keep my distance from people. Billy tells me it's safer this way, but I admit it feels lonely. If only I could have found a way to deflect any unwanted attention and stalking from Shana, then I wouldn't need to hit the treadmills this evening.

I've never been a runner who listened to music, but with all the thoughts bumbling about in my head, I'm starting to think looking into buying an MP3 player wouldn't be such a bad idea. I crank my neck around, loosening up before taking to the belt of the treadmill.

"Hey." I feel a hand on my lower back as a man whispers in my ear. My body seizes, finger lingering near the incline button on the machine. That voice, I know it. My arm reacts on its own, flying to the left of me, allowing the side of my palm to connect with the creep's neck. I spring off to the right of the treadmill, putting space in between us.

"Shit," Billy coughs out.

"Fuck! Billy, I'm so sorry." I clasp my hands over my mouth as my boyfriend doubles over in pain by the other side of my treadmill. I jump over, landing next to his side.

He waves his hand for me to give him a minute.

"I didn't know it was you. I thought—"

"Don't worry," he clears his throat, "it's okay." His voice is hoarse and painful.

"Are you sure? I think I tried to break your windpipe." I duck my head down closer to his neck for further inspection, but he covers it up in a protective motion.

"Back off, woman. I'm in pain already, don't insult my pride." I can't help but chuckle.

"I'm so sorry." I kiss his cheek. "I thought you were a creeper or that guy from the car," I cover my eyes. "Do you hate me?"

"No. Of course not." His voice is slowly returning as he coughs again.

"Are you sure?" I peek out between my first and middle fingers on my right hand. He's fighting the smile on his face. I possibly damaged his windpipe, and he's laughing at me.

"I know not to sneak up on you next time." He laughs and mounts the treadmill next to mine. "I'm glad to have a workout partner tonight, though. Even if you did kick my ass as a warm-up."

"Oh? Should we sign up for Judo, or should we just run?" I karate chop the air for emphasis.

"Let's stick to running." He rubs his throat, "I think you'll kick my ass again if I choose Judo. One ass-whooping a night is sufficient enough."

"Good idea," I chuckle. I watch Billy tap the buttons on his treadmill, and I hear the machine beneath him come to life. I hit the power button on my own device and start the pace of my jog.

"So, how was your day? You seemed tense downstairs."

"You were watching me, and you didn't come to help?" I scold, and playful raise my karate chopping hand to him as my breath begins to quicken.

"I couldn't help it. You look so cute when you're flustered. I wanted to watch." He waves his white gym towel in surrender.

"Man, it was tougher to get in here than Fort Knox with that lady running the desk. I thought I wasn't going to get in, and I need the run." I crank the speed up on the treadmill and increase the incline. The more my legs burn, the better this will go.

"Why?" Billy hits his speed button, trying to keep up with me.

"Long, long, long day," I pant as the resistance of the belt starts to do its magic.

"Paige disappeared for two days," I start my story to answer his quizzical brow, "and she came back this morning with needle marks up her arm." Billy doesn't seem surprised.

"That's not the worst I've seen there at Ramona's place," he answers, panting heavier than me.

"I guess not. She handled it like a pro, you know? Like it wasn't her first time with it. She even had me call Greta, a nurse from the rehab center to help her, and she was there within the hour, and she didn't ask many questions. She knew the motel as good as Ramona and me, so I'm positive she's been there enough through the years. I hope Paige can get clean. Ramona says she has Bambi's eyes, and somehow that means she's going to fail." I shake my head. "I don't know."

"What else?" He backs his speed down, competition against me futile and now forgotten.

"What do you mean, what else?" I tap for the belt to go faster.

"There's more to your day than Paige's track marks. I can tell." He shakes his head at my finger, still incessantly tapping for more speed and more pain.

"Yeah, but I don't want to talk about it."

"Come on," he pleads.

"Just memories of the past coming up like the stomach flu." I fake gag.

"All right." He turns his head away from looking at me and focuses on the TV to the right of him. Sports Center is playing. I can't tell if he's pouting or trying to hide the pain of running even half my speed.

"Do you think Stewart ever went to therapy?" I ask.

"What?" Billy flicks his head back toward me. "What's with your obsession of Stewart all of a sudden?"

"I don't know. The past is on my mind a lot lately. Maybe the last couple of months, I was in shock and am only now dealing with everything." I glance at the TV. "He told me time and time again that he would go to therapy and get help for his anger. Almost every time he apologized for hitting me, he used the line. Did he ever go when you were friends with him?"

"We never talked about stuff like that, Jane." His face takes on a severe nature.

"Yeah. I guess not."

"I bet he didn't." He turns his head back to the TV, and I follow.

"I bet you're right." I sigh. "How was your day?"

"Not good. I think I might be on to your attacker."

"Oh?" That should make Billy perk up, but instead, it draws the edges of his lips downward. "Is that bad?"

"He's been attacking more and more. He's on the warpath. I'm just nervous that I won't reach him in time." He grabs the bars of the treadmill after slamming the power button. He jumps off and leans over the handle of my machine. "Please lay low. I'm terrified to lose you."

"I will. I promise." I've never met a man dedicated to my well-being. I stop the treadmill.

"I think my day just got better. Do you want to go home with me?" I wink.

"Hell yes."

# Eighteen

My phone rings deep within my purse, and I shove my hand inside, trying to locate the cell before the tone stops.

"Ramona, what in the world could you need now?" I holler into the receiver. She has sent me out on errands and has called me damn near every five minutes since I left the motel.

"Why aren't you at work?" The voice booming on the other side is not the rasping, potential lung cancer tone of Ramona.

"Billy? Sorry, didn't mean to yell at you, babe, I didn't look at my phone when I picked up. You won't believe how many times Ramona has called me in the last half hour alone—"

"Why aren't you at work?" He repeats. There's an edge to his tone that sets my posture a little straighter. I promised him last night that I would be careful, and he's caught me breaking that promise in the morning light.

"I'm out running errands for Ramona. She can't leave Paige alone while she's detoxing right now, and these things needed to be done. I'm so sorry. I promise you that I'm going to be quick."

"Where are you?"

"Well, I went to the post office and mailed a few things for Ramona, bills, and what have you that she didn't make it out to the box in time with today. Um, then I went to the consignment shop and grabbed Paige some new clothes because she ruined them in a sort of rage that involved peroxide because she saw animals or something on them. I'm not quite sure about it. To be honest, I'm a little fuzzy on the details, and I didn't ask for it to be cleared up. Figured it was for the best not to know."

"Where are you heading now?" He's definitely meant to be a Detective.

"Uh, that grocery store that Ramona likes. Johnson's?" I ask for confirmation.

"Good, okay, stay in that part of town. Do you understand me?"

"Billy, what's going on? I'd hate to have our first fight right now, but I've had a shitty morning, and I don't much care for the way you're talking to me. I know that you asked me to lay low, but I can't be a hermit when Ramona needs things done."

"I'm sorry, Jane," he's softer now, no longer dictating. "I got a call about another girl being stalked while running, and I worried about you. I'm sorry. I don't mean to sound paranoid and crazy. I'm so close to catching him. So close."

"It's okay. It's okay." I scratch the back of my neck. "What happened with the girl?"

"She got away, but her description of the guy matched up with yours. I'm heading that way to check it out. I stopped at the motel to tell you, but you weren't there."

"Oh my god," I gasp. "He's trying to find me, isn't he?"

"I don't know, but until I can look into this, please stay on that side of town. It doesn't seem like he's hitting that area."

"Yeah. Yeah. I will. I'm going to run into the grocery store and head back at the motel. I swear. Twenty minutes tops until I'm behind the desk again."

"Good. Good. I'm sorry, Jane. I just... I worry, that's all. I don't want anything bad to happen to you." I imagine he's running his hand through his hair, frustrated by my stubborn streak.

"You like me, do you?" I tease.

"Maybe." He laughs.

"Hmmm."

"What?" He breathes into the phone. I know he's trying to calm down from not instantly getting ahold of me when the call of the attacker came through.

"I like hearing that."

"I like you, Jane."

"I like you, too, Billy." I laugh. "Now, go away so I can spend Ramona's money."

"Oh, have fun. Be careful, though."

"I will. I promise. Twenty minutes." We hang up, and my phone almost immediately rings again.

"Miss me?" I chuckle into the receiver.

"Get me some filtered cigarettes, too?" I really need to start reading the caller ID before answering a call, and Ramona needs to stop calling. It's the tenth call from Ramona with a new thing to add to the shopping list since I left the motel. She won't leave Paige's side, so I got myself nominated to do the shopping, and now I regret it, especially after Billy's phone call.

"So, you want filtered instead of your normal brand?" I pull into a parking space and slide the gearshift to park. I look all over the lot for any suspicious characters in blue cars.

"What the fuck is wrong with you? I don't smoke that wimpy shit," she coughs out.

"Then why the hell am I buying filtered cigarettes?" I slam my hand against the steering wheel, my patience thinning.

"For Paige. She needs something else to keep her hands busy." I imagine an inaudible duh following the sentence as if I should have already known.

"I thought that's why you were making me buy candy?" I pinch the top of my nose in between my eyebrows.

"I don't know what she'll want."

"Ramona?" I clench my teeth.

"Yeah?"

"Quit calling me." I hang up on her.

"Get candy. Get cigarettes. Get filtered cigarettes. Grab me some body wash and a new puffy thingie, oh I don't know what the hell you call it." I mock Ramona. "Don't go to that fancy food store where you buy your shit. I don't want to be paying out the ass for something they claim is organic. I don't give a shit if it's healthier for you. Go to my grocery store. It's cheaper."

"Don't go there. Stay in this part of town," I start to mock Billy. "Don't run outside. You can't breathe the fresh air. You have to be a hermit."

I scream as loud as I can inside my car and tear at the sides of my hair before opening the door and heading toward the store. I hadn't realized that getting Paige off drugs was going to make me long to start doing some myself. I kick the tire of the car parked next to me. It's childish to do, but I suddenly feel a little better, and I won't dare hit my own car.

"Ramona saved your life. Billy saved your life," I repeat under my breath. "Yeah, but they're both going to torture the shit out of it now." I yank a cart out of the return space and shove it toward the entrance.

The store smells of dirty diapers and body odor.

"Well, isn't that appetizing."

I push the cart down the aisles, determined to grab the shit on Ramona's list, and check out in record time. The items on the shelf are cheap, but who knows how long they've been sitting there or why they smell funky.

"Is it really worth saving a few pennies, Ramona?" I ask under my breath.

I grab the body wash and body puff, and then because of the price and because it's Ramona's dime, I throw in two more of each.

"Take that, old lady," I cackle.

"Hello, Jane." I jump and turn around to find Shana coming up behind me, her hollow eyes staring at me as if she's seen a ghost. What the hell is she doing in a dive place like this?

"Shana, what are you doing here?" I look around before whispering, "It's gross here." She doesn't look okay. Her eyes have sunken in, motherhood robbing her of her sleep, youth, and sense of smell in a place like this.

"I thought you switched grocery stores. I didn't see you, and I went every single day to see you. So, I started going to other places." She lifts her lips in a weak smile. "You go so often to the grocery store, and suddenly you stopped going."

Like a leech from the creek bed, I can't shake Shana no matter what. Why does she insist on seeking me out? I'm her husband's ex-wife. I don't know what game she is playing out, but if Stewart ever found out that she was following and talking to me, he'd quickly forget his apology and beat her senseless.

"Shana, you have to stop following me. We aren't friends." It feels mean to say, but I have to ward her off. Coming around me will only cause trouble for her with Stewart. Big trouble, the kind that breaks bones. I rub my wrist, remembering a day I irritated Stewart enough to receive that kind of pain. Now my right hand can tell me when the rain is coming.

"I know," her voice cracks. "Jane." It's barely a whisper before her resolve fades, and she's bursting in tears, fumbling to remain upright.

"What? What's wrong?" I glance around at the other customers who are staring at us. I turn Shana's body with mine to face the shelves and give us a little privacy. It doesn't feel as awful or as bile-inducing as I thought to provide Shana with a kind touch. She leans into me as a pillar of strength.

"He lied," she croaks. She lifts her sweater sleeve to show me a large bruise encompassing her forearm.

"Fuck."

"Help me, Jane. You have to help me. He's going to kill me. He's going to kill Delilah. Please, Jane."

# Nineteen

"No." I struggle to find air. "No. Shit. Shana. Shit. Shit. Shit." I kick the bottom shelf before me.

"We need a way out, Jane. Please, help us find a way out," she pleads. "I can't let him hurt her. He'll kill her. She's so small, Jane. So small," her voice cracks as does my resolve.

"I will, Shana. I promise." I flutter my hands nervously in the air, hoping that the movement will somehow pump an idea directly into my mind that will solve this colossal mess. I look down in Shana's cart at the car seat inside. Delilah is fast asleep, blissfully unaware of her father's evil intentions. Her face holds everything pure and wholesome left in this cruel world. Despite all the bad shit filling my life, I want to reach for her innocence and spare it.

She's going to make a mess of Stewart's mansion. She's going to make noise. She's going to break things. It won't take Stewart long before he can't stand it and corrects Delilah with his hand, no longer satisfied to only stomp out her mother's strength. She'll be a target before she's a year old.

"Jane." I look up from the baby to the face of her mother. "I know you don't like me. I know you don't want to do this, and you don't have to. I'd understand. I get it. I'm the dirty mistress, and this is what I deserve. It feels awkward asking you, it's unnatural, but please. Please, Jane, take pity on Delilah. I have to get her out of this mess. Stewart's abuse cannot be what she knows of life."

I raise my eyebrow at her. "I said that I would help."

"I thought that I could handle this on my own. I thought I had it, but my plan didn't work. It feels so weak standing here, begging you now." Shana pushes her tears off her cheeks, puffing her chest out to try and look brave.

"It isn't weak to ask for help, Shana." I rub a hand down her back, longing to comfort her and take the pain.

"It's not natural, and you know it. I screwed your husband. You're not married because of me. Why should you help me? It was unfair of me to put that on you. It's been unfair of me to try and track you down. Look at you; you don't want to help me."

"If I didn't want to help, I wouldn't be standing here."

"I yelled at you and said hurtful things."

"Yeah, and I've said things to you."

"I'm the reason you aren't married." A dirty mirror has been raised in front of Shana's face, and she doesn't like what she sees, but she doesn't realize how distorted that funhouse mirror really is.

"I screwed him when he was somebody else's husband." Shana stumbles as she attempts to exit and bumps her knee into the shelf. "I don't fault you for what you did because I did it, too. I was in your shoes once. Well, not all of your shoes." I look back down at Delilah, and in my peripheral vision, Shana follows my lead. "I never got to be a mom."

"I would have left by now if it weren't for her. He'll find me. Call it abandonment and take her from me." Her voice is the epitome of panic, rising in pitch, desperate for air. I bet she longs for the simple life she had before Stewart walked in. The life she had before I called her up and pulled her into this world.

"I'm betting he's all too happy to remind you of this daily before he leaves for work. A little reminder to stay put, and don't try anything smart."

She chuckles, but it's dry and flavorless of humor. "Jane—"

"Listen, Shana. I'm going to put my cards on the table here and tell you the truth so that you understand where I stand, and there's no mistrust between us, no more going back on this decision because I need transparency if I'm going to help you. You have to decide if this is what you want. You can't come to me in a few days claiming that he's going to change, and you're suddenly okay, and I'm the bad guy again."

"Okay."

"I am done blaming you for the loss of my marriage because it doesn't feel like a loss. Would I like more security and half of the financially sound life I had living with him? Hell, yes. Who doesn't? Right now, I have enough money to put food in my refrigerator, pay my bills, and set some aside for a rainy day. Where I grew up, that's fucking fabulous, and I'm trying to adopt that mindset back. I'll always be annoyed that I was in that marriage and wound up with nothing. I lost so much because of Stewart and his ways." I pause remembering the parts of my body he took, stealing away my chance of becoming a mom. "I spent five years trying and failing at being the perfect wife for Stewart and his image. I got nothing for my efforts, but that's his fault and mine for signing the prenup. However, I will never be able to turn my back on you or this child, especially her, after finding out that he's doing this again. So, you're stuck with me, and unfortunately, I'm stuck with you, but that's how this is going to be." I bite my tongue, my speech leaving me uncomfortable and vulnerable to one of my greatest enemies.

"I admire you, Jane. You didn't have to warn me that day when you came to pick up the trunk. I was such an asshole to you, and you still had the heart to try and get me out of it. When he threatened to hurt Delilah, I thought of you, and I knew you were the one with the answers." She stares over at me.

"I don't know what kind of answers I'll have for you." I peer down into the cart, and the baby inside of the car seat. Delilah. It's a beautiful name.

"He calls you a bitch," she whispers.

"Yeah, I sure can be." I brave a move and touch Delilah's socked foot. The sweet innocence underneath my finger cracks a small part of the cynic in me. I smile at Shana as if to say I just touched a baby's foot, but she doesn't understand the magnitude of this moment for me. She smiles back as if I'm a crazy weirdo.

"You warned me," she repeats.

"Yeah. You're too thick-headed to listen." I move my finger onto her other foot, and she jerks a little as if it's ticklish. This is amazing. I want this feeling forever.

"Well, I'm not now. I have a duty to Delilah, not to Stewart." I hear the conviction in her voice. There's something so powerful when women become mothers, the trivial things of their youth fade away, replaced by nourishing wisdom. They look to their partners for affection, but there's an unspoken rule that they have put them second from now on. The child takes precedence. The heartbeat that was inside of her takes over her thoughts before anyone else— even herself. She is forever attached to something higher than her, and she'll stomp any soul that tries to dim that fire.

"Can you get a copy of the prenup from his office and meet me tomorrow, or do you need another day?" I reluctantly let Delilah's foot go and turn my attention to helping her mother secure a safe way out.

"Where would it be?"

SHANA IS STILL WAITING in the check-out line when I make my way outside to my vehicle. She's repurchasing diapers, and it astounds me how many a kid that size needs. She just bought a box two days ago. I shake my head and dodge a small pothole in the parking lot. I hope Shana sees that over the top of the car seat. I look at the angle of the hole and where I know she parked her car. She should miss it.

*Listen to your thoughts, Jane. You're so worried about a grown-ass woman hitting a little hole in the world. She's not your child.*

I feel responsible for Shana's grief in a way because, without her, I would never have been freed from mine. Is the guilt the reason that I'm putting myself back in this tangled web? Billy warned me not to go up against Stewart because I would lose. Is he right?

Hell, he's warning me not to be out here because a maniac is on the loose and possibly after me. I should tell Shana that, give her a heads up of what she could be bringing her baby around, but with the way she flipped her mind to stay with Stewart last time that we spoke, I'm nervous about spooking her again.

I load the purchases into the trunk of my vehicle. Shana's car is parked three rows away, but she's still inside the store. I have to start taking in my surroundings, so I look around the scene, searching for blue cars. I don't want to be caught by surprise again. I spot it as I put the cart back in the return space. Parked diagonally from her is a black car that catches my eye. It looks familiar, and I get a tightness in my chest.

I wait until I'm safely inside my old Ford Explorer before I look closer. A man is sitting in the driver's seat, watching the door. I glance in the direction of the store just as Shana and Delilah are making their way out, and then I look back at him. At the sight of Shana, he sits up straighter and puts the book he was reading down in the passenger seat. He cranks over his engine and waits.

I duck lower in my seat. He never turns his sight this way, so I don't think he sees me or made a connection of who I am, but he's following Shana. There's no doubt about that. He watches her struggle with the groceries after putting the baby in the car, so I gather that he's not supposed to make his presence known. Shana doesn't even notice him.

Matter of fact, she doesn't notice anything around her. She's oblivious to the dangers of the world as she pushes the cart back to the cart return two cars down. There are at least three men that turn to stare at her and one man who is sitting in his car watching her every move, waiting for her. Yet, she sees nothing. It's no wonder she walked into Stewart's arms without warning signals.

I note the make and model of the car, nothing like the dilapidated red car housing a madman at the wheel that drove me from Stewart's mansion that night housing a madman at the wheel, but also nothing like the blue car that saw me while I was jogging. No, this car is luxurious. It has Stewart written all over it. I don't remember ever having a detail put on me when I was his wife, but then again, I was just like Shana, oblivious to the world and dangers around me. Is it because she has a baby and has already expressed that she wanted to leave him for the way he treated her? I never threatened to go.

Shana pulls out of her parking spot, and the man in the black car instinctively follows her, never looking my way. I pull out and make sure to put a car in between his vehicle and mine. Sure enough, he keeps a tail on Shana and trails her back to the development. I don't dare turn down that road, not wanting to be seen again. Instead, I park on a side street and watch as the black car creeps back out of the development once enough time has passed for Shana to make it home. Well, this just got a lot harder if Shana is being followed.

# Twenty

I'm earlier than our set meeting time, a half-hour early to be exact, but I'm not taking chances. If Shana is being followed daily, then they'll start noticing who she is around. New hair or not, it won't be hard to take a quick picture and show Stewart. My identity will be sold out quicker than a new iPhone model fresh on the market, and the horrible life that Shana is living now will get a whole lot worse and fast.

"Hey, Melinda."

"Hey! My girl. What's up?" She's cheering upon spotting my face. I wish I could offer her more than a half-hearted smile.

"Can I get one coffee, two bear claws, and a bottled water?"

"Of course." She taps the buttons on the register in a merry way.

"Hey. Can you leave a bear claw and the water here for when that girl arrives, then hand them to her?"

"Sure," she draws out. "Everything all right?"

"Just don't make a big fuss that I'm here when she arrives. Don't shout my name or anything." I lift my eyes to hers, searching for understanding, not wanting to explain the reason behind my vague request. She's a stray of Ramona's, so I'm banking on that fact.

"Got it." She knows the mission requires secrecy. There's a woman in danger, and she needs our help, much like we needed Ramona at one point in each of our lives.

I hand the money over and drop the change in the tip jar. I make sure to secure my usual table behind the half-wall, near the restrooms at the back of the shop. I drink my coffee and munch my pastry in outward silence while the thoughts inside rage, trying to settle on a plan for Shana's escape.

When I hear an average level voice level tell Shana that she'll find me around the back near the restrooms, I breathe easy knowing that Stewart hasn't found her out. Us. He hasn't found us out. The car didn't spot me at the grocery store, and he wasn't in the parking lot when I came here.

The registers can be seen from the front window, so I don't dare want any suspicion raised. A mother of a new-born, stopping for a treat, and taking a seat in the back away from everyone seems natural enough. There's no way she wants her baby to be that close to strangers, but she does want out of the house. It's the perfect scenario for any gawker because it looks natural.

"Hey. What's going on?" Shana pops up around the half wall with Delilah strapped to her chest in a wrap before setting her drink down on the table. She's eyeing me as if I've gone mental. I wonder if she wants to run away from her husband's ex-wife now, as well.

"Sit down and don't move your mouth like you're talking to anyone. Look at the baby and talk." There's a sudden calmness that comes over me. She's here. There's still a chance to save her and Delilah.

She quickly averts her eyes, having learned the conse-
quence of pausing with Stewart. As she peers into the wrap
at Delilah, fear beginning to dawn on her face.

"Is everything all right?" she asks me, using the baby as a
disguise for talking out loud.

"No. You're being followed. I saw a man in a black car
wait and follow you from the grocery store, and I'm sure they
followed you here. Judging by the car that he was driving,
Stewart put them up to it. I'd bet my life on it." I note her
trembling posture. "Don't panic. Soothe the baby."

She bounces her body, calming down sweet Delilah, who
must have stirred because of the change in her mother's demeanor. She senses her mother's fear, but she doesn't know
the real cause of it.

"Try and keep yourself calm. I've been here for a half-
hour, so they have no idea that you're meeting me. I double-
checked every angle before choosing this seat. They can't see
me from outside. I didn't take any chances, okay? I'll wait
long after you're gone to leave myself. Put your diaper bag on
me as if there is nothing in front of you."

She lifts the bag from her shoulder, dumping it on the
side of the booth where I am, then she finally takes a seat
across from me, clutching tight to the bundle on her chest.

"Is the prenup in here?" I ask and start unzipping parts
of the contraption she calls a diaper bag, coming up empty at
every corner.

"Yes." She says it to Delilah. There's hope for Shana yet
as she can take and retain simple instructions. "Side pocket."
She giggles at Delilah for an extra ounce of show. Her eyes
fight to look out the window; she wants to see who is follow-

ing her. She wants to confirm my suspicions or be able to tell me I'm crazy.

I find the folded papers wedged inside the side pocket as she said, and I open them up, aware of keeping my arms far on my side of the table so that not an inch of me can be viewed from the outside window. My eyes begin to scan the prenup, sending a prayer up to God that there's a loophole somewhere and that I'm able to find it for Shana.

"Jane, I'm getting scared. If he finds out…" She's on the precipice and dreaming of the fall. I pull her back.

"He won't. Take a deep breath and try to calm down, Shana. This is nothing. This is an extension of Stewart's security measures. I am hidden by this half wall and the plant on top here. I'm keeping my arms tucked in. I got here way before the black car, and you can't see me from the front window. I checked. It's going to be okay." I want to reach out and touch her hand, but I can't risk it; I pray the words touch her instead.

Shana bounces Delilah against her chest until the infant decides to stop fighting sleep and doze off. She looks so precious sleeping there. Shana looks around and takes inventory of the other patrons in the coffee shop. She can't fight it any longer. With a sleeping baby across her chest and the appearance of sitting alone at a table, there's no danger in her roaming eyes.

"What if they come in?" she whispers.

"He won't. He sits outside while you are grocery shopping, so I don't think Stewart hired him because he suspects you of anything. I think it's more of a measure to make sure you're safe when you go places."

"That I don't run." She confirms the other half of my thinking.

"Yeah, so you don't run," I sigh.

"Because I threatened to leave."

"Yeah," I whisper, matching her meek voice. I finish reading the first half of their prenup.

"Pretty much like the one I signed. So, you and I both know you won't be getting any money from Stewart. If you have a way to set aside a bit of cash from what he gives you for shopping or something like that, do it. It won't be millions, but every little bit helps."

"I've been doing that this past week." She smiles down at the slumbering infant in her arms. My body aches to have something of my own as precious as a child, but I force down the jealousy. There's no sense in being envious of Shana right now. She may have a child, but she's in the worst possible predicament that a mother could find herself.

"Good." I smile at her for being on the same wavelength as me and dip my head back down to remove the top page from the agreement and set to work on the second. "Only what you brought into the marriage. Yada yada. Same as me. This is probably his agreement for all his wives. It's ironclad, so why mess with perfection? You won't walk out of the marriage with any of his cash. Now, you were pregnant when you married, so here's a little extra clause." I fluff up the papers and bring them closer to my face. I don't like what I'm reading, so I read the paragraph twice, hoping to change the words somehow.

"What, what's wrong, Jane?" Delilah stirs and starts to fuss a little bit. She's hungry. Like a covert spy, Shana pulls the wrap and grants herself a little privacy while the child's head dips in for a meal.

I set the papers down and scrub my face.

"Shit, Shana," I hiss and smack the edge of the table on my side.

"What?" She does her best to avoid direct eye contact, but I know my pause only brings her worry.

"You signed away the kid."

Her gasp echoes in my soul, finding a dark place inside of my gut, rotting it with horror. The same feeling that she must be experiencing now. I wish I could change the words printed on that paper.

"What do you mean? That's a mistake. That has to be a mistake." A tear rolls down her cheek and hits the purple cloth that's covering Delilah's body.

"Under circumstances of a divorce, Shana Westwood will forfeit sole custody of the child or children. This is for the benefit of the child or children because Shana will not be able to provide the same as Stewart Miller." The words taste foul. I gulp at my empty coffee cup, wishing I had saved a morsel to help swallow this shit down.

"No. No." She holds Delilah closer to her, fearing the child will slip through her fingers. It is a real possibility. "Stewart said that was for my protection. That it didn't mean I wouldn't have my baby. It meant that he would still be the sole provider of money for her."

"Hate to break it to you, Shana, but Stewart is a lying manipulative asshole who made you sign over your future rights to Delilah should you divorce him. He made sure that you would feel that being with him, despite the abuse, was the better option." I scratch my forehead and slam my back against the wall of the booth side.

"What am I going to do?" Terror rises in her eyes. Glancing everywhere around the coffee shop for the answer. "How do I get out of this, Jane?" She chances a look my way. Her begging causes a deep ache inside of my chest, where I'm sure my heart is shattering.

I look around what I can see of the coffee shop, hoping to find the answer that Shana missed. I hope to hear something other than what my gut is telling me, but there's nothing, and the words keep growing stronger inside my mind. If it comes to it, Shana can't be a part of it. She has Delilah to think about, and she can't leave her alone. It's better if she's ignorant, but we're only free if Stewart Miller is dead.

"I'll find a way." My voice is cloaked in confidence that I'm sure my body language betrays. No matter what, Delilah will not fall prey to Stewart's hands.

# Twenty-One

"You got to start sleeping, kid." Ramona's ready at the door of the office with a cup of coffee in hand for me as I walk in the door to start the workday.

"How did you know?" I wipe at the inside of my eye, pushing the sleep from it, stifling a yawn. I steal the liquid heaven from her possession and grant her a grateful smile.

"You never take that long to get out of your car and get in here." She sips her own cup and shrugs — mind reader. Everyone has unique talents, and Ramona has always been reading people.

"I keep having nightmares about the night I came here." I pull tight to myself to ward off the shivers.

"Has Billy had any luck finding the man since you were followed that day?"

"No," I moan, "I'm afraid they're never going to find this guy, and I'm going to be a hermit for the rest of my life, or worse." I cringe at the thought of the driver finally locating me.

"Don't worry, kid, that boy of yours will find him. He's the best police officer that I know. If anyone can find that asshole, it's Billy." Knowing that Ramona has absolute confidence in Billy helps to ward off a bit of the fear in my heart.

"I'm glad to see that you are here in the office this morning, not cooped up in that room watching Paige. That's a good sign, huh? Must mean that she's feeling better if you're slumming it with me here in the work world."

"I wouldn't know." Ramona shuffles some papers on the desk, but the smooth action does nothing to fool me. She's worried.

"What? What do you mean you wouldn't know?" I grumble. "Where the fuck is Paige?" I growl looking about the room — days without productive sleep has left me irritable, and Paige's dives out of here are becoming annoying, mainly when they cause this grief on Ramona's face.

"She left," Ramona confirms my suspicions while taking my purse from my shoulder to lock it up in the desk drawer. "I printed out today's check-ins and checkouts. We are ready to go in here. We have six rooms to clean and four to check. Busy day. We better get going, kid."

"She left?" I sputter, spilling coffee on my hand and forearm. The burn feels somewhat cathartic this morning.

"That's all you got from that?" Ramona coughs, her lungs' only time to scold her for what she's done to them.

"Six rooms to clean. Four to check. Busy day. Paige left?" I yank a napkin off the coffee pot table and wipe my hand and the outside of the cup dry.

"Yes." She pushes past me to head outside, and I stomp after her, full of piss and vinegar.

"Left for good? Disappeared again? What? You're awfully vague, Ramona."

"I'm not sure." She lifts a shoulder and holds the door open for me. "Let's go."

"She wasn't ready to go yet. The bruises on her body hardly healed up. She was strung out on who the hell knows what just a few days ago, and she was so sincere about getting clean. How did her heart and mind heal already?" I yell at Ramona as if it's her fault. "We have to find her then. What can we do? You know she's not ready to leave here."

"You win some, and you lose some, kid. I can't force people to stay. You have to let people change on their own accord. Shit, just because they know it's the right thing to do, doesn't mean they're going to do it. We can't do anything, but hope she comes to her senses."

"She'll be back." I try to reassure Ramona, but it turns out that I'm one in need of the reassurance.

"Maybe." She opens the maintenance closet. "Maybe not."

"That's ridiculous." I stamp my feet like a petulant child.

"Jane, that's enough," Ramona barks. "I thought you didn't like Paige."

"I guess she grew on me," I mutter. "At least enough that I didn't want her lying in a gutter with a needle sticking out of her arm."

"If that's her fate, kid, you can't stop it. You have passion, and enough coursing through your body to adapt when it's necessary. But, that doesn't mean that your passion can change others. The secret is that only she can change herself."

"I could always help."

"I think you're confusing help for taking over the task and completing it for her. Those are two separate things, kid." She has a point, like always. I huff in annoyance.

"So is the room open for strays?" I lift my eyebrow.

"I'm warning you, kid, don't start that shit with me today. I am not taking on Shana and her child. They smell like trouble, and I'm too old to poke my head into that kind of a mess. I don't want that stinking up the joint."

"You were poking your head into Paige's trouble, and it came with needle marks," I counter.

"That's different." She ducks into the closet, pitching toiletries into a bin for the cart.

"How?" I watch her turn around from the closet and take a deep, cleansing breath before answering me.

"Listen, Jane. I can smell it a mile away that Shana is going to get you in a world of trouble. Let it go. Don't bring them around here and stay far away from that girl. That's the best thing that I can tell you, but yet again, that's up to you."

"Why should I stay away from her, Ramona? She needs help."

"I can sense these things. I'm telling you that I feel it in my bones. She's no good to be hanging around, and I don't want it at my motel.

"Can't blame me for trying." I set my coffee on the cart and check it over.

"Billy called."

"Yeah?" I perk up at the sound of his name.

"He said he would stop over around lunchtime to talk to you." She throws some extra sheets on the shelf of the cart.

"That doesn't sound good. Did he sound mad?"

"How the hell am I supposed to know that?" Her long yellowing acrylic nails scratch the side of her wrinkled face. "We got a lot of work to do that will help to keep your mind busy until you find out at noon. Now, let's get these rooms done."

# Twenty-Two

R amona and I make it back to the office in record time. This morning was not only our fastest workday but the quietest with neither of us longing to talk about our problems out loud. We can't grasp control over the situations we're battling, trying to save a woman in need from the demons of the world, and it's a painful shame to face. Things like that need to be worked out inside the mind, and it seems as if Ramona and I are no closer to solutions than when we started this morning.

I place my lunch on top of the desk and push the noddles around the plate with my fork, the absence of my appetite evident. I look to my left to see Ramona on the couch doing the same with her meal. She only appears relaxed about the Paige situation, but I know the last few days she spent curled up in a chair in Paige's room while she detoxed have her feeling slighted that the girl could leave without so much as a goodbye. Her past calls her in a way that Ramona and I can't understand or begin to wrap our heads around the possibility.

I throw my food in the garbage can, and find myself diving into someone else's problems— a book kept under the desk. One of Ramona's former strays left it here, a copy of a forbidden romance. Ramona blared her TV, and I took to a different form of entertainment to drown out the words of Shana ringing in my mind.

"You definitely made Melinda your friend." I jump at the sound of Billy's voice in the partition window. My papers fly off the desk in every direction at the slam of my hand on top of them. Ramona jumps in the background at my scream.

"Holy shit, Billy. You scared me." I grab my chest for emphasis. "Didn't you learn anything at the gym the other night about sneaking up on me?"

"Sorry. Couldn't help it. You looked so cute, focused on your book. I had to sneak up. What are reading anyway, some sexy romance?" He chuckles and pushes his head inside. "Hey, Ramona." I give the top of his head a shove.

"Hey, Bill." She waves but doesn't turn around from her soap opera.

"What did you say about Melinda?" I push his head again until he's outside.

"Come here and see." He winks and moves around the corner of the partition out of my line of sight. I shut the small window door.

"That boy is smitten," Ramona's singsong voice carries over the dramatic music in the background of the TV.

"No, my love, I think he's here because he wants a piece of you," I joke — all of a sudden, a handful of popcorn sprays against my back. I'm glad to see a better mood returning to Ramona, along with her appetite.

I laugh at her as I head outside, locking the door behind me. Ramona drilled the routine into my mind the first week that I was here. *Always lock the door behind you.* There was a need for safety here because of the women she took in and helped. They came to her for a sense of security, and she took the task seriously.

When I turn the corner of the building, Billy is holding a bag from Mitz in front of his face.

"Treats, my favorite." I grab the bag from him.

"Gifts from Melinda. She says she misses seeing you in the morning." He eyes me with suspicion.

"I've been sleeping late, not able to sleep much during the night." I chomp down on a cinnamon roll and let the icing rest on my lips a second longer before licking it away.

"New place jitters?" Billy grabs at the cinnamon roll in my hand, and I relinquish it to him for a bite.

"No, just a lot on my mind." I motion for him to follow me to the edge of the sidewalk to sit rather than park ourselves close to the front section and the partition window.

"So, what did you come here to talk to me about." I rest my body down on the concrete and kick my feet straight out in front of me.

"I need you to lay even lower," he whispers.

"Billy," I protest.

"I know, I know." He holds his hands up in surrender. "But, going out the other day was foolish, Jane. How can you stay safe if you keep on sticking your face out there for him to find?"

"Why do I have to lay even lower?" My voice holds a whining tone. I munch the last bit of cinnamon roll, and it tastes a little less sweet, knowing it was brought here under false pretenses. This wasn't a sweet conversation at all. This was more freedom being taken from me because of a madman. I was kicked out by one, only to be controlled by another one, I can't see.

"There's been more attempts similar to the one that happened to you. I swear I'm going to catch him, Jane."

"I'm practically a fucking hermit now, Billy. I changed my hair, isn't that enough?" I shove the bag back at him, pissed off that they were brought as a peace offering instead of a kind gesture. He can keep his damn cinnamon rolls. I'd rather have my freedom.

"I wish it was, Jane. I swear it won't be much longer. It's for your safety." I run my hands down my face and flick them out in front of me as if I can throw the irritation away.

When I close my eyes, I can still feel the clammy grip of the driver's hands around my neck and the wet asphalt of the alley beneath me, dampening my clothing. I hear the way his voice echoed, bouncing off the buildings that created the alley's space.

*"I know you're still here."*

The way he found me tucked by the dumpster, his eyes coming around the corner, that sight will never leave me. Sometimes I dream about it and wake up in a cold sweat as I hear the man's voice in my ear. There's no doubt his intentions were malicious.

*"I've always wanted to kill a woman."*

Billy stopped him, tackling him to the ground before the last of my oxygen could be stolen from my body. If he hadn't been so concerned about me, the guy wouldn't have been able to run away and escape his arrest. He could be in custody right now.

"All right, Billy," I sigh. "How low?"

"Motel, apartment, and gym. That's it."

"What?" I screech.

"Jane."

"How am I supposed to shop for groceries? What about the coffee shop? What the fuck am I going to do?" I slam my hands on my thighs. "This is not fair, Billy."

"I'll bring you groceries and coffee. Those are two places you can't ever go again." He pushes the bag from Mitz toward me. I cover my face in my hands and scream.

"Ever? That sounds a bit dramatic, don't you think? You mean until you catch him, right?" I ask, testing the boundaries of my new limitations.

"Yeah, that's what I meant." Billy looks away from me as if he's hiding something.

"So, until you find this guy. Okay, I can do it for a little while longer." I nod.

"Catching him doesn't look good, actually, because we have no leads." He scratches the back of his neck and stands up to leave. I don't understand. He said it wouldn't be much longer, and now he's saying forever. Something doesn't add up.

"You don't want to end up like Leona, do you?" He glares down at me. The name sends glass scraping down my spine.

"Fine." I snatch the bag and stand up, heading for the front desk office. Billy doesn't follow.

"I'll see you later, Jane." He's lying to me, and I'm going to find out why.

# Twenty-Three

"There," I say to my reflection in the mirror above my bathroom sink; only the woman looking back doesn't look much like me, and that's the whole point. I don't plan on stepping outside these walls looking like Stewart's Jane or even Billy's version. It hasn't even been a full day, and I'm already planning on breaking his damn rules. Tonight, I'm in disguise.

Billy doesn't know anything about Shana or that she needs out of Stewart's claws. He would go ballistic if he knew I put myself anywhere near that life again, especially after his warning on my balcony to never go up against Stewart. Billy escaped with his career, probably barely intact because of the gossip created by my ex, and I barely escaped with my life. And now my new boyfriend is lying to me, and I need to find out more because I won't be tricked again.

I need to do some investigating today. Things I can't do from inside the apartment. Things that I need to risk going in public to find out, so I've overlined my lips to make them look fuller and applied false eyelashes. It's incredible how makeup changes your appearance. I layered on my clothes to give my body a thicker appearance. I'm not the Jane that I've become accustomed to seeing in this mirror. I'm someone else entirely. Anyone looking at me from the outside wouldn't know that I was once the skinny blond ex-wife of Stewart Miller.

I lock the apartment door behind me and head to the lot where I've parked Ramona's car. I told her I needed to borrow it for the evening, and she didn't hesitate to offer it up when I came stomping back in after talking to Billy. *Girls stick together.* She didn't ask questions, and I like that about Ramona the most. She knows when just to let it be.

When I yank open the protesting driver's side door, my nasal cavities are assaulted with the scent of Ramona— a mixture of leather upholstery, cleaning products, and unfiltered cigarettes. The smell is horrible but oddly comforting. She didn't hesitate to loan me her sweet baby as she calls her car. She's more of a mother than my own was able to be.

I idolize her. Saving Shana and Delilah is a 'Ramona thing to do,' and I long to see her proud of such an accomplishment and feat of character.

I pull out of the lot and head for the library. It's not too far off. As a matter of fact, my apartment is an excellent location for all the things I could need in life, so I never have to go far. Billy couldn't have picked out a better place for me to live. I'm not from this area initially, Stewart brought me here, so I trusted Billy to help me find a home to call my own. Albeit, reluctant at first, much like Ramona, about my leaving the motel, he did end up delivering a location with stellar amenities and safety.

*"It's safe in this complex. I never get any calls out here. You'll be in the best little spot away from danger."*

And with a sales pitch like that, and a cute little balcony off the one-bedroom apartment, who could say no? It was quiet, just as Billy had said. My neighbors keep to themselves, and I'm happy to do the same except today. Today, I am on a mission to uncover some shit. Something is going on, and I need to find out. I want to expose the truth, starting with Stewart's past. A name that Billy's brought up a few times keeps ringing in my head.

Leona.

Leona was the first to marry Stewart and was the only one who didn't begin as a mistress. Their marriage lasted for over two decades. I became Stewart's mistress the last three years of that time, stealing from Leona what Shana took from me. When they divorced, she told him she didn't want anything, that his money was filthy, and to keep it safeguarded against me because I'd be gunning for it. I believed that line when it passed Stewart's lips, but now after reading a near-identical prenup to my own from Shana, I don't think he was telling the whole truth. Not much of what fell from Stewart's lips was ever truthful I'm finding out.

I pull into the library and park as close to the front door as I can. I'm breaking a rule of Billy's by being here, so the faster I get this done, the better. I can only imagine if he finds out I'm here, the fury will be double when he discovers that I'm trying to unravel his lies. I climb the steps to the front door, swinging the heavy oak door open, exposing myself to a rush of cold air coming from inside.

The lady behind the counter smiles at me when I make my way over to her.

"Hi. I was wondering if I could use the computers for some research."

"Certainly. Do you have a library card with us?"

"No, I don't, but I'd like to sign up for one." I put my name down as Jane Voss, Billy's last name — how it is at the gym and my new driver's license. I hand over the lie to her as proof of my name, and she doesn't question it. She has me fill out a form and takes my answers as the truth. Billy said the name change was for my protection.

She produces the little card for me to sign, then she directs me to the location of the computers.

"Just go straight down and to the left. Beyond those shelves is an open area lined with computers. If you need to print anything, let me know." She sits back down in her chair, having completed her duty.

"Thank you so much."

I walk down the shelves lined with books, classics and new releases until I come to an end. I turn left and find the computer area without trouble. A middle-aged woman with graying hair and a similar color sweater is sitting on a computer typing in a chicken peck style. I suppress my laugh. She reminds me of Ramona at the keyboard. Aside from her, no one else is around. A breath that I didn't realize I was holding escapes my body. I can't live like this, on edge all the time. No one should I have to wear a disguise to come to a library.

I tap the keyboard of the nearest computer and watch as the screen jumps to life. I sit down, the bulk of my clothing making the task a bit uncomfortable, and wait impatiently as the home screen comes into view. After clicking the internet icon, I begin my research. If Billy is lying to me, I'm going to find out real quick because the internet holds damn near everything.

I type in Leona Miller with the keyword Pittsburgh into the search bar and watch the hits fill up the page. All this information available at my fingertips and I never utilized it before.

*Millionaire's ex-wife found slain*

I click it.

*Leona Miller, 53, was found dead this evening on Bedford Street at around 11:07 PM. Officers say the victim died from her throat being slit, and that drugs may have been involved.*

*As many know, Leona is the ex-wife of the prestigious defense attorney, Stewart Miller. The couple had recently divorced at the beginning of the year, but Mr. Miller did call in his comment earlier today.*

*"It saddens me greatly to hear of Leona's passing. I know she was fighting some demons, and these things helped lead to the end of our marriage, but I hold no ill will. I still wanted her to win the battle, and it hurts to hear that she didn't."*

*Leona Miller has been hinted at being a recovering addict, her ex-husband admitting to keeping the news out of the papers for years. There have been no arrests in the case.*

Drugs? Leona didn't do drugs. They divorced because of me. I hit the back button and search for more articles.

*A drug deal gone wrong finds ex-wife of attorney Stewart Miller dead*

That doesn't make sense at all. It takes five pages of articles with similar titles before I find a more objective piece.

*Stewart Miller moves on with younger woman as ex-wife's body grows cold*

The author is clearly not a fan of Stewart's or mine. I click the article. The webpage linked to the material on the search page is more of a blog than a news website. The owner states at the top that he provides his opinions and the part of the news that people want to glaze over.

Interesting.

*Leona Miller lays cold in the gutter from a knife sliding across her throat while her ex-husband is moving in a new wife. Coincidence? I think not.*

*Come on, people. It doesn't take one meeting with this man to smell the stink of his abuse in power. He's one of the prestigious lawyers in the area, and he didn't get to his position without help. Look around at the articles that boast about his ratings, the money, and the famous people he helps escape jail time. They're all over the place right now, smacking you on the nose before you've had breakfast. They discuss those matters rather than the cold dead body of Ms. Leona Miller. What about her? They aren't out to get the killer. The newspapers are out to boost their ratings by mentioning his name.*

*Do you honestly think that a man like this has no dark secrets? Do you think someone can rise to this sort of level of power on good morals and merit? Don't you smell the bullshit from a mile away? With all that money, and his "heartfelt" sentiments toward the news of Leona's death, don't you think he would be helping by funding a proper investigation?*

*Am I the only one awoke and pissed here?*

*I'm here to report what the newspapers are too scared to say out loud or even hint. Stewart Miller left his wife with nothing. Nothing. His charade is up.*

*It wasn't because he feared she'd squander the money on drugs. The man has a tight-knit group of lawyer friends— in short, someone drew up a pretty lovely prenup for Leona to sign. She was on those streets because he put her there. Simple as that.*

*Want to know something else that didn't take months or years of investigative journalism to find? Leona Miller has never been in a facility for drug use. She's never been to the hospital for any near overdoses, as Mr. Miller has claimed. She's clean as a whistle. The woman even volunteered at anti-drug charity events.*

*The police can try and cover it up for them and change the articles around to fit the new narrative, but I still remember the line about her bruises. She didn't receive all of them from the attack, and she sure as shit didn't get them from drugging herself up with heroin.*

*I'm not saying he held the knife himself, but I've seen Stewart Miller shake hands with a lot of people, and any one of them would have been happy to keep her quiet from exploiting his secrets and theirs. How does a woman who calls up the news station to sell her story end up dead in a day?*

*Wake up, Pittsburgh. We have a murderer defending murderers.*

I push back from the desk, yanking at the collar of my top shirt. Holy shit. Did Stewart know that Leona was going to sell her story? Could he kill her?

*"He says he'll hurt her."*

Shana's reference to Delilah's safety sends a chill down my spine. Stewart could very well be the man that this anonymous blogger thinks he is. I click on his article page. He hasn't written a thing since his article about Stewart. I click the about page.

Franklin Myer.

I open a new tab on the internet and type Franklin My-er's name alongside the word Pittsburgh. If I can find him, perhaps he'll meet me. He might not have been my biggest fan five years ago, but I don't look the same as I did. I can fool him into thinking I'm someone else. I need answers. Some-thing is going on that will help me free Shana.

*Blogger found dead in a hit and run accident while walk-ing in downtown Pittsburgh.*

"Fuck," I hiss.

"Shh." The lady at the other computer scolds me.

"Sorry." If only she knew.

I exit out of the tab and go back to looking up Leona's name. She never told Stewart that she didn't want his dirty money; he never gave her a chance to have any. Selling her story was her way to get back at him and finance her new life. She didn't do drugs. Stewart had her killed and the drugs planted. And now he has a car following Shana.

There is one last thing that I need to check on before I leave this library.

# Twenty-Four

I clear the search bar and type in *Driving App Murderer Pittsburgh*. Nothing pops up. I strum my fingers on the desk. I need better keywords.

*Attempted murder Jane Miller.*

Nothing.

"What?"

"Shh."

"All right. I get it." I roll my eyes at the lady in the corner. Billy would like her; she isn't one for breaking the rules. She slams her first finger against her lips, a physical reminder of what she wants me to do. I throw her a thumbs up. *All right, lady. Calm down.*

I place my chin in my hand and stare down at the screen, tapping my elbow that's resting on the table with my other hand. How could there be nothing about the attempted murder on me? I filled out a police report. Billy assured me that with Stewart's last name attached to it, there would be stories about it all over the paper, and they'd find the guy within a couple of days.

Did Stewart have them buried because of Shana? No doubt the gossip surrounding an ex-wife being nearly murdered doesn't look well when your latest mistress of the mansion has an ever-growing belly, and your first wife died not long after she left your home.

149

I square my shoulders back, resting my hands in my lap. *Think, Jane.* My eyes flutter closed, and images of that night come rushing back at my command with ease. I'm there in the backseat once again, and I can see the back of the driver's head to my left. It's funny how the smell stays in your memory, too, because I swear the tree car freshener is dangling near me once again.

*"What hotel did my husband pay you to take me to tonight?" The bag holding my shoes pushes into my shoulder as we take an unexpected left turn.*

*"No hotel tonight, sweetheart."*

*"What?" I glance around, but there is nothing but darkness. I don't think I've ever been to this part of town before. Stewart usually has a driver who takes us places, and I'm afraid to admit that I've never paid attention to the streets or my surroundings.*

*"Don't worry, sweetheart."*

*"Jane. My name is Jane." I hate to be called sweetheart, especially by this man. The name is not a term of endearment from his lips. It sounds more like a death sentence.*

*"Yeah. I guess you can call me... well, shit. You won't be talking after tonight, so you can know my real name. I'm Lance."*

*"What do you mean I won't be talking?" I grip the door handle and pull against it, but it's locked.*

*"I'm going to kill you." He laughs.*

I jolt in my seat, shivering as his voice surrounds me. *Lance.* I forgot he said his name until now. I should call Billy; this could crack the case for him. I can be free. A laugh escapes my lips as my hands continue to rub the chill away from my bones.

I reach for my phone, my thumbs poised to type out a text to Billy, but they don't fall on the screen. He lied to me today. He told me that I didn't want to end up like Leona, dead in an alley. That was almost my reality. I for damn sure don't want to end up in the grips of Lance once more. With me gone, Shana and Delilah don't stand a chance.

I grip my phone in the left hand, using my right to chicken peck in the search bar like my neighbor has been doing on her computer this whole time.

*Lance Pittsburgh car accident*

Enter. The internet page spins over several times, without success. I hit the refresh button several times out of impatience before I get the results of the search.

I gasp at the fourth headline on the page.

"Oh my god," I whisper.

"Shh."

I click the close button on the screen and stand up.

"That's a good idea," I say to her as I leave. I should stay quiet.

# Twenty-Five

Running has always been my solace. As a child, I didn't have the best home life. My father left when I was young, launching my mother into a single parent lifestyle that she wasn't ready to handle. We were poor, a product of her decision making rather than a lack of jobs and funds for a woman. She had the means and will power to make cash; she didn't know how to delegate it.

We argued a lot about it in my teenage years; that's when I discovered running. I took off from the house one day after a particularly bad argument and kept going down the block. My legs felt as if they were being punished, but the pain started to clear my mind, so I went down another block. Suddenly, the ache turned to fuel, and I ran at least three miles that night. I went until the pain became too much to bear in my side, something I learned to harness and control. A kind old lady brought me home in her car.

After that, I ran every day. I exhausted my body so that the jittering of the day stopped leaving me restless. The crawl of anxiety didn't linger under my skin when I took to the pavement. I ran the bullies, my mother's stupid decision making, a failing grade, a horrible friend out of my system. The habit continued in my adult years when I moved away from my mother's house. She died without me there, and I put my feet to the concrete over that as well.

Today, I'm running to gain a clear mind so that I can plot my next move. The library proved to be fruitful with information, shit bursting at the seams with it. I went looking for it, and there it was, but I wasn't ready for what I found—more lies. Lies don't bother me as much as the reason behind them, and I'm going to need a lot of exercise to sort these out. Fuck, drawing a map might help if I wasn't afraid of the paper being found.

One answer is evident in all the questions floating in my mind as I hit the power button on the treadmill — I can't trust a soul. Their pasts are wrought with lies, dangerous ones that have the powers to get me killed if I'm not careful. Believing anyone at this point is too risky.

I crank my neck left and right, relishing in the delicious crack each side gives. The soles of my feet pad against the belt, and I feel the stress beginning to admit defeat to my brand of therapy. It won't be long now, a few miles maybe before I can look at all this new information with fresh, bright eyes. The gym is a perfect idea after this long day.

"I figured you'd be here." Or maybe not.

"Hey, Billy," I pant, trying to push the annoyance from my voice so that Billy doesn't hear it.

"You always run when you've had a bad day."

"That's accurate. Yes." I laugh. It's fake, but it gets the job done. Billy suspects nothing.

"I'm sorry about this afternoon. I want to keep you safe is all." His eyes hold the truth. Billy is genuine when he tells me that he wants me to be safe, but it's what I found in that last article today that has me questioning his reasoning. Reason means everything.

Did Billy like to play the hero so much that he lied to me? Did he think he needed to have a white knight personality for me to notice him? He saved my life that night. Lance was in full character to kill me, but where does this charade end?

"Billy, I'm a little nervous. How safe is my apartment building?"

"It's safe, Jane." He hits the power button on the treadmill to the right of me, and I wonder if running as the same effect on Billy as it does me. He looks like he hates every second of it.

"I know, but I'm terrified with that driver out there. He's a scary man. I can still see his face when I go to sleep. I don't know how much longer I can live like this." I watch him closely for signs that he's about to expose the truth. The charade needs to end. He's already in the relationship with me for God's sake, just tell me the truth.

"I understand. I wouldn't let anything bad happen to you, Jane. I would tell you if it wasn't safe to be there. Right now, it's one of your safest places." So, it's denial again.

"You don't have to take that burden on, you know. I can take care of myself." I reach out and touch his shoulder, but to my surprise, he recoils.

"Sorry. You startled me," he laughs. He's nervous.

"How can I startle you when I've been talking to you this whole time?" I peer deeper at the lines on his face. He looks years older than me. Lies take on an entity of their own when you've held them in for so long.

"I was going over your apartment in my mind, making sure you had everything as secure as you can. Making sure everything is as solid as it can be. I guess I was just in my head is all."

"And is it?"

"Is what?" He looks over, confused.

"Is my apartment secure?"

"Oh yeah," he waves his hand, "It's the safest place."

"Good." I click my tongue and turn my head to face forward. I tilt my head left and right, but my neck doesn't give up any more popping sounds. My whole body has tensed up during this entire conversation. Thanks to Billy, this will be the first time in my life that a run hasn't solved my mood.

"You know, Jane, I don't think you're going to have to worry much longer. I am close to solving this case. I can feel it." He smiles at me. I force my lips to match his. When he turns his head forward, I let it fall.

I can't believe I'm sleeping with the enemy again — what a fucking liar.

# Twenty-Six

It's two in the morning if the clock hasn't stopped working. I know that it hasn't because I've watched it turn over the last eighty-six minutes, one by one. I can't sleep. My mind plays back the driver's abuse every time my eyes close. When they're open, I only see Stewart's hands coming down on me in anger, and suddenly my face turns into Shana's, and I'm holding a baby. When I attempt to find a happy place, Billy comes into view, but before the sweetness settles around me, the headlines of his betrayal zoom past him.

Billy has made it his life's mission to be my knight in shining armor, deeming my safety the number one priority above everything else, going so far as to isolate me from the world. Shana doesn't even have a fifth of his overbearing protection going on against Stewart's anger. He's the real monster out there. Not Lance. Not Leona's killers. Stewart is the one threatening the life of an innocent child. I'm surprised Billy wouldn't want to be the hero of that day rather than playing the role far past it's prime with me.

No one, *no one*, was looking out for Leona. I spin in the bed, punching my pillow, willing it to fluff up. It's not the pillow that is the problem; it's my part in Leona's murder that's making sleep evade me. I believed Stewart's words, every one of them when he said that Leona didn't want any money and left peacefully. When news rang out about her death, I held his hand at the dining room table while he sobbed tears, screaming that he wished he could have helped her.

He'd rip the newspaper up every morning, pissed that she was on the front with no sign of police catching her killer. A tantrum and rant about the unjust evils of the world shortly followed each day. At least, that's the act he wanted me to see, and I ate it up. What a heart he had, that though his marriage had fallen apart and they spent the last couple of years like strangers with her running around on him, he still cared for her — what a beautiful human being.

What a load of shit.

Stewart didn't care about Leona. He cared about his money, and he designed her exit so that she couldn't grab at the one thing that Stewart Miller loves. He wasn't sad to see her name in the papers every morning. He was up at the crack of dawn, waiting for the delivery so he could make sure he hadn't been caught over his morning coffee. He probably had a good laugh out in the driveway every morning after retrieving it from the box. It was the best way to start his day.

He shoved my ass out the door without so much as a few dollars that he threw in my direction and a shitty car service that he made a guy at work find for me. The man offered him discretion when he suggested the app. He told him how he used it for all his mistresses, and his wife never found out. How lovely. I went from mistress to wife to nothing in a few years, and I thought I would be the one to change him.

That's what Shana thought when she met him, too. I wonder what sob story he fed her about me so that she would take pity on him and entertain the thought of getting involved with not only a married man, a much older one at that. Stewart chose his career wisely as a lawyer. He could talk anyone into believing almost anything. I watched through the years as he would change people's steadfast beliefs on their head using his charisma to convince them they had it wrong.

The blinders have been torn from my eyes, though, and the thought of Stewart writhing in pain for all the misery that he's caused warms me. My stomach flops, threatening to spill everything I'm holding inside. My hatred for Stewart grows as the lies come to light. He's going to hurt Shana. There's no doubt in my mind. She's already threatened to leave, and that kind of tenacity is something Stewart longs to stomp out in people around him, just like he did to Leona. He has Shana under his thumb for now with the threat of hurting Delilah, but he knows she'll make a move. She's bold. There's something inside her that will threaten the precious throne Stewart sits on, and he won't wait until she plays her hand to react. No, Stewart Miller is already conducting his own plan to get rid of Shana.

I'm her only hope to be successful now. I'm the only one on the outside that knows the truth, not just from experience but from what she's told me. I won't turn my cheek or look the other way. Silence will not imprison me. I have to get her out of there. It's all I've thought about tonight, but it doesn't matter what plan I come up with; there's a glaring flaw in all of them.

Well, all except for the plan where Stewart no longer exists. He's the catalyst in everything. Without him, stress falls away from all involved.

I'm not like Stewart, though. I don't hurt people for sick pleasure. It's immoral, disgusting, and wrong. That's not what people were put on this earth to do, hurt one another. I remember so many times being shoved by a vacant hand in the streets simply because I found myself homeless due to my mother's poor decisions, or in the halls of the school because I found myself too broke for new clothing, and it was the butt of their game. I didn't lash out violently. I kept my calm. In a way, I believed my bullies to be lower than me because I didn't strike them back.

Stewart is the first person I've thought about pushing back. In our marriage, I never thought about taking my hand to him. I felt superior that I never stooped to his level. No matter how angry he made me, I didn't become him. Now, I wonder if it were the right choice. At the time, I believed that it was the way to show him love.

"*Cowards hit.*"

Ramona's words come to me, and I close my eyes to remember that day, standing in the motel room bathroom after throwing everything inside of it around in rage. She knew what to say then, and I push my memory to bring those words to me now.

"*Cowards throw things.*" *She demands eye contact with a single look on her face.*

"*Sorry, I—*"

"*Victims always apologize.*" *Her voice is steady, sure of each syllable.*

"*Listen, I—*"

"*You're no coward, Jane. You wear the bruises of a coward, and those will fade.*"

*I yank at the short sleeve shirt, aware of the purple finger-prints high on my shoulder showing now.*

*"The way you flinch when someone yells will fade when you realize that not everyone is out to correct you with their hand."*

*I peer down at my cheap sneakers, Ramona's words stripping me bare right here in this bathroom.*

*"Look at me, kid." Her voice is soft and kind. I wipe at the tears that are abandoning the security behind my eyelids and face her.*

*"You've heard his words delivered in your voice inside your head, and that too will fade. You won't believe the things he told you about yourself. You'll find that he lied about everything he called you. But, if you don't stick up for yourself, kid, you're going to fade. You will always be his victim if you can't find a way to allow this to strengthen you and your purpose in life. You can play the part all you want, but this isn't something you can fake until you make it. You have to work at recovering."*

I can't become Stewart. There's a way around this, and I will find it. I shut my eyes and force myself to try and sleep. The vision of his last breath leaving his body while I stand over him floods my mind, and I fight the smile begging to break out on my face.

I'm a monster.

My stomach clenches again, and I run to the bathroom and release its contents into the bowl. Once I'm sure the last of it is in the toilet, I lean my head against the cold porcelain as my leg bounces on the tile floor. The coolness of the room does nothing to stop the growing heat in my face. Thinking about murder makes me ill. How would I ever manage it?

No, I need to come up with a plan. I need to figure out a way to get Delilah out of there.

*There's another way, Jane. There is.*

Stewart is much older than Shana and me, plus he has a heart condition, so there's no way he'll last forever. Evil never dies, though, and wishing for someone's death is sick inaction and a wrong juju builder for karma. I flush the toilet and make my way back to the bed. I lie on the opposite side of the queen bed, having worried sweat stains into my usual side of the sheets.

I'm meeting Shana in just six more hours, and she's hoping I'll have a plan. I told her I would. I told her I would take care of this and find her a way out. That was before I knew the truth. Now, look at me. I'm lying in bed praying that my ex-husband dies because I want the mistress he knocked up to survive with her daughter and all his money. I want justice for them. I want justice for Leona.

I have to think of something.

Imagine what would happen to Delilah? Not only that, how would she feel about her mother knowing that she never tried to get away. And what if her mother tells her about me, what if we keep meeting? Delilah will know me, and she'll see that I'm aware of her situation. Three adults will let her down. That's too much to bear. I can't be one of those idle people.

They'll live with me.

I adjust my head on the pillow and curl the other pillow into my chest. I don't have much space, but I'll take care of them, and this is the last place that Stewart would think Shana would be. He'll never look for her here. Billy assures me this neighborhood is safe. Maybe it's secure against Stewart, as well. Then we could save up enough and move states. Far away from here.

That's what we have to do.

I drift off to sleep finally, but there's a nagging laugh in my dreams.

# Twenty-Seven

It's now fifteen minutes past 9:00, my meeting time with Shana, and I'm terrified more than I've ever been in my entire life that she isn't going to show. I let her down. Stewart knows we've been meeting. The black car had to have told him. They probably saw us at the coffee shop together.

I scour the headlines on the newspapers near the front of the store for the tenth time, look for anything about a woman and her child missing or being found dead. There's nothing. That doesn't mean she's alive or coming today. She could be trapped in the house. She could be crying for help at the top of her lungs, begging to the gods to free her from her hell, and no one hears her. When Stewart finds out that she wants out of the marriage, being locked inside the house will seem like a paradise to all the ways he will think of punishing her for such a heinous act. Or worse, Delilah.

"I'm here. I'm here." I hear her voice behind me pushing a shopping cart, and I nearly run to hug her before I remember that she's my ex-husband's mistress, and that's awkward. We shouldn't do things like that. However, we share a kinship that no one else around us can understand. We have been at the mercy of Stewart Miller. I can't help but smile that she's alive and pushing a cart with a baby seat inside.

"Sorry, Jane. Sorry. Sorry. Delilah threw up on herself and me. We both had to change. It was a messy and good

God did it smell awful. I debated about taking a shower, but that's a whole other ordeal with her right now. So, I cleaned myself up the best that I could with a baby wipe, and I'll have to get a shower when she naps today before Stewart gets home. I hope I don't smell now." She takes in my face. "What? What's wrong? Are you okay?" She grabs my arm.

"I just..." I go with the urge inside of me and encompass her. She hesitates before hugging me back. She has no idea the danger that's lurking, seeking to find us out. We may be ahead of them now, but it's not by a large margin.

"Why does it feel like you're wearing a fat suit?" She mumbles in my ear, and I release a chuckle and Shana at the same time.

"Because I need to look fat right now, and that's all I can say about that." I pat the sides of her arms and smile. I can't tell her about Lance; she's already worried.

"Okay," she draws out and starts to push the cart toward the baby aisle.

"You look horrible, though." Shana does a double-take of me as I lean against an etagere of diapers fighting the droop in my heavy eyelids now that the adrenaline from thinking she was in danger has left my body, suddenly making me aware of how little I rested last night.

"You, too," I shoot back.

"I didn't sleep." She flattens down her hair and wipes under her eyes like she can make the under circles go away that easily. Instead, it only rubs the concealer from them, exposing the dark shadows underneath, making them more prominent to the naked eye.

"Neither did I, but you got a baby to take care of at least. I have no excuse but my thoughts." I pop my head off the etagere and follow as she pushes further down the aisle.

"She slept excellent last night. She only woke up twice to eat." So, Shana had more on her mind than waiting for the next cry from Delilah's nursery to come over the monitor.

"Have you ever heard of karma, Jane?"

"Uh, yeah. That's a dumb question to ask me." I draw my eyebrows together.

"They say what you do in this, and previous lives, decides your fate in the future and all other reincarnations." She rattles off the definition that she no doubt preached when she was a yogi.

"Stewart better stop while he's ahead then." I almost laugh. Only the fucked-up people of the world who have seen the darkness could find the joke funny. Shana's lips curl up into a quick smile before they fall into a frown just as fast.

"What about me?"

"What about *me*?" I echo. I think Shana is quick to forget that I didn't grab money with clean hands, either. I watch Shana's face scrunch up in disgust at the thought of me being served a wrong dose of karma.

"How could you have any rotten karma? You work tirelessly to help Delilah and me, and I'm the one who took away your security."

"That doesn't mean I've never done wrong." I hum against my lips, feeling the tickle reverberating between them. "Maybe karma takes things into account. Maybe, I'm supposed to be in charge of your karma since I'm the one you wronged, and Shana, I think you've paid enough."

She looks my way but says nothing before she bends her legs, turning her head to the bottom shelf to examine the baby wash. I can tell that she needs a minute to take things in, but unfortunately, what I found at the library tells me that we don't have that kind of time.

"Come live with me," I whisper, as I duck down next to her, pretending to browse choices as well.

"I thought of that," she sighs, and I watch the relief hit her shoulders and allow them to come down away from her ears. "We would be a hassle." She glances back at the shopping cart with Delilah inside.

"You would be in the last place that Stewart would look." I smile at her. This is the first time I feel as if it could work. "Load up on whatever you need and leave now. Come back with me. We can find a way to give that damn black car the slip. My apartment is a safe place."

"Really?" She looks at the diapers on the aisle. "I don't have my clothes."

"We'll get you new ones. It's worth wearing a discounted shirt than to be living in that house for one more minute, isn't it?"

She smiles and nods in agreeance. Shana may have changed her simple ways for the more lavish lifestyle, but she's not too far gone that changing back would be hard. Despite Ramona's warnings that she'd miss the luxurious lifestyle, I don't believe Shana would long to take Stewart back just to have a more substantial residence.

"It is." She grabs my hand and squeezes. "Jane, I can't thank you enough."

"It's nothing." It's a lie, but one we are accustomed to handing out. In reality, it's a lot to ask of me. It's a lot to take on. The decision, however, is nothing. We stand up and start putting in stuff, around Delilah, that we know the baby will need. We can use Stewart's dime to pay for this last bit before we toss the cards away.

"You have to leave your phone here, Shana. He can track it. And we will dump your car in a different parking lot far from cameras, so he can't get the security footage to find out who's with you. I'll tell you the route to go to lose that black car."

"Okay, Jane." It's turned severe, but we haven't an inch for a mistake if she's to get out and save Delilah's life and her own. She must give the black car the slip. If my research proves anything, it's that Stewart Miller will not have his dirty laundry aired out, and Shana threatened to leave him, so she's in danger of doing just that. If the black car notices one hair of hers out of place, he'll scream to Stewart.

"I feel a weight lifting from my shoulders," she says. I watch a carefree smile dare to touch her lips. She can see the other side, but I have to get us there first.

"You know what? Me too."

We turn the aisle to grab a few more things when a familiar face catches us.

"Jane?" His face takes on a level of confusion when he looks upon my companion. "Mrs. Miller?"

"Hi, Billy." It's not my voice greeting him, and the words slip from Shana's lips with an ease that makes me uncomfortable. How does she know Billy? He stopped hanging around Stewart three years ago, and that was long before Shana.

They had a falling out. No, he hates Stewart. Why would he be addressing Shana so properly as if he...

Billy's skin flares with embarrassment when he notes the confusion on my face as I try to place the pieces of the puzzle together. He has a secret he's waiting for me to discover. He doesn't make to assist me, which could only mean one thing. He's still in the inner circle of Stewart Miller, and he's still working for him.

"Billy?" I back away from Shana and watch his head bow in admittance. He's still associated with Stewart. He never stopped being friends with him. Billy simply kept in the shadows so that he wouldn't see the abuse on me. "No, Billy. Stewart?"

"You girls sure look friendly." He scrubs down his face and shakes it at me. He's sad. "Excuse us, Mrs. Miller." He grabs hold of my arm and drags me away from Shana, who is leaning over the cart, holding on to Delilah's foot, afraid she'll slip through her fingers.

"What's going on here, Jane?"

This can't be right. Billy fought with Stewart. He stood up to him over the abuse. He told Stewart that he wasn't a real man for the marks on my body. There's no way he's kept himself associated with such evil. Sure, Billy was part of the downstairs meetings, the sin that surrounded Stewart's rise to power and money, but he couldn't still be there. Yet, he's calling Shana the same thing he used to call me when I was married to Stewart. *Mrs. Miller.* Stewart had all the employees, and other men call me that.

"You're still friends with Stewart," I spit.

"We aren't friends. I work for him," he whispers.

"No. No, that's not true. You work for the State Police Department." I wipe the sweat from the back of my neck.

"I do." He turns into the shelf. "I also take money from Stewart to make sure..." the rest of his sentence falls to the linoleum.

"To make sure of what?" I nearly scream in the middle of the store, drawing attention to us.

He lifts his head to me, and a tear escapes his eye. "To make sure his bad deeds are covered up and kept out of the paper."

"Oh my god. No."

"What are you doing with Shana?" He grips ahold of my arm and squeezes. "I told you to let this die. Don't get involved with anything of Stewart's."

"You're going to let her die for his money?" I flinch against the pain in my arm caused by Billy. He realizes what he's doing, and lets go.

"You don't know what's going on here, Jane." He looks back at Shana. "Leave now. Go home. You have enough to worry about than letting Stewart find out you've been hanging around his wife and child."

"So what if I have," I push his chest defiantly. He leans in toward me.

"Leona was no accident," he whispers the truth I have already figured out in my ear as I stare back at Shana.

"I know," I grit out.

"Leave, Jane," he pleads.

"Shana," I call to her. "Call Ramona at the motel if you need me." I turn and glare at Billy.

"I knew you were lying, Billy, but I didn't think this was what I was going to find out."

I walk away. If Stewart finds out about our friendship, it won't just be Shana on the front page news; it'll be me as well.

# Twenty-Eight

"Jane Voss." The last name of Billy leaves a film of sour grapes on my tongue, but the lady behind the gym desk doesn't notice.

I need to run. It's the only thing that calms me down and lets me think. I'm not done getting Shana and Delilah to safety. I'll run all damn night if that's what it takes to figure this mess out. I can't stay in that apartment surrounded by Billy's enclosure for a second longer. I know he'll show here tonight, and we need to talk. I need him to explain himself. Why would he pursue a relationship with me if he was harboring such a horrible lie that he knew would be a deal-breaker? Did he think I would never find out?

"You're all set. Go ahead in and have a great workout." She's perky. I want to punch her.

"Thank you." I stomp past her and up the stairs to the gallery that holds the treadmills. It's one of the safe places Billy told me that I could go, and with this gun still tucked in my waistband, I don't fear anyone right now. Let Stewart himself walk right in, and I'll lay him out.

I key in an incline on the treadmill and start it up. As my feet pound the belt, my mind races to sort out all the information that has been dumped before me. First things first, Leona's death was no accident. Stewart had it planned because he couldn't risk her sharing any secrets about the people he had in his pocket. Billy confirmed that today in the store.

She didn't fight her attacker, though. There were no signs of a struggle. I read that line repeatedly in almost every article. Leona Miller didn't fight back when someone was taking her life away from her. Did she know her assailant? Why would she accept her fate even when someone grabbed her and placed the knife to her throat?

My feet give way underneath me, and I grab the bars on either side of me to keep my face from meeting the treadmill. I didn't fight the driver. When his hands were around my throat, I gave in. I gave up. Leona was conditioned just like I was to be submissive to Stewart's attacks. He abused her.

*"I never had to hit Leona. She was the perfect wife. I left her for you, and this is how you repay me by acting like trash? Someday you're going to learn, Jane. Eventually you have to get this through your head. I'm the one with the power, and everyone needs to obey."*

Who killed Leona, though? Who made the final mark of abuse on her? Was it Billy? The thought doesn't sit right in my mind, and it doesn't match up with his confession in the grocery store today. He is paid to make sure Stewart's evil deeds don't end up in the paper. Did he cover up for Stewart? Was he one of the officers on the scene? Did he make it look like a drug deal to save Stewart's face and collect a paycheck? Is that why the police didn't investigate further?

How does he sleep at night? How can these two different people be the same person? Billy can't be a bad guy and my hero all at once. He's caught in Stewart's sticky web, with no way out. Shit, after knowing what happens to people when they dare try to expose Stewart, how can Billy escape?

I could turn him. He hates Stewart. I've seen the disgust encompass his facial features when Stewart's name is mentioned in the conversation. If I tell him what I'm trying to do with Shana, he could help us and cover up our tracks so that we can get away. Maybe it will help his karma, or perhaps it will motivate him enough to get out from under my ex-husband's thumb.

I run some more, but my head is still filled with cobwebs, so I deem the mission futile, and I make my way to my apartment for the night. Billy never showed up at the gym like I was sure he would. He's chosen his side, and it isn't mine.

I stare at the complex before me. If that's the way that it's going to be, then I'll make sure I'm ready for the attack. I dip my hand inside the waistband of my leggings and pull out the gun that Billy gave me. I hold it down at my side, concealing it inside the sleeve of my jacket.

When the elevator dings to let me climb on, I check all the corners before going inside, feverishly tapping the closed button. When the motor begins to roar to life, drawing me upward to my apartment, I lean my head back against the wall. I'm almost there.

The ping alerts that I've reached the fifth floor, and I grab the gun in both hands, still covering it in my jacket sleeve. I lean outside of the doors, checking left and right.

"Go away. I don't want to talk to you anymore today," I scream at the drunken lump in front of the door to my apartment.

"Where were you?" Billy slurs.

"I was at the gym. Isn't that a safe place for me to go so that the driver doesn't find me?" I air quote my words, then push the key in the door above Billy's head. When the doorknob turns over, he falls inside, having relied on the wooden door to hold him up.

"I knew that you'd be there." He smiles at me.

"You never showed," I bite out.

"I'm sorry, Janey."

"Go away, Billy."

"Forever or for now?" He's begging like a dog dying to be loved by its owner. I have nothing for him.

"You lied to me, Billy." I slam my bag down on the kitchen island, yank the refrigerator door open, and grab two water bottles. I hand one to Billy, still lying on the floor. He better sober the fuck up for this conversation because I'm not waiting to have it. We have wasted too much time as it is with all his lies.

"I had to," he grumbles as he shifts his body inside the apartment and kicks the door closed.

"No, you didn't."

"What was I supposed to say; 'Hey, Jane, it's nice to see you again. I still work for the asshole who kicked you out on your ass and abused you. Can we still be friends?'" I watch him push himself off the floor and sit with his back against the wall, stability that I can't tear away from him. "I'm sure that would have gone over splendidly." He opens the water bottle and chugs half of it.

"How about: 'Hey, Jane. Remember that driver who tried to kill you the night that I saved you, well, he's dead. He died of an overdose a week later, and I was the officer on the scene, so I knew it was the same guy.'" His mouth pops open in shock.

"How did you know?" His water bottle tilts in his careless hand, spilling some of the water into his lap.

"Instead, you used your hero antics to make me believe that I was in danger so that I would run to you." I slam the kitchen cabinet, taking my frustration out somewhere. I toss a towel at Billy to dry himself.

"Jane, I—"

"Oh, save me, Billy. Save me. You're the only one who can protect me and keep me safe. Wow, Billy, you're the white knight. Oh my god, I'm falling in love with you," I mock.

"I wasn't like that. I just thought—"

"You fucking thought that when I found out that you still work for Stewart, and that you help him cover up his shitty acts that it wouldn't matter because I was moony-eyed over the fact that you are my protector."

"Not exactly. You don't understand."

"Did you honestly think that these months of cultivating a relationship between us was going to be enough to withstand this lie?" I pace around the kitchen, running my hands through my hair and gripping the sides of it. I place the gun on the kitchen island.

"I was hoping you wouldn't find out." He tries to stand up but stumbles back to the ground. *Don't come close to me, Billy.*

"How'd that work out for you?" I stomp to the front door and pull it open. "You need to leave, Billy. Our relationship is done, and we are also done with this conversation."

"Jane, you don't understand." He makes another attempt to stand, and this time, he's successful.

"I don't want to." I shove him out and lock the door behind him. I won't sleep with a liar again.

# Twenty-Nine

I sink into my chair behind the desk of the motel office, gripping my morning coffee tightly to my chest. Ramona hasn't spoken a word, and I'm okay with it. I have plenty on my mind as is, talking feels too tedious at the moment. I turn away from her constant newspaper rattling to glare out the partition window at what dares to be a bright day. Fuck that.

Ramona keeps shaking the paper behind me, and it's getting on my nerves. I'm about to tell her so when I turn around and see her face. The color has drained from cheeks as if she's seen a ghost.

"Well," she whispers, "she's dead." Ramona shakes the newspaper and wipes a tear from her eye, breaking our silence with her sad admission. I scramble in my chair to wheel myself over to her, flinging coffee everywhere.

"Who? Who's dead? What are you talking about?" She waves her hand in front of her face trying to gain some composure to talk.

"Give me that." I rip the paper from her hands and read out loud. "Woman found dead in an apparent homicide-suicide. Paige Garrison..." I breathe a sigh of relief not to be reading Shana's name, and an immediate breath of pain follows to be reading Paige's name. "Shit. No. No."

*There was drug paraphernalia at the scene, and officers do believe that drugs were involved in the deaths.*

I wanted more for Paige's ending, more for her fight. I swore she would come back and prove Ramona wrong.

"I couldn't reach her. Those damn Bambi eyes," Ramona screams, standing she throws her chair against the wall.

"Ramona, it's not—"

"My fault? It is. I could have been softer. I could have held her here. I could have fucking locked the door from the outside so that she couldn't leave and throw her life away. I should have learned." A haunting sound, like a feral animal, comes from deep within Ramona's body.

"You couldn't have held her against her will. You told me that everyone has to do it for themselves."

"She would have been safe, Jane. Safe. I offer protection here. I failed her."

"She wasn't here, Ramona. She left. You kept her safe when she was here."

"No. No. I didn't. I failed her." I rush to embrace Ramona.

"No, you didn't," I say, but she pushes me off.

"I need a walk."

After her retreating back fades from view, I look down at the paper again. Paige didn't make it out to the other side. Her boyfriend sucked her back into the life of drugs and abuse. No matter how Ramona tried, or what she offered Paige to start a new life, something about the past pulled her back. Something in the past always pulls you back.

"Jane." Speaking of the past.

"Go away, Billy," I groan at the familiar voice behind me through the partition.

"Jane, we need to talk."

"This is not a good time, Billy. Not a good time at all." I'm facing away from him, looking at the door that Ramona exited not too long ago. "I have work to do."

"I heard about Paige."

"Good for you, you can read the newspaper." Ramona's sarcasm must have worn off on me as I let the words fall from my lips without care.

"Fine, if you aren't going to come out here to talk to me, then you can sit there and listen." He pauses, waiting for me to turn around, but I refuse to look at him. I can't look upon his lying face. A face I've kissed, hoping for a future.

"Shana slipped up last night and said something about you to Stewart. He knows you guys have been talking, what about she wouldn't tell him. She told him she just bumped into you at the grocery store, and that's all, but it was enough to get him riled up. You can't go to that grocery store anymore. He's going to be looking for you there. He's pissed, Jane. Don't you understand?" The plea in his voice turns my chair.

"Well, sounds like you need to go home and think about how you're going to cover up my death like you did Leona's," my words are venom, and he flinches at the sting of them. "Make sure they don't use drugs this time. The line is getting old." I look at the door that Ramona left unlocked this time. I walk over and turn the deadbolt.

"That's not fair, Jane. I'm your friend."

"Friend?" I felt insulted having been more than that not but a handful of days ago, or at least that was the part he let me play in this lie.

"I protect you."

"You protect me? From what? The driver is dead. Lance is dead." I throw my hands to my hip, daring Billy to challenge me and dispute what I know to be fact now.

"I know. I should have told you, but it was the only way that I could keep you safe."

"Do you hear yourself? Are you even listening?" I walk toward the partition and lean in. "Lance is dead."

"Yes. I know."

"The driver who tried to kill me is dead."

"Yes," he agrees again.

"Keeping me terrified that I'm going to be jumped at any time by a dead man is sick, Billy."

"No. No, it isn't. It was the only way." He clenches his fist in irritation.

"Whatever."

"Listen, Jane. Stewart's pissed. He'll be looking for you."

"Yeah, yeah. Lay low." I mock one of his favorite commands.

"Leona was given a week, and she decided to talk. Think about it. If Stewart knows you are interfering with his new life." He taps the partition ledge. "Get out of town, Jane."

"Shit." I slam my head on top of the desk.

# Thirty

The carpeted floor in the office wears a hole from my feet pacing for hours awaiting Ramona's return. When I saw the doorknob turn, I couldn't hold the information inside any longer. I blurted everything out at once, and she made me slow down and tell it to her again.

I divulged everything. She took it in, her eyes growing wider with each revelation that I shared.

"Billy?" Ramona can't believe what I'm telling her. It doesn't fit what we know of his character. Hell, I'm still puzzled that he turned out to be under Stewart's wing still.

"Yes," I reluctantly admit.

"Works for Stewart? Or worked for Stewart?"

"Yes," I shout. "Same thing. I thought he decided he didn't want to be part of Stewart's team, but he stayed."

"He saved your life, though. When that guy tried to kill you, he put his life on the line to get that maniac off you. He can't be a part of the bad guys." Ramona wants to champion for Billy. He's been good to me, to Ramona, to everyone we've seen him touch. The amount of work that Billy put into fooling me about what team he was playing on tricked the fuck out of not only me but Ramona.

"That was after Stewart, though. Maybe he knew Stewart was kicking me out, and he followed me. What doesn't make sense is the driver died a week after the incident, and Billy was the officer on the scene, and he never told me. I found out at the library, searching the internet. He has spent months telling me that I need to be careful or the driver will find me." I scrub my chin. "He thought if I needed him, a relationship would form. It worked. It makes me sick. He wanted to cover up his sin and have me all at the same time. It blew up in his face last night at the apartment when he came over drunk out of his mind, telling me that I didn't understand."

"Hmm."

"What?"

She sighs. "Sounds to me like Billy was using it as an excuse to make you stay low."

"Yes, that's what I'm saying. He was playing the part of the hero, abusing that night, and lying about it to make me fall for him."

"No. No, that's not it."

"That is it. What the hell are you talking about? You're not making any sense."

She leans up in her chair, grabbing both of my knees. "He can't expose his boss's secrets, the secrets he is trained and paid to cover up. Something about you, though, caught his eye, and he couldn't sit with watching you have an accident like Stewart's first wife."

"Oh my god, are you saying—"

"That driver was hired to kill you, Jane. No doubt in my mind. Billy didn't follow you. He had the inside track because he works for the monster." Ramona leans back and checks that the door is locked. I spin around, pushing against the partition window double-checking that it is closed as well. I stare out into the parking lot.

"That maniac was hired?" I ponder.

"I would bet good money on it. Why else would Billy say that the driving app didn't have his information? Stewart ordered that car and not from an app. He wanted a scummy creature who could be dazzled by money to sign up for the job and kill you."

"Shit."

"Big shit."

"Triple shit." I peer out into the night, but nothing looks suspicious enough to cause an alarm, only the fact that I just connected the dots and found out my ex-husband was trying to have me killed.

"What about the car that followed me when I was running. That doesn't make sense either if it was Lance."

"Open your eyes, kid. You're still acting like Billy will turn good, and Lance will rise from the grave. If there's a car detailing Shana, Stewart has people scouring the streets daily looking for you. You didn't die in that car like you were supposed to, and if Billy was the officer on the scene of that man's death, then Stewart was pissed that the maniac failed, and sent people to deal with him for making a mistake. Stewart doesn't sound like a man who stops trying when his first idea fails."

"No, I agree, he wouldn't. So, when the guy saw me running, he decided to follow and see if I was me."

"It's a good thing you changed your hair, kid. That may have helped you."

"Yeah." I glance over at the side of the desk. I can't believe it. All this time, I was worried about Lance discovering my whereabouts and finishing the job of killing me, but it was Stewart not finding me that I needed to focus on. I left him in my past, but he didn't want to stay there, too worried that I might share his secrets with the world and knock him off his pedestal. Stewart doesn't leave things to chance, and after Leona threatened to tell her story, he wasn't risking the next scorned ex-wife doing the same.

"Makes sense now," Ramona breaks into my thoughts.

"What does? Oh man, what else?"

"That boy always wanted to make sure you were in an apartment that he found for you and that your phone was a throwaway one without a contract, and why he told you to sign up for things with his last name attached. Man, he sure as shit is good at covering up things. He wanted to make you invisible to Stewart, and he almost did. If Shana never saw you in the grocery store, you'd still be hiding like that."

I sigh, "I don't know how I should feel toward Billy right now." I sink into the chair, exhausted and emotionally drained.

"You need a beer, kid?" Ramona hobbles over and unlocks the small closet near the corner of the room. I always wondered what she hid in there, never being allowed to peer inside. She expressed it to be off-limits. Hers only. She opens it now to reveal a mini-fridge stocked with beer cans.

"You asshole. All this time that I have been here, and you're just now sharing this with me?"

"Eh," she lifts one shoulder, "I couldn't let you drink all my stash." She hands me a can and sits down with one for herself.

"Well, cheers to my fucked-up life getting even more fuckier." I tap my can against hers.

"Are you going to listen to Billy?" She pops open her beer and takes a sip.

"I suppose I should. Every piece of advice that he's given me has been for the best." I follow suit and drink half of the can in one gulp. It's terrible, but beggars can't be choosers right now, and discovering the guy you liked helps your ex-husband cover up murders is not something water will help swallow.

"Come with me?" I beg Ramona.

"I'm too old to move, kid."

"My life won't be the same without you, though," tears start to form. "It's not fair that I have to leave and lose everything again because of Stewart."

She wiggles in her chair closer to me and pats my knee. "That's true. Your life is much better now for knowing me."

I release a small tear-laced laugh at her, and we share in the merriment until the nagging ache fills me again. *Shana*. What am I going to do about Shana? I promised her that I would find a way out for Delilah and her. As I sit here in the company of my friend, she's up in her house, wrought with worry about not escaping a monster.

"Well, I hate to say it, but you know that you want to hear it: You were right, Ramona. I got myself into a whole mess of trouble now by talking to Shana." I slump down in my chair.

She gulps down her beer and tosses it into the trash can, then leans back as far as the computer chair will allow her to go. I wish I could be as relaxed as Ramona is toward the entire situation. If I had listened to her and not gotten involved, I could have been.

"I hate being right." I know she's thinking about Paige and her Bambi eyes right now.

"I know," I whisper. "Now, I'm more terrified for Shana and Delilah than I've ever been."

"If you could get the eyes away from her long enough, you could probably give her a chance to run." It is interesting to hear Ramona is on my side now about Shana, having been so adamantly against me even talking to her. Having Ramona in my corner strengthens my resolve to find an escape for them.

"Where would she go?" I don't have much time before I needed to run away myself. I'm sure the pressure will be on Shana now to spill the beans about me. I don't blame her for doing so, considering what Stewart will do to her, or God-forbid, Delilah, to get the answers. "And how would I ever get them to look away from her now?"

"I don't have those answers, kid."

"Well, let's sit here until we do." I gulp down my beer and toss it in the garbage.

"Go home," she orders.

"What?" I screech, but it doesn't faze her one bit. She turns on the little TV in the corner and glues her eyes to it. Half the time, I don't think Ramona is even watching what's on that tiny thirty-inch screen. It's more of her thinking spot to zone in and focus.

"It's late. You just discovered that your ex-husband hired someone to kill you and that your cop boyfriend lied about his involvement and that. He's been trying to hide you from the wrath of his boss for months. You need to think about yourself for a moment. Go home."

"But you could help me. If I stay here, then we can bounce ideas off each other until one sticks. We could save them, Ramona. Please."

"Listen, kid. I'm not sure I can help you solve this one. That girl has Bambi eyes, and she's either selling you short right now or submitting to never leaving that property again. You could be in danger sitting here right now and not even know it, what with the crooked cop that has a crush on you and an ex-husband who has everyone in his little pocket. You're fucked if you tangle up with it. So, throw your hands up. Get out of it. Go home and pack your bags. Start a new life." This wasn't like the Ramona I believed I found when I first came to the motel or the one who laced every comment with bitterness at my leaving. This was the failed Ramona talking, the one that couldn't save the girl before me, the one who feels like she couldn't save Paige, the one who doesn't see any point in trying anymore.

"Another new life." I roll my eyes. "What about Delilah?" I beg and plead to her good nature one last time before I call this a night.

"Well, in the morning, I could make an anonymous call and have someone check out the place, but we both know they're going to make it through the inspection. We could call the cops, but you already saw them today." She sighs. "I want to help, kid, I do, but I just can't. This is a tough one."

"That last girl chose her fate, Ramona, and so did Paige. It was nothing that you did. It wasn't the way you pushed them or the way you went about trying to heal them. It was the only way they saw out. Hell, maybe it was the only way out for them. They just wanted the pain to end, and that much has been accomplished. If you didn't pull the trigger, why blame yourself?"

"Because they were my responsibility, Jane. You just don't get it." She shakes her head and wipes a stray tear from her face. "I took them into my home, my motel, and told them that I would help. I promised them."

"I do." I stop her and place my hand on her knee. "I do understand, Ramona. Shana and Delilah feel like my responsibility. I'm the only one on the outside that knows what's happening, and I can't be another person turning my head and looking away. I can't break my promise to Shana that I'm going to help her get out of this. I can't break the promise I made to that sweet innocent life who doesn't know the evil inside of her father."

Her wrinkled hand encompasses mine. "I get it. I do." Her face lifts in a small, sad smile. "Go home and sleep, kid. You'll think of something. I have yet to see you give up. Those two are blessed to have you. I've taught you well."

"That you did," I whisper.

I stand and kiss her forehead. Something I have never done before, but Ramona feels like a mother to me. She's something I haven't had in a long-time— family.

"Goodnight, Ramona." I walk to the door of the front office. I look back and see her staring out her little partition window, as if a guest is going to come by at any moment to book a room for the night.

"Goodnight, kid." She calls as I lock the door and shut it behind me. I sigh and let my body relax. I'm going to figure it out. Stewart won't win.

As I leave, the parking lot looks like a ghost town. Only Ramona's car and mine sit in the back lot. The customer parking lot holds four cars, none of them the black car that followed me during my jog. I look for the blue car that follows Shana, but I don't find it. No one here in this parking lot, but empty vehicles. Paranoia creeping over me once again. I laugh it off.

This is how my life will be now, how it has been the last couple of months, looking over my shoulder to make sure no one is reaching out to grab me. Only I was looking for the wrong madman. What a shitty way to live. Not nearly as shitty as sleeping next to the monster.

# Thirty-One

The clock turns over minute after minute under my careful watch. No sleep again tonight. After an hour of watching it, I give up and decide that it's no use. No one can sleep with this much shit hitting the fan, so I might as well throw on makeup and start the day.

I took the long way home last night and made sure that no cars followed me. When I pulled into the complex, I waited with the engine off for ten minutes, but no one else showed. Still, I'm frozen as I stare at the couch against my front door, terrified to open it and find a monster behind it.

A cardboard box sits empty on my bedroom floor. I couldn't bring myself to do it. I thought about it, and I should have packed last night and left, putting myself five steps ahead of the devil, but I won't. I cannot continue living my life out only in the shadows, turning every corner, wondering if they will find me. I won't walk down every road, expecting to find someone that Stewart hired to kill me waiting.

If Stewart doesn't find me, there's one thing that will, without a doubt. Shana. I won't sacrifice Shana and Delilah for false security. I'll still be looking over that shoulder if I get them out, but I want them next to me. I can't selfishly take myself out of the equation, driving with only my taillights for them to see.

My fingers trace the butt of the gun tucked in the waistband of my pants. On tiptoes, I creep to the peephole and find nothing on the other side when I lean in over the loveseat. I push the couch away from the door, causing a little more noise than I'd like. I look outside the peephole again— just an empty hallway.

It's time to put my plan into action. The deadbolt turns under the weight of my trembling hand. With the door open, I find nothing popping out to greet me. No Boogeyman waiting in the midst for me. The possibility of Lance's face returning never brought this much fear inside of me.

I need to get a message to Shana through Ramona or one of her contacts. The three of us need to leave this city. The sooner, the better. Tonight. It has to be tonight.

My car sits close to the entrance of the apartment building. I lucked out last night that this spot was free. Parked next to me, Billy leans against his truck, sipping his hot coffee and watching me. My heart picks up the pace with fear, and I reach for the gun.

"No need for that, Janey." His eyes are lined with darkness. Perhaps a lack of sleep. "I would never hurt you. I've given so much to protect you, why would you ever think that I could turn on you?"

"I don't know what to think anymore. My life has been one lie after another these past few months.

"I hope not everything." He means our relationship; the one started with a lie.

"Why are you here? Are you following me now?" I tilt my head to the side.

"I came here to see if you listened to me for once and left," he says.

"Nope. Still here."

"You're too stubborn, Jane." I frustrate him. Never listening and always wanting to do things the hard way.

"Yeah, well, I have a few things to do before I leave."

"So you are going?" He looks surprised. It's what he wanted, but he can't cope with the reality hitting him that I won't be near him anymore. It's safer, but we're all greedy when we find someone we like.

"Isn't that what you wanted? Isn't that what's safest? Isn't that my only fucking choice?" I throw my hands out to either side of me.

"It's not what I want. It's what's going to keep you alive, and that's the thing that I want above everything else, *everything* else."

"Because you like me? Or because you don't want to live with covering up my death?"

"Both," he swallows hard.

"Aren't you risking being found out by being here?"

"No, they don't follow me." He kicks a stone near his shoe.

"How nice to have the devil's trust," I bite.

"It's helped to keep you safe," he spits back.

"Safe. Oppressed. Unaware. In Danger. All sounds the same." I roll my eyes. Before they settle back in the middle where they need to be, Billy leans over and kisses me. My hands push hard against his chest, effectively breaking the contact of our lips.

"What the hell, Billy?"

"I had to." He starts crying. "You're about to hate me more."

"Why? What happened? Shana? Delilah?"

"Get in your car, Jane." He sniffles.

"No."

"Don't you need to go to work?" His voice cracks.

"Why? What's waiting for me? You sold me out, didn't you?"

"No," he growls and flicks his head to me in disgust. "I would never. I'd give them the entire world before I gave them you, and I won't apologize for saying so." With that, he spins on his heels and climbs inside of his truck, motioning for me to do the same.

I head out of the parking lot, and sure enough, as I'm waiting for the traffic to clear, Billy pulls up behind me and waves as I look back in my rearview mirror. Dickhead. I slam my head on the top of the steering wheel. I tap the gun jutting into my stomach. Have I lost him entirely to Stewart?

I pull out, turning to the right and head toward the motel. The road opens to two lanes, and Billy takes the opportunity to pass me. Shit. What is he planning on doing? I hit my brakes and duck down. Does he intend to kill me on the road this morning? Oh my god. He wants me safe from Stewart, but has his mind warped into believing taking me out himself will be the best way?

As Billy's truck comes up alongside me, I push my head back in line with the middle portion between the driver and backseat. He has a gun, and I can't let him get a clear shot at me. I peak over, but he keeps his head straight, never once glancing over at me or breaking his concentration from the road ahead of him.

When the truck passes my car, he steers back in front of me. He wants me to follow him. He's crossing Stewart by leading me somewhere safe again. I let go of my clenched breath with relief. The motel comes up on the right side of the road, and suddenly his turn signal flicks on for the entrance. I instinctively turn my signal on as well. Billy is a lot of things, most of which have turned out to be wrong, but he has always had my safety at the forefront of his mind.

I expect him to turn in, but when he comes to the entrance, he keeps going and turns his turn signal off, picking up speed. Odd. He runs the red light, no longer wanting me to follow him. He was making sure I got here safe and didn't go anywhere else. I let a cleansing breath of oxygen fall from my lips — another extension of Billy's protectiveness.

I turn into the parking lot of the motel, but instead of circling around to the back lot, I park in front of the main entrance partition because a sign on the front of it catches my eye as it waves in the breeze of the morning — bile races to my throat at the mere sight of it. I undo my seatbelt, making sure the coast is clear before running over to it.

*For Jane.*

The handwriting is familiar. I saw it on every 'I'm sorry' present in the first year of marriage and then the horrible beatings after that. I rip it off and flip the paper over, but that's all it has written on it. There's nothing remarkable about the piece of paper. It's an everyday piece of computer paper. It looks the same as the stuff we use here at the motel. The black ink comes from Stewart's favorite fountain pen in his office. I can see the damn thing when I close my eyes, and I imagine the monster sitting there writing this note for someone to post here.

"Oh, God. Ramona." I scream into the morning and slam my face and hands against the partition, cupping my hands around my eyes so that I can see inside. My eyes fearfully devour the awful scene before me.

Lying on the floor of the office, in a pool of blood, is my dearest friend. There are papers thrown about her, and the chair is tipped over, lying close to her hips, indicating a struggle. She's staring up at the ceiling. I slam against the partition and call her name again. There's no answer.

I run to the back of the motel, fumbling with my keys along the way to unlock the door of the office. She could be alive. She could be dead. The knob gives way as soon as I touch it. Unlocked. Ramona would never leave this door unlocked. How did they get in?

The room smells of copper and death, the mixture entering my brain and stealing away all good memories with Ramona. She's gone. I know it before I touch her, but I do it anyway, and she's cold to the touch. Stiff from the life leaving her body.

"Ramona, wake up. Ramona. Ramona, please wake up." I shake her gently, but her throat is cut, and there's so much blood around her. I slam backward onto my butt and bang the back of my head against the wall, gripping the note in my left palm.

*For Jane.*

If it's murder Stewart wants, it's murder he'll get.

# Thirty-Two

I wait for the cops to arrive out on the sidewalk of the motel. I give them a fake name. I stop anyone else from looking inside and seeing Ramona in that shape. The frigid cement stiffens my joints and makes them ache, but it's nothing to be upset about because I can still feel the ache in my body. Ramona can't. They took her out because of me. To send me a message for daring to mess with anything of Stewart's. Why didn't they take me when I left?

My black hair covers my eyes as I bow my head. I don't look like the Jane they all know, so I was probably not even a blip on their radar, just an employee leaving for the night. I guess the more important question is, how did Stewart find me here? How did he know about my connection to Ramona? And who told him?

*"I'd give them the entire world before I gave them you, and I won't apologize for saying so."*

I stuff the note deep into my pocket, where the cops won't find it. I won't give my past away and play Stewart's torrid games. Stewart has entered *my* world now, and I won't stop until he goes down. There's nothing but good inside the woman lying on the floor in the motel, yet evil is the one that gets to live. That's not fair, and I want what's fair above all else—an eye for an eye. Only I'm not a coward like Stewart, I won't send someone else to do the dirty work, and I won't bother taking out things next to him when what I want is his blood spilled.

I see the truck pull up and park next to my car. I catch his eye behind the steering wheel as he eases his way out and holds the door open for a while. He's gathering his thoughts, debating about the best way to approach me. I bet he's rehearsing the lines that Stewart wrote down for him. My ex-husband can't let go of the charade of God he likes to play; he must control every little aspect. Still, those words will be easier to say than anything Billy can muster himself. He knew Ramona. He knew how good she was, but he traded her in for his career and loyalty to a scumbag with money. He knew that she was dead before I did.

*"You're about to hate me more."*

"Hey, Billy," the cop standing before the entranceway greets him.

"Billy," I bite out. My mascara has run down my face and hardened the skin. Speaking words makes the tightness crack, and nearly shatters my resolve, as well.

He nods to the officer on the scene already. "Hey, Chuck." Billy points his chin toward me in question, and Chuck shakes his head.

"She came on the victim this morning and called us. Her name's Melody." Chuck motions for Billy to come closer to him so that he can disclose some secret information. He's a poor whisperer. "She's been a bit difficult, cussing out Joe for doing his job."

"Joe is a dick, and he talked about her like she was nothing. She's not a fucking case file," I bite at Chuck.

"I'll handle her, Chuck," Billy intercedes as Chuck pushes his chest toward me, ready for another argument.

"We're old friends." I want to laugh at him as the lie quickly passes his lips. I was stupid for believing a single word that has passed Billy's lips in the last couple of months.

"Get her to leave, Billy, or I'm hauling her out of here myself." Chuck stomps off down the sidewalk to cool off, none the wiser that his case could be solved by looking at the person here with me.

Billy groans as he lowers himself to the ground next to me. He doesn't say a word but places his hands together between his knees. I feel the uncomfortable tension rising from him. Tears start to fall from my eyes all over again. For Ramona and for the relationship I thought I had with Billy, I weep.

"If you want to remain anonymous with the fake name and all, you better stop instigating Chuck." He sighs.

"She was a good person." I scowl as the sun is just beginning to rise, and already the light is gone for Ramona.

"If I warned you about them coming last night, they would have killed you and me, too. I know you wouldn't have left her side if you knew what was going to happen." He sighs with frustration, half at the fact that I didn't understand his position and reasoning, and the other half at the fact that he put himself in this position.

"They. Don't you mean *you*?" I turn my head slowly toward him. "What's wrong, Billy? Don't you want to go in and see your handy work? Isn't that why you put your turn signal on for me this morning?" If looks could kill, Billy would combust right in front of me all over this parking lot, and I'd play volleyball with his fucking head. I have never felt my trust betrayed so harshly before him.

"I didn't do it, Jane. I didn't do any of it." His eyes stare out into the parking lot, not brave enough to face me. He wants to free himself of guilt by placing the blame on others because they were physically there, and he wasn't. I won't let him.

"What's your job, Billy? To commit the crimes or to turn the other way?" I watch the veins in his neck pop. "You sure as shit aren't a cop. How dare you even call yourself that. You don't serve or protect a community. You turn your head so that one man can rise to power by exploiting other human beings. You let murderers dine at your table, Billy, and what's worse is you serve them." Billy's head falls lower with each word catapulting from my throat.

"I don't like what I've gotten myself into, Jane. I never wanted this to happen. I liked Ramona, but I couldn't stop it last night. If I did, I would have been in deep shit myself, and I couldn't have come here today and warn you to get out." He dares to let a tear fall from his eyes, and it's all I can do not to turn violent.

"Would you like me to slit your throat right here, and get you out of it, Billy?" My voice is low and haunting, sending shivers down my spine and his. His head pops up in shock at the sound of my voice. "What would Stewart do if I pushed the blade into your esophagus? Would he find another right-hand man to take down the people who question the shit he does? What if I sent him your head in a box to let him know that his crimes won't be so easily hidden anymore? Do you think he'd feel sorry for you, and pause in his day to think of you?"

"Jane." I can't tell if it's a warning or a plea.

"What's that saying — snitches get stitches? You snitched on me, Billy." I pull the note from my pocket and throw it in his lap. "Now, tell me who the fuck did this, or I'll make you bleed all over this sidewalk before stealing your truck and getting myself inside that mansion with no fucking problem, and pay your boss a little visit."

"Fuck, Jane." He picks the note up like it's going to bite him.

"Guess who's handwriting that is, Billy?" I place my chin in my hand and squint at him. He's nothing but a fucking pea to squish.

"Stewart," he answers.

"Who else does he have working for him?" I grip my knees, white knuckles blazing in the light of the rising sun, it's taking all I have not to punch Billy in the face. Did he honestly think that being in the company of Stewart would keep his name clean?

"I don't want in on this anymore, Jane. I want it to end. I didn't tell them about Ramona. I swear. I was not the one to let it slip." He turns to me with pleading eyes. Perhaps Billy was always what I saw, an ethical and moral cop, or at least that's what he set out to be. We don't ever get what we set out for in the beginning. He was dazzled by the powerful man inviting him to dinner parties with grand ideas of how he was going to support the force or get Billy a position he's always dreamed of having. Stewart groomed Billy until he was in too deep that he couldn't pull out. He had his own type of prenup to consider now.

"I'm getting Shana and Delilah out of there. He's not hurting that baby. Grow a set, Billy, and help me, or you'll let him hurt an innocent little girl. That will be on your hands and let me tell you something – if he so much as raises his voice to that little girl, and I find out, I'll kill you on the fucking front lawn." I've never felt so volatile in all my life. I didn't know I had such a wretched side to myself. I thought it only lived in Stewart. I don't think anyone can fight a monster as strong as he is without becoming one themselves. I don't feel my stomach turn over at the thought of murder now.

"Didn't you hear me? I'm not the one who sold Ramona out to Stewart. Think, Jane. Who does that leave?" I already knew who told Stewart about Ramona long before Billy pulled in here, long before I called the cops to report her murder. It was Shana, and I can't blame her. I just can't because she had her child to think of when he came down on her, questioning her about me.

"She didn't have a choice, and you know it." I push a tear off my cheek.

"You were never trying to get Stewart's money," Billy muses, allowing the insults and threats I've thrown to roll off. He's earned them, even if he wasn't the one to give Ramona's name.

"No, you absolute dumb fuck. How could you ever think that that was my intention meeting with Shana?" My words beam off his body as if I have thrown knives instead. "I couldn't give a shit less about the dirty money that he robs

from people. I want to get Shana and Delilah out of there."
I scoff. "You believed the worst in me so fucking easily, and
I was stupid enough to see the good in you. You're right; I
do that wrong. I shouldn't look for it anymore. I should do
what's easiest. Maybe then Ramona would be alive."

"No, you can't change, Jane," he pleads.

I don't have time for his fake friendship or delusional
insight into my personality from a liar. I crumble the note
that's sitting in his lap and hold it up to his nose. He takes it
from me.

"Who the fuck is working for him?" I bite every word
out, making sure the spray of spit hits Billy's face. I want him
to feel my words, not just hear them. They need to rever-
berate in his mind and stay deep within him where he can't
shake it or drown it out with noise. Where late at night,
when he thinks he's falling asleep, they echo from within,
never letting him rest.

He shifts his glance back out into the lot, past the cars to
the road behind. People getting on with their days and lives
not attached to Stewart. "Leave them to me. I'm sure they
left fingerprints here. They've been getting sloppy." He lifts
himself from the sidewalk and stares down at me with the
note still in his hand. I watch him take the lighter from his
pocket and set it ablaze.

"I want them," I seethe. I'm bloodthirsty and looking to
quench the craving. Revenge will be mine.

"No, you don't."

"Yes, I—"

"You want Stewart." Those three words echo around inside of me and linger all around outside. It's the truth, and Billy isn't stopping me from seeing Stewart this time around.

"You'll be free tonight. I'll take the two who did this into the station." He looks down at me.

"Don't lie to me, Billy. I have no problem killing you or everything you love." What they've made me scares me, but I choose to embrace it. I'll play their game, and I'll win. If I don't, who will stop them?

"I know, Jane." He lets the paper fall to the ground on the sidewalk. "I know." With that, he walks into the building to find Ramona's killers. I press the gun against my side under my shirt. I'll find the coward who couldn't bother to kill Ramona himself. He sent other people to do his dirty work, but I'll come and do mine all on my own. I lift a cigarette from my pocket that I took off the desk inside. They were Ramona's. I push the end to my lips and lean forward to the paper burning on the ground to light it.

"I'm coming for you, Stewart," I whisper as the nicotine ignites.

# Thirty-Three

Powerful men are impossible to take down, mainly because they have the needs of others clenched in their fists, creating loyalty out of fear. Fear is a powerful emotion. Stewart built his throne by making sure he had something everyone needed or wanted, and that their secrets were hidden in his back pocket so he could ensure their loyalty. He found Billy's naïve nature as an exposable weakness, playing on that until he built a friendship he could manipulate and spoil. When you create fear in others, you create a barrier of protection for yourself. Stewart's wall is miles thick.

He gained my loyalty in the same way. My misguided love for him was the first slippery slope, then his money and security the second. When he told me that Leona didn't love him, I remembered the feelings of a father who didn't bother to see me as anything but a nuisance, and my heart reluctantly opened to him out of pity. Once I became aware of his fortune, I allowed myself to be blind to his flaws to gain what I thought was a secure future. He sealed the deal, and then I was locked in with nowhere else to turn. He never feared repercussions for the marks he left on me. I never posed a threat. That was then. Women who are scorned and fresh out of fucks to give are harder to deter. Stewart's reign ends now, and I'll be the one gaining power by fear.

I snub out the butt of my cigarette on the concrete. Officers are surrounding the area, and I need to leave before the gawking of the press comes with this chaos. I don't need them to identify me. They'll all know my name soon enough because I don't give a fuck if I shoot Stewart down in broad daylight with a thousand witnesses, at least that motherfucker will be dead. My best friend is gone, my other friend is a liar, and I have one last friend who is fighting a monster.

I push off the cement. Stewart wanted to send me a message. *For Jane.* The same way he wrote it on every gift that he left out after putting a souvenir shiner on my face for me to hide with a pound of makeup. The same way he would write it on lavish Christmas presents I had to open in front of a crowd so that they could see how spoiled I was, and how he doted on me.

"Jane."

I turn my head at the desperate plea from Billy's untruthful lips.

"I don't have time for your shit." I walk over to my car.

"Wait. Please wait." I yank the car door open as he closes in. He slows and holds the door so that I can't close it.

"Billy," I warn.

"Listen to me." He looks around the parking lot, and it's then that I realize he does it a lot. He's always been worried about being found. He lives a life looking over his shoulder, and it's miserable, so why did it want that for me? Just to stay alive? What a horrible life.

"Who are you looking for?"

His eyes set on mine in a funny way. "You don't get it, do you? You're really that blind."

I don't like his tone. "No, I see things a lot clearer these days. I've had drivers hired to kill me, and a crooked cop hiding me." I've solved that puzzle. "I'm just wondering what part of the past are you afraid of today, Billy."

"Jane," he sighs. "Listen, please."

"No. You had your chance. If you get in my way, I will fuck you up." I spit at him.

"I won't get in your way." He lets go of the door and comes around to lean onto the passenger door in the back. "I like you. I always have."

"Aside from your misconstrued view of how to protect me, what good does your affection do me?" I slam my hand on the roof of the car.

"I—"

"It doesn't make me want to be a better person, and it doesn't seem to keep friends for me." I tilt my chin to the front of the motel office. "What good is it?"

"I fucked it up. I know, but I..." He pauses and looks out toward the back end of the vehicle, at the sky brightening into the afternoon.

"What?" I'm annoyed that he's holding any of my attention. I have work to get done.

"I want to do right by you. I don't want to be Stewart's puppet anymore." Billy turns toward me, and I watch a tear cloud his eye. My heart lurches against my will, and I turn my head away before he gets back inside.

"Then stop being so easily manipulated. It's hard; sure, no one said it's easy to get out from underneath a thumb as oppressive as Stewart's. But, here's the secret. You have the inside track to take him down. You hold more power. What turns the head? The neck."

He nods, staring back at the motel before deciding to give in.

"There are two men that do his bidding. There used to be more. They're criminals, and I keep them out of jail. I have fingerprints here. I can call them into the station tonight." He taps the door and starts walking back into the building. I shake my head in confusion.

"Did you hear me, Jane?" He pauses at the headlights. "Tonight, everyone but Stewart will be at the station. His security cameras will be down on the kitchen entrance of the house. If anyone came in by way of the neighbor's backyard, they wouldn't be seen, and no one is going to be watching or following Shana if she's at home." He waits until I lend him my eyes. "Or you. They still don't know where you are, and I'm never giving you away." He walks off, back into the building, never turning around again, but I watch the way his back bears the weight of all his wrong decisions.

If he is leading me down the wrong path, I'll be fucked. I'll be walking right into an ambush. It doesn't matter what my gut tells me as I duck into the car and shut the door behind me. I'll need to follow Billy to make sure he follows through with his end of the bargain. I don't trust anyone. I turn the key in the ignition. The clock reads 11 a.m. I don't have long until night falls to come up with a foolproof plan to break into the house that once imprisoned me, but I'm not sure I have much of a choice.

I'll need to gather a few things from home and make sure that I dress appropriately for the funeral tonight.

# Thirty-Four

I love the feeling of black clothing against my skin. It's always been my favorite color, probably for the slender effect that it lends to the body against the intrusive naked eye. It certainly was the color I chose to have most of my clothing. Black felt demure when I was wealthy. It felt powerful to wear the color of no-nonsense. I loved the elegance it presented when paired with any sequin overlay that added sparkle. I made sure every gown was black. Perhaps, I was attempting to show everyone around me what kind of relationship Stewart and I had by my choice in color for those events.

Tonight, though, tonight I wear black for the camouflage it provides in the dark unknown of the night. I wear the color to conceal my presence. I cloak my body in black tonight because I will be playing the role of the reaper. I am the executioner this evening — Stewart's executioner, and the first to attend his funeral.

Sneaking back into my apartment set my nerves on fire. I can't escape the feeling of being watched, and paranoia slips in. I grabbed what I needed and ran back here, back to the motel, back to safety. Work still needs to be done, life goes on, and all the guests want to check out early. I can't say I blame them, or that I'm sad at the refunds I need to write to save the property's face. It gives me the night off from work. It gives me invisibility.

Billy remains a constant vigil as all the other officers go back to their jobs, and Ramona's body is taken away. Whenever I look out any window facing the customer parking lot, his truck is still there. Is he remaining to watch over me or to stall for time before he attempts to take down a giant? He remains a permanent structure on the sidewalk, far from me, all afternoon while I fulfill my duties here. No more words are spoken between us. I have nothing left to say until Stewart's body starts to decay.

I linger at the office door a couple of times, but I never go back in.

Ramona should never have helped me. It became her demise. She lay here, breathing her last breath in pain and fear, and it was all because of me. I should have stayed and ignored her commands to go home. They would have had no choice but to come in with both of us there. I could have fought them with her. I sigh, knowing that my help would not have secured our lives. Tonight, I might still lose my life. Stewart could win.

I grab the permanent marker and smear the word 'closed' on the stark white sheet of paper, much like the paper Stewart left the note on for me to find. I grab a roll of tape and head out of my makeshift office to the front partition. I can hear Billy talking on his cell phone around the corner, so I tiptoe closer and eavesdrop on his conversation.

"Did you identify the fingerprints?"

"Send me the address. I'll pick them up."

"No, backup won't be necessary."

"I know it won't. I've dealt with these thugs before."

"Thank you."

I tape the sign on the front partition. I sneak over as he pushes off the structure and saunters to his truck. I duck into a nearby room with my skeleton key, and I gaze out into the parking lot as Billy tries to make up his mind concerning his next move, or maybe he's trying to get up the willpower to do it. Before he can turn around and spot me, I make my way to the back of the building where my car sits next to both of Ramona's vehicles, only this time, I don't climb behind my wheel. I choose the car of Ramona's that I didn't take to pick up the trunk from Stewart's house. Stewart doesn't know this car, and neither does Billy. Ramona just got it last week from a house auction. It's a classic model precisely like the one her father used to drive when she was little.

Earlier, I snuck into Ramona's room and snatched the keys off the hook near the door. I didn't hang around for the emotions to well up from the nights spent in there crying in her lap, begging for the answers to life. That's something I can't waste time dwelling on now. Emotions drain from me as I prepare for battle. I prepare my mind for revenge.

After turning over the car's engine, I walk to the side of the building; the light in the sky has begun to dim and set on this awful day. I sneak into the bushes and rest while Billy lingers, fighting the internal struggle of being a good man.

It doesn't take long before the decision comes to him, and he hops into the truck. I break away from the bushes and run to Ramona's car. I back up, making sure the headlights aren't on, and drive toward the front lot, jumping out of the car to peer around the edge again. He turns right out of the parking lot to the main road. I rush back in and floor it to follow him.

I cut off a van that no doubt is harboring a family, but I can't be concerned for them right now when my life rests on finding Billy's truck in the handful of cars out on this road. It doesn't take me long, and I slow the car down to keep myself from gathering attention as the maniac driver behind everyone. The van comes up alongside me, and the male driver kindly shows me a one-finger wave.

"Same to you, babe." I hit the radio's power button. Ramona had it dialed into an oldies station, and Brenda Lee sings through the speakers and into my soul. I feel her words of apology resound in my heart.

Billy shifts into the left lane to take the turn across traffic at the red light up ahead. I pull down the visor to conceal my face, although it's unnecessary and dangerous during dusk. I grab Ramona's driving glasses and hat from the passenger seat.

"Sweet Jesus, she was blind." I dip the glasses on the bridge of my nose so that I can peer above them. The light finally turns green, and Billy doesn't once turn his head toward the rearview mirror; he keeps it forward and focused on the task he is assigning himself. For once, Billy doesn't feel it necessary to look over his shoulder.

The fucking question is, what did he decide?

I turn behind him, watching his taillights begin to glow like an amber fire on a winter's night, and I park the car behind a few others on the side of the road and kill the headlights.

"Are you slowing down to park, Billy?" I shed the glasses but keep the hat on and the visor low as I wait to see what happens next. I lift my hand to my lips and gnaw on the hangnail poking out from the first finger.

Billy parks his truck in a driveway near the end of the street, and I watch the clock as it takes him two whole minutes to step out onto the busted concrete of the house's drive. Dusk is settling into the night as the streetlamps flicker on. Instead of knocking on the door, Billy walks right in.

"Motherfucker! This is his house." I slam my hand against the steering wheel, punching it over and over. "You cock-sucking, lying sack of — wait a minute." I squint as his form reappears, and another follows him. It's large like Billy, but a hair smaller and full of cockiness. I roll down the old window as fast as I can and stick my ear out. I wish I had risked it and parked closer.

I only hear bits of the conversation, the parts they allow to rise in volume, but it's clear by the body language that the man Billy retrieved from the house is upset with him. Billy begins to pace back and forth from the truck to the edge of the neglected driveway as the man with him keeps throwing up his hands and hollering. From what I gather, it's frustration about loyalty.

Loyalty, motherfucker? Try marrying the devil, and upholding vows.

Billy pulls his gun out, and the man freezes, the same as me. I hold my breath, waiting for Billy to pull the trigger. *Take him out, Billy. He killed Ramona.*

The insides of Billy are rotting away as the corruption of his employer takes over his waking hours, and I don't think he has the strength that Ramona talked about needing to survive. I attempt to conjure up Billy's eyes in my mind, comparing them to a deer in headlights.

"Get in!" Billy shouts it loud and clear, and my heart and body jump in the Buick. The man does as he's told, respect and fear for Billy's position evident.

I'm not sure who it is, but I can do the math, and one doesn't equal two. Where's the other criminal Billy spoke of today? I watch as Billy backs out of the spot, and I duck down in the seat. I didn't think about the fact that he might come up this way on the street. Fuck. I look in the backseat and plan to jump and lie down when the taillights of Billy's truck flash my way. I sit up in the driver seat and breathe a sigh of relief. I need to be smarter. Every step needs to be calculated. I shift the car into drive as Billy turns left at the end of the street.

Time for Round Two.

# Thirty-Five

The white tailgate of Billy's truck intermittently glows as the streetlamps hit it. I keep my distance, and when he turns on the road that I know like that back of my hand, I tap the gun against the gear shift faster as the sign for the development comes into sight. I won't go in there with the car. I turn off onto a side street and park. There is no sense in continuing the charade of following Billy when I know exactly where he's heading next.

Stewart's house.

I depress the cigarette lighter in the car. Ramona bragged for days that her car was better than mine because the lighter was built-in. *They don't make them this good anymore.* I can still hear the scruff in her voice from smoking one too many of these damn things. I search for the pack inside the pocket of my jacket. There's only one left.

"Here's to you, Ramona." The cigarette lighter pops and I depress it down on the end of the cigarette and breathe the sweet nicotine in until it catches fire. I inhale a deep drag and puff the smoke out of the driver's side window. I click the gun against the gear shift three times, wishing I could run this energy off.

I flick the ash of the cigarette out the window before inhaling again. Things come back to you, just like riding a bicycle. I used to smoke as a kid, bumming cigarettes from the other outcasts of our school, some who saw me the night before running down the street. Others who watched the bullies choose me instead of them for the day, so they figured they owed me a smoke.

I toss the cigarette out the window when the heat touches my pinched fingers and ease the door open with a loud creak, signaling the age of the vehicle. It's time to claim my soul back. I close the door behind me, making sure to do it with ease. There's still a walk ahead of me before I can make it to the house, but I don't need to alert the people living on this street that I'm here. I don't want to make a habit now of collecting witnesses. I'm invisible, just like Billy made me.

I tuck the gun into the waistband of my black jeans and lay the black t-shirt carefully over the top. I pull my matching jet black hair half-up behind my head with a ponytail holder. I've appropriately dressed for Stewart's funeral tonight, and I won't be leaving until the last breath leaves his lousy body. It's time to go to war.

I duck down the sidewalk to the opening of the development. The house is down the first street and at the end of the cul-de-sac. It consumes the cul-de-sac is a more appropriate description for the estate. I saunter down the road until the house comes into view, then I duck behind the home of the third neighbor to the right. There will be no fences in my way, not until I reach Stewart's house. He's the only one on the street that insisted on sheltering his personal space to inform the neighbors that he wasn't up to being invited to silly barbeques or making acquaintances.

I roll my eyes as I push through the last shrub of the neighbor's yard, butting up against the fence. I shimmy between the shrub fencing of the neighbor and the black iron fencing and landscaping of Stewart's. One neighbor wasn't to be outdone by my ex's unfriendly ways. He handed them right back with greenery you couldn't see through. I used to find it helpful to hide us, considering we lined the inside of the fence with hedges as well, but now as I try and jam my body in between the space, I find it fucking ridiculous.

I make it to the edge and drop to all fours crawling the rest of the way to reach the driveway. I see Billy's truck parked out front; at least he gets to exit out of the front door, not the side door that I was physically thrown out of that night. The night Stewart decided I should die.

*"Jane. It's done. We both knew when someone better came along that this would happen."*

*He drops my suitcases on the brick driveway.*

*"Stewart, I don't understand."*

*"Shana is coming in an hour, and I don't want her to see you here. You need to leave. This marriage is over, Jane."*

*"Stewart, I can be better. I swear, I can."*

I grimace at the desperation in my voice, floating up from the past. I thought Stewart and his rules were the only chance I had at living. It turns out that he was the grim reaper, seeking my soul for the repentance of his sins.

There isn't a soul inside of Billy's truck now. I knew it! He brought them all here to plan against me. I scan the windows, duck around the edge of the entrance, and wedge my body underneath the hedge and continue back around the backward "L" shape until I come to the side yard where I was kicked to the curb just months earlier. With a quick sweep, I note no one is outside, so I dart to the house and lean against the foundation, pushing my butt against the brick until it meets the ground. I make sure to tuck my legs in as close to me as possible.

If Billy lied about the security cameras not working on this side of the house, they'll all be coming out to get me in a matter of seconds. I remove the gun from my waist and hold my breath and wait. I hope my gun can kill all four of them because that's what it's going to take.

No one comes. I melt into the wall, releasing my fear and tap the gun as a check, even though the feeling of the steel against my skin makes me feel safer than anything has these last couple of months. Soon that feeling will be replaced by seeing Stewart die. There's no turning back now. I'm here. I hear yelling from inside the house, and my body instantly freezes. The voices trail toward the front door. I've relaxed too soon.

I chance a peek around the edge of the house. As soon as my eye rounds the corner, the front door swings open and I jump back against the brick.

"This is ridiculous, Billy. I don't pay you good money to embarrass me this way." Stewart's voice hasn't filled my ears in months, but the shrill pitch hits the back of my spine and burns against every vertebra in an angry way.

I peek back around the corner again to see the man I saw at the house earlier coming out the front door with an equally cocky delinquent walking beside him. Billy shoves them both forward toward the truck. Their calm demeanor is irritating and getting the best of him. They aren't taking it seriously because they believe they're untouchable. That's the world that Stewart has created.

"You hired them. They embarrassed you. I can't make fingerprints magically disappear, Stewart. That's not how my job works." Billy opens the passenger door and thrusts one of the criminals inside.

"I am here without my official car to save you face, and now I suggest you quit screaming if you don't want the neighbors to know." Billy nudges the back of the last guy's head before he relinquishes his fate and steps inside the truck. He shuts the door behind the two assholes. My fingers burn to choke the life from them. They stole Ramona's last breath, and they don't show any remorse.

"I have a plan to clear them, Stewart, but it involves a ride downtown to make it legit. You don't want this to link back to you, do you?" Billy stands before Stewart with a tall, straight back, a stance I never saw him take before in Stewart's presence. Billy must have worked his way up the ranks in Stewart's army since I last saw him at that dinner party to talk to him this way. Disgusting.

"Get rid of them, then. This is the third time that they've screwed up. They're out." The breeze of the night carries the sound of Stewart's hiss to me, and I shiver at the coldness of his words. He orders executions with ease.

"They'll sing like canaries, don't say that," Billy pleads, but Stewart is adamant.

"Their little friend couldn't take care of Jane when I gave him a chance the night she left, then they couldn't find her, and when they take out the old lady, they don't wear gloves?" He dips his voice lower and pokes a finger into Billy's chest with each syllable— "Take. Them. Out."

"Stewart. That's not my job." Billy's straight posture slumps forward.

"It sure as fuck is if you want to keep the position that I got for you." I bite my hand to keep from screaming. The ride that Stewart secured for me the night that he put my ass out on the street was a set up to kill me. I knew it, and Billy didn't confirm or deny it today in the parking lot. But to hear from the devil himself confirm it burns me in a new way.

"Stewart." There's a whine to Billy's voice. He doesn't want to agree to it, and he doubts I'll succeed tonight, so lamenting to make Stewart happy is much more weighted in his favor of survival.

"And you have people, why can't Jane be found?" I shiver, waiting for Billy's response. He knows where I am. He has always known where I am. He saved me from the driver.

Billy knew that Stewart planned to have me killed. He probably sat at that table, at one of Stewart's basement meetings, agreeing with the decision while plotting in secret to save me. Stewart, however, overlooked Billy's affection for me as an infatuation that burnt out the second it was called into question at that last dinner party. Billy went against orders to save me.

Fuck.

Billy is scum, but he's the reason that I'm still alive today. Every time he told me only to call him and not to tell anyone where I was, or when he would say to me which roads to take home, he was protecting me. I thought Billy was helping me avoid traffic, or he was a natural worrier by nature as a cop. He always used the excuse of the maniac driver being on the loose to get me to comply without question. When I found about Lance's death, I assumed Billy was securing my affections with his hero act. I was naïve.

He's the one who found me the place with Ramona, and he knew she would help me and keep me safe when he wasn't around. My heart aches at the twisted choice Billy made not to save Ramona last night.

"She's evasive," Billy answers. "I haven't been able to track her down, only her employment at the motel like Shana said, and she's since quit. She wasn't at the crime scene once, and I stayed all day waiting. I doubt she'll come to the funeral. Perhaps, Ramona wasn't a friend of hers like Shana thought." The lies flow through his teeth with ease, practiced and precise. Stewart doesn't see through them like I do. I watch as Billy's heart breaks, struggling to act like he feels only indifference toward me, that Stewart talking about me being dead doesn't hit him emotionally.

"Find a relative, any of them. Take them out. She'll show up to that funeral."

I gasp into my hand. He'd hurt anyone to get to me, and he doesn't care. How many lives has he been responsible for signing the death warrant for if he jumps to this solution so easily? I need to kill Stewart. I have to become the monster so that we can all escape him.

"Don't worry, boss. I'll take care of it. Go rest. You don't look so well." Billy walks toward the driver's side of his truck.

"It's all this fucking stress." He waves to Billy and waddles back into the house. Stewart has dark secrets to keep, and he plans on making messes to keep the view away from him. Little does he know that the newspaper headlines will once again conjoin his name with mine tomorrow.

# Thirty-Six

Billy's truck heads down the road, and I stare, long after it fades from view, at the furthest spot I saw it before it disappears. I send a silent prayer to God that Billy finds peace. I don't know if God will listen to me anymore for what I'm about to do, but for all the wrong that Billy committed, I can't forget that he saved my life. He stuck his neck out to keep me safe. Even after all of his secrets were exposed, he was willing to do it again tonight. I can use that to save Shana and Delilah. Billy will be free to save himself. After tonight, though, I don't want any part of him.

He's not even afraid to be in the truck with those guys. That's how close he can sit to murderers and feel at home. Maybe it's a side effect from the job, which job I'll never know. I'll have to sit with a murderer all my life after tonight, but there's no other way to find justice for Ramona or safety for Shana or — fuck, even my own life if I don't commit this crime. Stewart won't rest until every finger that can point fault at him is underground.

I scooch my body to the side door off of the kitchen. There's no time to waste. I kick myself into action. The front outdoor lights go out, and I wait in the bush beside the side door for Stewart to make his way into the kitchen and flick it off as well so that I can make my move.

Stewart is a man of habit, guarding the idea that once you find a routine that works, you stick to it and never waver. He likes things that way, anything spontaneous pisses him off. So, I know he'll come into the kitchen shortly, look out the window, and search the driveway for anything suspicious. When he confirms it's safe, he'll shut the outdoor side light off.

The bricks on the driveway glow from the power of the bulbs overhead, hand-laid by workers so it could be the very best, and I watch them shine. Once Stewart turns off the light, he'll pour himself a nightcap of scotch. *Better than any sleeping pill that the doctors can give you.* He'll greedily gulp it down, not wanting to loiter with it; the more he consumes in a single swallow, the faster he thinks it will work. He'll rinse his cup out in the sink and head back to the front entryway, flicking the kitchen light off on his way to double check that the downstairs is safe. He'll turn on the alarm by the front door before heading upstairs to bed.

I have a small window, and no time to waste. That's the time frame left to make my move and get inside. I check to make sure my phone is on silent and wait. The lights flick out, and I feel my chest tighten. This is it. There's nothing but the sound of my rapid heartbeat pounding as I slide my body over to the three stairs leading up to the door, squatting beside them ready to jump up and get inside. I run my hands over the outside feeling for the crack in the cement.

Stewart never knew I hid a key here. One of the worst beatings at his hands was when I locked myself out of the house and had to wait for him to come home and let me in. There was nothing like an inconvenience and a loss of money to get him in the mood to hand out a punishment. I didn't plan on going through that again, so I made a second key to the kitchen door and hid it here.

I feel along the cement until the crack makes its presence known under my fingertips. I swallow a large gulp of air before pushing my fingers inside. Bingo. I hit metal. I pull the key in between my fingers, but the sweat on my fingertips fumble the key, and it falls into the mulch. Shit.

I hear the pipes under the house groan as Stewart rinses his glass out. Fuck. I slide my hands around on the ground, gathering splinters from the wooden mulch, but no access to the inside of the house. I take a deep breath, but then the light in the kitchen goes out. Fuck. My right hand finally hits the metal and grabs it, along with a handful of dirt and mulch before I stand and mount the steps, quickly brushing the debris from my legs and popping the key into the handle as fast as I can with no light. Come on. Come on.

I feel the pin tumblers click underneath the key's weight, and I twist the doorknob open and slip inside as fast as I can. I lock the deadbolt behind me and pray as I slide down to the floor and take my shoes off – part old habit, part fear of getting mulch from outside in here. I don't hear the loud whooping noise coming from the alarm. Silence surrounds the house.

I purposely slow my breathing down to slow my heart rate, and I hear the familiar beeps of the alarm keypad. I made it. As the alarm sounds that it's secure in the house, I feel a small chuckle in my throat. It's not protected at all. That alarm used to signal my imprisonment inside these walls, now it feels like a song of redemption. I peek around the island as I watch my ex-husband mosey toward the stair-well. He looks older than I remember, but in no way like someone's soft grandfather that they'd run to with open arms.

He resembles a mean older man you'd find in the movies living alone and inciting rumors of being ax-murderer. Un-like the films, though, he wouldn't turn out to be a misun-derstood soul who was quite friendly. No, Stewart is a snake through and through no matter how many times he sheds his skin. He never sheds his species.

I know Shana will already be upstairs, putting Delilah in bed or climbing into bed herself. The second that Billy arrived to discuss business, Stewart undoubtedly dismissed her. She is only to be seen as a prize when he wants the world to know that he landed a catch; otherwise, she needs to wait for his next command, somewhere far away from him. I hear his feet slowly mount the stairs one by one.

Revenge will be mine. I lay my head against the island and squish my body to get comfortable. I'll wait until Stew-art falls asleep, which won't be long, and then I'll sneak Shana and Delilah out before ending his life. They need a good head start in case this doesn't go the way I envision, then I'll satisfy my ache to even the score. The main objective is to get her and that baby out of this place, so that's what I'm going to achieve first.

Stewart could easily use them against me if he's awake when they run. The result is death for Stewart, but it doesn't mean I need to get sloppy. I pull the gun out of my waistband and give my stomach some relief from the awkward way it pushes against me. I hate waiting, but it's the only way. The main light in the house over the stairway goes out, and I glance at the clock. In a few hours, Stewart Miller will be dead.

# Thirty-Seven

I jolt awake. Fuck. Where am I? I look around. I'm in the kitchen at Stewart's house. I look at the clock on the stove. Three hours! I slept for three hours. Shit. I jump up from the floor in the kitchen, my body protesting the fast movement from the stiffness it endured from sleeping in such an awkward position on the floor.

I crack my neck in the silence, but it does little to relieve the ache in my head. I shake it off and move, I've wasted too much time already. I grab my gun from the floor. I walk around the island with ease — having memorized the space in this house for five years, I don't need a light. Billy better still have the two guys locked up at the station. I peek through the slit of the front window, and there's no one in the driveway. They aren't here. I still have time.

I grab my gun from the pocket of my pants and feel for my phone. Maybe I could text Shana awake. I push the side button with my thumb and see five missed calls from Shana and a voicemail. Fuck. She needed me, and I was asleep in the kitchen. He probably beat the shit out of her, and I couldn't help. She was calling for my help. I debate about hitting the voicemail button or rushing into the unknown. Fuck. Curiosity gets the better of me, and I hit the voicemail and check the voice to text message.

**Jane. Come quick. I think ... dead.**

Dead? Who's dead? Stupid fucking phone. I run up the stairs, skipping some, and hitting the landing in record time with a steady breath. Running the stress away has made me stronger.

I pass by Delilah's nursery and peek inside. She's sleeping soundly in her crib. Still alive. I listen to her quiet breathing. *Don't worry, sweet girl. You'll grow up safe.* I shuffle my way down the hall carpet to the main bedroom with my gun poised in the air. When I make the slight corner to the entryway, the door is shut, but the light is on underneath. Shit.

I lean my ear to the door, and Shana's crying flows through the wooden space between and fills my ears.

"Oh, no. Oh, God, Stewart. Stewart." She begins yelling his name, but I don't hear his response. He's inflicting her with unbearable pain, I know it. I turn the doorknob slowly and ready my gun. Here goes nothing. I can't turn back now. I look behind me at the nursery one last time. I should have shut her door. Fuck. I stand there, debating against her mother's cries and saving her from hearing them.

I twist the knob and shove it open, letting it hit the wall, and I hold my gun up. I startle the hell out of Shana, who falls to the floor immediately at the sight of the weapon.

"Jane," she sobs into the side of the bed, Stewart's side, as she clings to the comforter. I lower the gun and put it in the pocket of my jacket. There's no threat — on the bed in the bright light of the lamps is Stewart. He's not moving, and he is a sickly shade of death.

"Is he... Is he dead?" I ask

Shana peeks up from the space between the bed and the wall. When she sees I've put the gun away, she runs to me, clinging to my upper arms as the tears rack her body. I can't focus on her; all I can see is Stewart's body.

I shake Shana from me, and she falls to the floor, clinging to the carpet. I step slowly toward Stewart. I smell the final release of his bowels, the natural process of death, but it doesn't satisfy my mind. I shift closer until I'm right next to his head. I stare at his chest, waiting for it to move, but it never does. I poke him in the neck.

"Wake up, asshole," I shout. Nothing.

"Jesus, Shana. What the hell happened?" I look over Stewart's body. There's not a drop of blood to be seen, and it's as if he just went to sleep, and that was that.

"I did it, Jane. I did it." She rocks back and forth on the floor, pulling her knees in as tight to her chest as humanly possible and falling over onto her side in the fetal position. I look back down at Stewart and then at her.

"What do you mean, Shana? It looks like his heart finally gave out. He is old, you know?" I feel nothing. Well, not nothing, I'm pissed that he got to go in such a peaceful way when he's caused so much hell for others. I peer down at his sleeping face. He dares to look peaceful. I glare at him, but ultimately decide to walk to Shana and comfort her. I sit down on the floor in front of her, tilting my head so that her wide-eyed stare is in line with mine.

"I switched his medicine," she whimpers.

"You what?" My voice is loud, and I hear Delilah stirring on the monitor on the nightstand, so I lower it and whisper. "What did you do?"

"I switched his medicine." She looks up at me, her eyes are wild, and they look just as Ramona said–Bambi. "I couldn't take it anymore. When you were here getting your trunk, I heard you in the medicine cabinet, and I thought you were fucking with his medicine, so I cracked the door open a bit. You had them in your hand. You were looking at both of the bottles. I thought, 'She's going to fucking switch them and kill him.' I shut the door and banged on it so you couldn't. You didn't switch them, and he didn't die, so I was happy. Then he hit me." She clenches her eyelids tight, and I watch the tear of her top eye trickle over the bridge of her nose and hit the floor.

"Holy shit." I lie down on the floor beside her. "I didn't know you saw me."

"When I told him that I was going to leave, he said he'd hurt the baby and me, remember." I stare into her eyes as she recalls the scene. "I was pregnant, Jane."

"What?"

"He hit me while I was carrying her." She moans into the carpet as the next wave of sobs comes over her.

"Oh my god. Then what?" I dare to ask, even though it's a scary story, and I'm not sure I want to hear the end.

"Then, I went to the medicine cabinet. I felt so sick. I needed something to calm my stomach. And there was his medication, and I remembered what I thought the day that you were here. I remembered what your back looked like when the trunk lifted it. I put two and two together that you were trying to warn me. You wanted to get me out before it was too late, but I was so stupid. You weren't thinking about switching his medicine and killing him because you were better that he had a new life. You wanted to kill him because he was a bad man. I was so, so stupid. A rich guy was looking at me and had knocked me up. I thought I was in love. I signed the prenup by then, and we were set to get married. He wasn't going to hit me again. So, I put the thought out of my mind. Only, he wanted to get married the next day. The actual wedding was just a big show for family." I close my eyes with the sound of her voice. "He hit me on our wedding night, and told me that I couldn't run now."

"I know the feeling," I mutter.

"So, when he went to sleep, I took his pills out of the jar. They look like that shit he gets for his headaches from the store."

I nod. I know, it's the same thought I had.

"So, I swapped them." She snatches at the carpet.

"That doesn't mean that's what killed him, Shana. He got a new prescription, and that was months and months ago." I open my eyes and hold hers in mine, but she shakes her head vehemently.

"I swapped them again. And again. And last week when he got a new set—"

"You swapped them again." Shana saved Delilah and herself.

"He took a simple pain killer tonight before he went to bed, not a beta-blocker, not something that would prevent his arteries from closing. Nothing. He's been taking nothing for the past five months."

"How did that make it past the doctors? Surely, he started to feel ill?" I ask. "It would show up on the blood work that he didn't have the medication in his system."

"He was supposed to have an appointment last month for just that. Only I told him they called and canceled the appointment. And I called them earlier in the day to cancel it for him." Her face is a wreck of tears and fluid leaking all over the carpet.

I'm stunned. "He believed you?"

"I changed the subject after that to something about spending money on new nursery furniture, he skimmed right over the appointment and went to being pissed off at me and in a mood." She glares over my head, where she knows his lifeless body is lying. I yank myself up into a seated position, and she follows me.

"Fuck. That was smart." I peer over at Stewart. He's dead. He's finally gone. Shana can live in peace. "But why track me down? You had it handled. It was just a waiting game."

"He didn't die."

"Well, he did now."

"He just wouldn't fucking die and leave us alone. I figured he'd never fucking die, and maybe that whole coronary artery disease was a big fat lie of his."

"Well, it turns out that it's the only thing Stewart Miller didn't lie about."

"Yeah." She sniffles.

"Call 911, Shana." I climb off the floor and reach my hand down to help her up, but she doesn't move to take it.

"What?"

"You have to report your dead husband, girl." I scratch the back of my neck and look at the mess. "I have to leave."

"Don't leave me, Jane. Stay here. I've already called your phone. It's not like you shouldn't be here. I called you here." She grabs hold of my arm now, threatening to drag me back down to the floor instead of using it to haul herself up.

"I snuck in before the alarm was set. I didn't drive to the house, Shana, my car is parked outside of the development. Don't you think the police might put two and two together that I came here tonight to kill Stewart? Especially when they find my gun?" I pat the pocket of my jacket.

"You can't leave. They're going to know that it was me who killed Stewart. They'll know. They'll take Delilah away." She's frantic, bounding to her feet and pacing around the room. She's a deer running wild in the forest. She's Bambi.

"Shana. This is the best thing possible in this situation. Stewart died in his sleep. He has a history of coronary artery disease. He's sixty years old." She couldn't make the connection. "Shana, you saved Delilah." The name stops her.

"I did?" She looks at me, and I look anywhere but her fucking eyes — those Bambi eyes.

"You did." I go to her side of the bed and grab the monitor to take it to her. I place it in her hands, and she peers down at the sleeping baby on the screen. "You saved her. You saved yourself. He can't hurt you anymore. He won't ever be able to hurt her."

She nods and smiles at her sleeping baby.

"I have to go, Shana." I go to the alarm pad by the doorway of the bedroom and enter the code to unlock the system. "Call the police." I watch her nod at the screen of Delilah, but she doesn't make for her phone.

"Shana."

She looks up at me.

"Take a deep breath." I smile. "You're going to be okay."

"They'll know, Jane." Shana starts to back away, looking to escape.

# Thirty-Eight

"Shana, they won't." I grab her arms and pull her back, forcing her to look at me. "Tell yourself that I did it. I wanted to switch that medication the day I came for the trunk. I did it. This is my fault, not yours."

"You? Jane, I switched the pills." She's confused.

"I thought of it first. If I never went into that medicine cabinet and thought of swapping those pills, you wouldn't have gotten the idea. It was me." She can't handle the responsibility, and I won't let her burden that shame. I can handle it. I'm the one who thought of it. I am the one who began the entire idea. I did it. I look at her eyes. I can't lose someone like Ramona did. *Stay with me, Shana.*

"You?"

"That's right. I did it. Not you." The words calm her. She needs to place the blame on someone else. Strength is too much for her to endure, I understand now what Ramona was saying, but I'm not going to give up on Shana. If I can convince her that it was all my doing, I'll take it away and add that sin to my name, so she keeps her mouth shut.

Delilah starts to cry on the monitor, but Shana makes no move to get her. She stares at her phone on the bedside table. I pull mine out of my pocket and hit the side. I offer the phone to her, but she shakes her head.

"I'll use mine." She's calm, finally. She's cold under my touch. I peer around the room for a robe, but the only one I can find is Stewart's, and I don't think wrapping her in it will help her mental state right now. I shed my jacket and wrap it around her, taking the gun from the pocket.

"Call them. I'm going to get Delilah." I rub her shoulders and take her face in my hands.

She nods at me and smiles. She points to a bottle next to the entryway of the bedroom.

"Mix it?" I ask.

She nods again.

I set my gun down on the table, twisting the cap off the little Tupperware of powdered formula, sprinkling it inside the bottle. I give it a good shake and watch it come together.

"Okay. I'm going to go give Delilah this bottle, are you okay?"

She's sitting on her side of the bed, staring at the phone in her hand. "I'm free." She laughs.

"You're free. Delilah is safe, and you're safe. We're going to be all right, Shana. Call the police." I smile at her. This night could have gone worse. I could be on my way to the police station now for murdering my ex-husband, but instead, I'm heading to the nursery to calm Delilah while Shana calls the police because it looks like Stewart died of natural causes. And she invited me to help her, I don't have to leave, but I should get my car or lie and say I parked that far because I was scared of what Stewart would do to her.

I walk down the hallway and turn the corner of the nursery, fearing to turn on the light because I'm not sure of the routine Shana has for these moments. Shit, I look back toward the master bedroom, I should have asked a few more questions before taking this task on, but I know she's in no state to take over.

"Hold on, baby. I'm coming," I whisper in the darkness. "I'm out of my element here, Delilah, just give me a second." I don't know the first thing about calming a baby in the nighttime, but I'm so scared Shana is going to drop her or go crazy at any second that I can't delegate her to the task.

I hear Shana's voice from the other room talking to the 911 dispatcher. Thank God, she called them. Everything is going to be just fine.

"My husband is dead," she cries into the receiver, and I can tell she's thrown her hand over her mouth by the way the sound is muffled. She's had to say it out loud to the world, and it's hitting her.

"Everything's going to be okay, baby." I scoop Delilah out of the crib, and to my surprise, she calms down in my arms. I know she's hungry, so I settle down on the floor with her in my arms and offer the bottle to her, which she happily accepts. I'm doing it. I'm feeding a baby. I smile down and stroke her little hand.

I did it. Well, Shana did it. She protected her child from the worst of all evils. She handled the devil and gave him his own death warrant. She didn't even need me. I grin down at Delilah.

"Your mommy is so brave. She loves you, sweet girl. You're going to be okay." I rock my body back and forth while Delilah suckles on the bottle, and I hum to her like my mother used to do on those cold nights when I couldn't sleep. It helped to lull me off, and by the light of the small nightlight, I watch the humming work its magic on Delilah's sleepy eyes.

Her eyes close as the end of the bottle nears. I did it. I can do this. I can help Shana with her, no problem. That is — if Shana lets me. She doesn't need me now. She's free to go to her parents' house. She doesn't have to hide out of sight of the watchful eye of Stewart. She can live her life peacefully as a widow. Delilah will have all the money she can imagine. Someone finally gets to touch Stewart's money.

I chuckle under my breath.

"I'm glad it's you," I whisper to the sleeping infant as I kiss her head. I pull her up on my shoulder to burp her, and she gives it up almost immediately. I bounce her a little more, not wanting to part from her. It's true what they say about a baby's smell, but I have to move my car, so I reluctantly set her back into her crib.

"Shana," I whisper to get her attention from the doorway to the bedroom. I motion driving a car and point to the floor as I mouth that I'll be back. Her hair wildly flies about her as she nods. The 911 operator doesn't seem to be calming her down with all the questions.

I run out the front door and down the sidewalk until I reach Ramona's car. I don't have much time to catch my breath before I need to put the car in drive and get to the development, but I make it before the ambulance or police. I climb the steps to the top floor once more, only this time it's with relief. Stewart is gone.

"Yes, ma'am. I hear them." Shana ends the conversation with the dispatcher. I press play on the voicemail from Shana after I step on the landing because it still shows I didn't listen to it for some reason. If the cops check our story, that could hurt.

*Jane, Jane. Jane, you have to come. Stewart is dead. Jane. Stewart is dead. I killed him.*

The time on the voicemail was just an hour before I found myself waking up on the kitchen floor downstairs. I was closer than she expected, but not there to help her when she first found out. I delete the message. She gave herself away at the end. The missed calls will have to do for evidence.

"I'll open the door, Shana," I say down the hallway, but she doesn't answer me. I walk toward the bedroom door. "Shana? Did you hear me? I said that I'll go get the door for them." I pause and wait for her voice. "Shana?"

I step into the room, but the only response is the sound of a gunshot and a searing pain in my shoulder.

# Thirty-Nine

"**S**hana, what the fuck are you doing?" There's a piercing pain in my upper arm. I grip it with my other hand and glare toward Shana. She's holding my gun and pointing it directly at me shaking her head wildly.

"You're going to tell on me, Jane." She sobs, and frantically wipes the tears away from her cheeks and grips the gun as it shakes in her hands.

The noise has woken Delilah, and I hear her screaming from her nursery. Shana doesn't register the screams. She's in some sort of shock, and she hears nothing around us. I can't pull her back into the light with me.

"Shana put the gun down. What the fuck? I'm not going to tell anyone. I mean, I am going to fucking tell them you shot me, though. I can't lie about that one. What the fuck? We're in deep shit now." My mind is racing to settle things down and cover them up. Shana is holding my fucking gun. Now I look like an intruder.

"Stewart said you were talking to the police about him, saying he hit you, he said you planned to ruin our lives and hurt Delilah. I didn't want to believe him at first, but you came here tonight to kill him." She's calm in tone, but her body betrays this notion as she shakes.

"What? I came here tonight to save you." I bound forward, but her jiggle on the gun stops me. "Shana, he lied to you. I didn't tell anyone about it. Stewart was trying to have me killed. He knew you saw me in the grocery store that day, and he wanted you to give up my location so he could send his goons to kill me."

"No. No." She shakes her head over and over. She is ignoring the cries down the hallway or the ones at the front door. She's too far away to hear any of them. I make to pull her back to me.

"Shana put the gun down. We have to open the front door. The EMT needs to get inside. My fucking arm hurts." I feel the pain jolt down to my fingertips.

"Why?" she spits. "So that you can tell on me?"

"That you shot me? Yeah, sorry, no way around that one, is there?" I motion with my good hand that she still has the gun.

"You're mad at me," she cries.

"Well, I don't know if anyone has ever shot you before, Shana, but it's not a warm fuzzy feeling that I have at this moment about it. I get that you're upset, and considering you're still holding the gun at me, I'm trying to be calm." I want to scream, but setting her off doesn't sound smart.

"You're mad."

"Shana, I am not going to tell on you about Stewart's pills. Remember? I told you I did it. I did it, Shana. It was me who killed Stewart." I try again for the calming effect of those words. I take a careful step toward her, but she catches me, jutting the gun out hard toward me.

"Your bruises were probably fake when you came for the trunk. You wanted Stewart dead. You were using me to get closer to his money, weren't you?" I can't believe the flip in her mind. Stewart worked her over mentally.

"He said not to trust you. Look what you made me do. I killed my husband." She screams, and I shush her, glancing behind me. No one is there, but sound travels, and I'm not sure how much they can hear through the front door.

"Shana, he lied to you so that you would hand over Ramona's name. He wanted anyone that was close to me to suffer so that he could hurt me."

I watch the gun lower in her hand. "Oh my god. Is she all right?"

"He killed Ramona. He had her throat slit last night," I spit the words out, but like sour milk, the taste still lingers.

"What?" The gun is still at half-mast.

"She's dead, Shana, just for knowing me. He wanted to hurt me any way possible. Don't you see? He hired someone to kill me the night that I left here. Imagine if he knew we were friends. He'd end all three of us; you, Delilah, and me."

"We're friends?" The gun drops to her side, and my body begins to relax for a second.

"Well, I think we might need to work on your trust issues—" I wave to my arm— "but yes, we are friends, Shana. Fuck, you're my best friend."

"I shot you. Oh, god, Jane, I shot you." She steps toward me, but I hesitantly step back

"It's fine. It's fine, Shana. I need to get the door for the EMT, so give me the gun." I hold my hand out toward her.

She stares at it in her hand and back at my shoulder.

"I'm okay, Shana. Give me the gun." I wave my hand for it. "Give me the gun, Shana. It's going to be okay. You are in shock. It's fine. They'll understand. I understand. We will tell them that I scared you coming back in the room."

"I'm sorry, Jane." Tears flood her cheeks.

"It's okay, Shana. I forgive you. He got to you. It happens. Give me the gun," I whisper, terrified to raise my voice while she's still holding the weapon.

"He took away your chance to have a baby, didn't he?" She asks.

I drop my hand and nod. I hear the EMT opening the door downstairs. Delilah hasn't stopped screaming over the monitor. Chaos surrounds us, but Shana is still and waiting patiently for me.

"Yes, he did."

"He used to joke about it when we were dating. It made me feel good that I had something you couldn't have, that I could give him something you weren't able to. Then after he started abusing me, I started to wonder if it wasn't incapability that you had, but one that he gave you."

"He gave it to me," I sigh. "I lost our first child to an ectopic pregnancy, and when I broached the subject of children a while later, he made me go to the doctor. They found that my last ovary was full of cysts. That wouldn't stop me, but it pissed Stewart off to know that I was 'defective' in any way." I scoff. "So, he hit me until one ruptured, and then he paid the seedy doctor who took my ovary to be quiet about the bruises. He had blackmail against him if he said anything." That's how Stewart worked — blackmail.

"I thought he loved me, Jane," she sighs and peers back to Stewart.

"I thought he loved me, too, Shana. It's okay. He's gone now, and he can't hurt us." The EMTs make it through the downstairs, and I hear them calling to us.

"We're up here," I holler behind me.

"Give me the gun, Shana." I hold my hand out to her. "It's better if I'm holding it."

"I don't feel any better, Jane. I thought I'd feel better."

"You will Shana, you will."

She furrows her brows together. "You can have Delilah."

"Shana?" I hear the sound of the EMTs rushing up the stairs as Shana lifts the gun to her head.

"NO, SHANA!" But, it's too late, she pulls the trigger as they enter the room and I lunge forward for her, but she's gone.

# Forty

"**M**a'am, can we ask you a few questions?" I stare up at the ceiling of the ambulance, aware of the cops' presence before one of them decided to speak.

"Yeah," I sigh. The EMT on my right side works on my shoulder. I'm the only person at this crime scene that he can save.

"Thank you." He climbs into the ambulance and takes a seat on the left of me. The EMT doesn't look happy about his workspace being infringed. The cop's partner notices and takes a position somewhere by the edge of my feet. I can't see him.

"I'm Detective Sanders. How are you feeling? You doing okay?" The cop next to me asks.

"I feel like I've been shot." The EMT stifles a giggle.

"How'd you get shot?" Sanders ignores him.

"Shana," I gulp at her name, terrified that I've released some of her memory by speaking it out loud, "she shot me."

"Why?" I keep my eyes trained on the ceiling.

"I was trying to stop her from killing herself." I can feel the tears slide out of my eyes and run down into my ears.

"She wanted to kill herself?"

"Well, she's dead, isn't she? And I watched her take a round off in her skull, so I would say that yes that is an accurate statement." The sobs shake uncontrollably from my body. The EMT stops work on my shoulder to stroke my hair for a while. "I'm not a flight risk for some mental ward. I don't need to be handled with kid gloves. My," I swallow, "my best friend just killed herself in front of me, and I couldn't stop her."

"What's your name, honey?" Sanders is soft.

"Jane."

"Jane, why were you here tonight?" He has to get this out of the way.

"Shana called me. She woke up and found her husband dead, so she panicked and called me. She didn't know what to do."

"Why wouldn't she call the police first?"

"I don't know. Probably should ask her," I deadpan.

"We need to ask these questions, ma'am, to understand what happened here tonight. I'm sorry they seem insensitive."

"Then let me tell you and save you some questions," I wince from the pain in my neck, turning it toward the officer. "Shana called me tonight, upset and I couldn't understand her, but I heard the words dead and please come, so I got into the car and came here. She let me in and took me upstairs, where she showed me her husband dead in his sleep. She was in shock, frantically pacing the floor crying. Her screaming woke up Delilah, their baby, so I told her to call the police, and I would take care of the child's feeding. She was calm at this point. She called 911, and I fed the baby. When I came back into the room, I saw she had a gun to her head." I pause. The lies are hard to get through.

"It's okay. Take your time," the cop whispers.

"I told her to put it down," I sob. "She wouldn't listen." I break, giving another minute over to my tears. "She shot me when she thought that I was going to take it from her. Then we argued a little bit. She felt awful for shooting me. I told her it was all right, just so long as she put the gun down. Then she told me goodbye." I press my face into the cot and squeeze my eyes shut. I will never forget this night. Shana will be in my mind every time I close my eyes.

"Okay. Okay."

"What's your full name, honey?" The EMT asks me.

"Jane Voss." I look up at the officer. The last name hits him.

"Voss. Do you know a police officer named Billy Voss?"

"Yes. He's my cousin." The lie falls easy from my lips. If Billy is excellent at covering up things, then he can fix my involvement here tonight and keep the eyes away from me. He owes me that. Shana killed herself and shot me with the gun he gave me. He'll have to explain it away, not me.

"I'll give him a call. Let him know what's going on."

"We need to take her to the hospital now." The EMT tells the officer so that he'll leave.

"No," I shout. "Where is Delilah?"

"Who?" The officer asks.

"The baby." The EMT tells him. At least someone was listening to me.

"I'm not leaving here unless she's with me. You're not putting her into some crazy home for the night." I grab his hand with the arm not shot.

"Does she have grandparents. I'll call them. What's their number?"

"It will take them hours to get here. What happens to her in the meantime, huh? She lost her father and mother in one night. I'm the only person she knows."

"In the meantime, she'll be with you at the hospital." He nods. "Though, it doesn't make sense, because if you need surgery, who will hold her then?"

"I will." I hear his voice from the back of the ambulance.

"Hey, Billy. I was talking to your cousin here." Sanders points to me.

"Yeah, I heard about it on the radio and couldn't stay away. I'll go with her." I sit my head up and see that he's holding Delilah.

"Okay." Detective Sanders gets out of the seat and shuffles to the back. "I'm sorry for your loss, ma'am."

"Thank you."

Billy quickly takes the vacant position, and the EMT's partner shuts the door behind the departing cops. We head to the hospital, Billy holding my hand while I hold Delilah's.

# Forty-One

"Jane. Jane, wake up."

Billy's voice rouses me from sleep, and I shift in the hospital bed, grabbing at the bundle on my chest. My arm sends a stinging reminder that it's still injured, launching my mind through visions of the events of the last few hours. A whimper escapes me, remembering that my friends are all dead.

"Sorry. She's fine. She's fine." He whispers.

I grip tight around the sleeping infant on my chest — her small breaths puffing in and out in peaceful succession. The bullet went straight through my arm, so surgery wasn't needed, but the hospital did want to observe me for the night. I refuse to give up Delilah until her grandparents arrive. It's been Billy's duty to track them down while we rest. It's the most peaceful sleep I've had in days.

I stare up into Billy's face. He's tired. No, worse than that, he's exhausted. His face looks like my heart feels after tonight. The abuse from Stewart has stopped on all accounts — to Shana, to me, to Billy, to the way he still wanted to hurt me and everything I loved. The abuse of being with him will always be inside of my mind. I'll walk, carrying those scars deep in my bones for the rest of my life, but no longer out of fear. Instead, it will be with a purpose.

"Shana's parents are almost here. They just called the desk to make sure you were still at the hospital." He didn't need to come and tell me this. I would know when they walk through the door and identify their grandchild sleeping on my chest. He craved any reason to break the silence and talk to me.

"Okay," I mumble and kiss the top of Delilah's head. I meant what I said when I told Billy that we were over. I don't want anything more to do with him. His lies are unforgivable, even if his intentions were honorable.

I lift my head some to see the door, nearly yelping at the pain in my right arm. I hope the pain helps to give me a reason for a quick goodbye to her. A long drawn out one will only break my heart. The life that I was starting to build is gone. One of the lives that I wanted to save took fate into her own hands, and now the other will leave me forever, without my involvement in her growing older.

"How're your buddies doing?" I leer at Billy. I don't give a fuck what his sad eyes make me feel, or the fact that I can understand his position, Billy can fuck off. I've stood over the bodies of both of my friends in twenty-four hours, something he played a lead role in doing both times.

"They are officially under arrest for the murder of Ramona Johnson, and they won't be posting bail. They confessed to it, as well, stupidly thinking they were talking to Stewart's friend, so I don't see it going in their favor at trial." I notice now that he's holding a cup of coffee in his hands, swirling it around dangerously as it's filled to the brim.

"Is that for me?" As much as I love Delilah being comfortable on me, my ass hurts something fierce. I move again in the bed, hoping for relief. It won't come, but I do manage to sit up a little on the thin wafer cot.

"Yeah." He hands it to me, and instinctively I reach out with my right hand, but it hurts too badly. I whistle through my teeth in pain, waving off the idea of coffee.

"Oh, Jesus, Jane. I'm sorry." He looks around for something that will magically fall out of the sky and be able to help my arm while not finding a place to set down the coffee.

"Billy."

He stops and turns to me.

"Knock it off."

He deflates like a kicked puppy. I roll my eyes. Why do I feel guilty? Because I see the good in people, I always have, but I'm done ignoring their bad.

I lower my voice and turn to him. "You aren't one of the bad guys, but you aren't a hero, either. You're shaded gray. I know you have stuck around here waiting to see where we stood, so I won't make you suffer any longer. We aren't going to be friends, Billy, or anything else for that matter."

He falls into the chair along the wall, propping both elbows on respective knees and tilts his head toward the ceiling, fighting tears. His back caves as he exhales a deep breath.

"It doesn't matter that I can see your soul and know that it isn't a bad one, that's not enough for me," I continue to explain my position to him.

"We can't be friends ever?" he whispers.

"I won't rat you out, and I will never wish evil on you, but I will never call you up and ask you to hang out." It's something that needs to be said, but it doesn't take the bitter sting out of my words.

"Why?" He chances a look in my direction to find me staring down at him. I'm glad he can look at me when I say this and feel the words with every one of his senses. I want him to not only taste the stale coffee but smell it when he remembers these words, the way I looked at him, and how they left him aching for the human touch to glue him together again.

"I spent five years loving someone who thought that laying their hand on me every single day was okay. Not only okay, but he thought he had the right to do it to keep me in line. Meanwhile, he waited for someone else to control. When he threw me out, I was heartbroken and shattered, only to be driven in a car with a maniac, who I found out was hired to kill me. Miraculously, I made a friend with an old lady who loved me dearly and showed me how to find the strength within myself, love myself, and assure my future on my own, not relying on the old ways. You're part of those old ways. The time when everyone saw, but no one spoke up. I don't want that life to touch me. It doesn't matter what you do, that shit is stained on your soul. I want to help women who are like me. I wanted to save Shana. I want to save all the Shanas of the world. So, when I tell you that you and I cannot be friends, it's because you stand in the way of that—"

"I would never—"

"You stand in the way. What am I supposed to do? Tell a woman she can come to speak to you about her husband beating her face in, only to find that he's rich and has you in his pocket, so now she's fucked through and through?"

He grimaces at my words, a physical blow rather than a verbal assault. "I've given that up." He wants the words to convey the truth, but he doesn't know his future. He found himself easily manipulated. What's to say that he won't stumble down that path again?

"It follows you, and I don't want it near me." Delilah stirs with my motion, and I bounce her back to sleep the same way I watched Shana do it in the coffee shop and at the grocery store.

"Look at this baby, Billy. She's an orphan now because her mother's mind was beaten down by a coward who pretended to be a man. Her mother put a gun to her head and pulled the trigger. My friend pulled the trigger on that gun in front of me, and I couldn't convince her to put it down because of the way he mind-fucked her." I long to swipe the tear falling on my face so that Billy can't bear witness to my weakness, but my arm won't move to do it, and I won't give up my hold on Delilah for it, so I let him see my pain.

"I'm sorry, Jane. I don't know what I can do to prove to you that I won't be going back to that," he pleads.

"I hope you don't, Billy, but don't worry about me. Prove it to yourself. I hope you reach the day that the mirror doesn't hold something distasteful anymore. I pray that someday, when you open your eyes and see yourself staring back, that you're proud. I know you can't do it today."

He shakes his head.

"I wish you nothing but well, Billy. I know what you did for me. I'm truly grateful to you for it. I probably should tell you that we can be friends because you saved my life repeatedly, but I can't. I wouldn't mean it."

"I understand." He stands and throws the coffee in the nearby trash can. "If you need me, Jane, I'll always be a phone call away."

"Thank you, Billy." I watch his sad eyes say goodbye to me.

"There she is. Delilah! Jane!" I hear Shana's mom screaming for me as I watch Billy fade away into the background of the hospital.

# Forty-Two

I hadn't realized that Shana's parents lived two hours away. It makes sense that Stewart would want to have a wife that didn't have an immediate connection with her family. He didn't want someone to notice the changes and alert the victim before they realize themselves.

I didn't imagine our first meeting to be this way. When I thought about the future and getting Shana and Delilah closer to her parents, I didn't think it would involve more than a car ride there. Now, I'm going to be the one to hand over Delilah physically.

And I don't want to do it.

I don't know if it's because of the investment I have spent making sure that Stewart couldn't sink his teeth into her, or maybe it's because I feel responsible for the bullet in her mother's head, but Delilah is an extension of me, she is a piece of Shana, and I don't want to let go. Not yet. I kiss the top of Delilah's head as a new tear forms beneath my eyelid and slips down my cheek.

"I have to let you go, sweet girl. Your grandparents are here." I know if I don't remove this child from my body, I'll run out the door with her and never be seen again.

Shana's mother runs straight toward me. She looks like an older image of her daughter, right down to the correct shade of dirty blond her that Shana had the day that we met.

The vision of her blurs with my tears when I remind myself that it's not Shana walking toward me. I tuck my lips in and nod her way. *Yes, this is your grandchild. Yes, she is safe.*

I've done what I promised Shana I would do, yet it's hard to hand Delilah over. Are Shana's parents good people? Will they take care of her? Anyone could do a better job than Stewart, but are they the right match? I know that I'm not.

"Hi, I'm Jane," I whisper as they close in around me. I indicate that although this moment is essential, we should let Delilah sleep through it. If I see her eyes look into my face, I won't make it out of this door. I stir my arm a little on purpose to feel the sharp sting surging through my body. If I hand her over, I can go back to sleep and this nightmare can be over.

"I'm Betty. This is Harold. We're..." Her voice cracks and I give her a moment to regain composure. She needs to say it. I believe that that's the first step to healing — acknowledging the truth, no matter how bitter the pill is to swallow. "We were Shana's parents."

"I know. You look just like her." Her mother's sob breaks. I have so much I want to blurt out, so many words dancing around my mouth playing devil's advocate with my tongue. How could you not notice the bruises on Shana? Why didn't you teach her not to mess with older men? Why didn't anyone teach me? Why did money hold so much power over my good sense and hers?

"She looks comfortable on you, darling. Best not to wake her." She offers me a sad smile. I'm not sure she knows my role in any of this.

"Can we talk?" I look her dead in the eye. "Let's go for a walk in the hallway." I motion to Harold to sit down in the chair and take Delilah. The movement irritates my arm, and I grimace in pain.

"Oh, my dear, you're hurt. Are you sure you're up to a walk? What happened?"

"I..." I reluctantly hand Delilah over to Shana's dad, but he holds her like a pro, so I know he's hands-on. I kiss her sweet little head before finally letting go. The bitter cold hitting my chest where there was once her warm body is a harsh reminder that I'm nothing to her. I'll be a lady who held her until Grandma and Grandpa arrived to take her home. That's all my role will be. I won't visit her while she's growing up. Hang out with her mother in the kitchen and catch up when I visit.

I push off the bed with my left arm, letting my body settle before touching my feet to the floor. I yank my IV machine's cord from the outlet in the wall, pulling the contraption near me.

I'll be nothing but a simple shadow in the past, but that's what I want to be. I could never sit without shame on my face and tell her about the way I failed to save her mother or worse — lie to her.

"I'm fine." I finally mutter to Betty as she begins to mother me and look at my arm as if she can do anything for it. "Let's take a walk, okay?"

She stops trying to touch my arm and turns toward the door. She lets me take the lead, and we step out of the hospital room. She takes a quiet step close by me, giving me lead a hair farther than her foot dares to hit. I'm in charge here. I'm the one who has the answers to the questions that she doesn't want to ask this early in the morning at a hospital housing her daughter in the basement.

"Betty, I don't know if you know who I am," I puff out, not sure where to start.

"You're Jane. You're the one who was going to get Shana out." I stop dead on the sidewalk and whip my head toward her.

"She mailed me a letter, dear. I just got it today. She told me everything. I was going to come get her in the morning." I've never been held so tightly as when Betty catches me in her arms on my way down to the floor. I didn't get Shana out.

"I'm so sorry," I whimper into her chest. I let her down. I let Shana down. "I shouldn't have left her in the room. She didn't handle it well. She wasn't built for it. I let her down."

"No. No. No." She pulls me off her and makes me face her eye-to-eye. "You helped your ex-husband's mistress. Listen to me." She shakes my protesting eyelids open and upon her face. "I know what my daughter did. I can't say I'm proud of it, but I can say that I see in you all the wonderful qualities she told me about. Her death is not on you. She pulled the trigger. You did all that you could for her."

"But—"

"No. All that you did was beyond what most women would do for a mistress. You recognized her danger and put yourself in the fire because of it, despite the wrongdoings she committed against you. I will be forever grateful to you, and so will Delilah."

"I didn't save her," I whisper.

"She was free, honey." Her tears mingle with mine as she pulls me to her chest to hug me. "She was free. It was no longer up to you."

# Forty-Three

"**R**amona, you old bat, why did you do it?" I yell out into the air as I stand at her grave. I paid good money to have her tombstone looking like it belongs to a movie star, and there's a giant crack running down the middle.

"I know it was you," I hiss. "Just take my gesture and leave it alone." I throw the flowers I brought down on her grave, then I immediately regret it and swoop down to pick them up. I place them softer this time.

I touch the crack in the tombstone, running my finger down the length of it and whistling.

"When you do something, you sure don't half-ass it. Even dead," I sigh. "Too bad for you, I bought the insurance policy on this bad boy. They have to replace it, fix it, keep it looking good." I laugh. I can almost imagine her scowling face now, perched on her small frame puffing a cigarette.

I pat the top of the tombstone. "I'll see you tomorrow, Ramona. Like always."

It's been three months since I buried her, three months since I buried three people. I look up toward the top of the hill. Despite my best efforts, Stewart's will was as reliable as the prenup. He got a fucking mausoleum; not only that, he had them build it on the top of the hill years ago so that he could look down on everyone, even in death.

I shake my head. I won't ever be climbing that hill to leave flowers for him, but a petty part of me wants to climb it farther, stick out my tongue and tell him that I'm now higher than he is. His funeral was barren after people found out that being his friend never meant to him what it meant to them. They got nothing. He left all his money to a single person.

Delilah.

For that, I couldn't fault him. That's the way it was supposed to be, and even an asshole as massive as Stewart knew it. Shana's parents tried to offer me some money when the precise amount came after his expenses were paid off. I didn't want a dime. I smile at Ramona's cracked tombstone. I don't jump at the thought of grabbing easy money now. It doesn't matter much to me.

Well, I can't say I'm a complete dumbass. I did jump for joy, hearing that he never changed his life insurance policy after we divorced. I was still the beneficiary.

Ramona left me the motel. The life insurance money Stewart left helped me move into a house and get out of my apartment. I used the rest to revamp the motel and keep it running at the standards of today. No more disgusting comforters on the bed, I burned them all in a ceremonious heap on the backlot. It cost me a fine that somehow disappeared. When I turned the money in to the police station, I was told the fine was taken care of already.

I want to ask him about it at the gym while he runs silently beside me almost every night, but I won't go back on my word. Billy and I are done for good.

I hired people. Unlike Ramona, I didn't want to stay at the motel and oversee everything day in and day out. I volunteer at the shelter most days and make sure the donation box has something in it every single day. And I come to see Ramona every single morning.

There is someone else that I need to see today, though — a visit I have been putting off. I feel the wind at my back, shoving me some.

"I'm going, Ramona. I'm going." I shake my head and sigh. I walk down the row five graves and go up six rows until I come face to face with the one friend I didn't expect to have.

Shana's parents had left flowers before they went home, faux ones, so they wouldn't lose their color. They wanted to bury her closer to them, but ultimately decided she'd be better looked after here with me. I told them when I got up the courage that I would come and put fresh flowers there instead. I dip low and clear a few stray weeds that cloud the front of the stone. I remove the blue and pink faux bouquet from the vase and replace them with the six pink carnations I brought with me.

"Hey," I whisper. It feels strange for the words to leave my lips, which is stupid considering the conversations I have with Ramona every day in this same cemetery.

"Fuck, Shana. I knew I wouldn't know what to say when I got here today. I wrote this." I pull out the folded letter from my pocket. "Now, I don't know if I should leave it or read it out loud." The squat of my thighs suddenly burns, and I sit down next to the grave.

"I guess you want me to read it." I smile.

*Dear Shana,*

*We weren't supposed to be friends. I don't think a soul in the world understands why I cried so hard at your funeral, except maybe your mom. You told her about your plan to escape, and that you would see her soon. I'm sorry that it never happened.*

*I never got to tell you how proud I am that you showed such bravery on your own. I thought you needed me to do it for you. I guess I took over and pushed you too hard. I blame myself for what happened, for the gun, for everything. I will never let a soul think that you had any part in the death of Stewart. It was all me.*

*Delilah is safe now. You saved her from a life that she no doubt would have had to endure alongside you. You were a good mother to her, Shana. Know that. She'll know that as she grows older. I won't ever utter a word against the thought, neither will your own mother.*

*You helped me see my purpose in life. I even started a foundation in your name, donating to women and children of abusive households. I hope to help others like us. I hope to make a difference in at least one person's life as you have in mine.*

*I'll spend years on this earth missing you and wondering if it could have all gone differently, but I'll never regret reaching out to you and becoming your friend. You may have been Stewart's mistress when we first met, but you were my friend at the end.*

*Love,*
*Jane*

# Epilogue

*Six Months Later*

S      I loathe Thursdays.

Shana and Stewart used to meet up on Thursday mornings, and he'd make her feel special. Then, Shana died on a Thursday. I got kicked to the curb on a Thursday. The awful raw energy I wake up with on Thursdays is dumbfounding.

Running is the only thing that helps. I haven't taken to running outside again. Even if the most significant threat of my life is gone, Billy's words still echo in my mind. *It's not safe, Jane. Go to the gym. You can get a membership under my name.*

I think of Billy's face, and I pound up the stairs of the gym, up to the walkway where the treadmills sit. I will run until the pain makes me too tired to rage inside. It doesn't matter that Stewart is gone, or that I'm now free and safe from his clutch. The demons still surface, begging to be smashed back down inside.

I refused to go to therapy. It was too dangerous to sit on a couch and confess my sins to someone because I was bound to let it all fall out with the dangled treat of healing right in front of my face. Then where would that put me? Where would that put any of us holding on to secrets? It would smear Shana's name and destroy the progress Billy was making. No, this was a sin I planned to take to the grave.

I hate myself for checking up on Billy, but sometimes my car goes that way home, and I can't leave until I catch a glimpse of his face in the window. The hardness has faded some, and there's genuine joy starting to form around his eyes, but they're still sad.

Shana's family didn't have any connections in Pittsburgh anymore, so they asked if I could be in charge of selling the place. I said yes. I was an idiot, but it looks like we finally have a buyer, and things will go through. That money is going straight into the already inflated college fund for Delilah, but at least she'll have her options open when she gets there.

She deserves a more luxurious life than money can buy, and that's what she'll get with Shana's parents, I'm sure of it. The letters come weekly, updating me on Delilah's latest milestones and mischievous activities. She has love wrapped around her, and it is better than money. Money strangles the life out of us when we hand that part over to it.

I hit the walkway, determined to run the fuck out of these feelings, but there's a new woman running on my favorite treadmill. I hate people. She's a rich woman, too. I can tell by the clothes she wears on the treadmill that probably haven't seen the light of day until just now. I kick my worn sneaker into the mat. Between running the motel and selling Stewart's house, I don't have time to buy new clothes.

I shuffle over to the treadmill next to the lady and give her a head bob hello, but she doesn't see me. Rude. I look closer, and she's glaring down over the railing. What's she looking at? I follow her gaze and land on our gym trollop, Anna. I gag, but she still doesn't give me the time of day.

I hate that blond, and I don't usually feel that way about women. There's something evil about her, something I saw in Stewart when I first met him and couldn't place my finger on. Now, I know better about what that quality is, and that bitch is straight from the loins of Satan.

I see her eyes, even from the side — she's pissed. Someone like Anna must have done her wrong, and now she is going to run it out. Good for her, that kind of fucked-up therapy is what I like. I shake my head and stretch my arms out. She's hitting the treadmill hard, and those new sneakers are going to be worn out soon if she keeps at that pace.

My right arm protests the early morning, so I spend an extra minute stretching it out and giving it a slight massage. The wound is reminding me again why I hate Thursdays. I growl. Still no notice from my neighbor. Hmm.

"Oh, that's our town trollop in the gym. She'll fuck anything that walks, and spends more time taking selfies on the workbench than actually pressing something," I bellow at her.

It works. She loses her step on the treadmill and slams the emergency stop button on the machine to keep from falling face-first on the belt. When her eyes hit me, I take note that they don't look like Bambi.

"Excuse me?" she pants out.

"That blond." I tilt my head toward Anna. "I saw the disgust on your face, shared your sentiments, saw you were new, and figured I'd welcome you to the gym." I smile, but nothing but confusion passes her lips as an exchange. "She won't try to be your friend; she's harmless to the vaginas in here. Unless your husband is here." I laugh a little when the shock on her face tells me that I've hit the nail on the head. Her husband is a cheater. I can spot them all a mile away now. "I'm sorry; I was just kidding."

"I just..." She debates on what to tell me. I watch the wheels in her mind turn over, and at the same time, I can hear mine cranking away. I shouldn't put myself in this situation; the pain of Shana still raw in my heart. I can hear Ramona in the back of my head telling me that this girl needs help, but I want to step back. She can handle it. She doesn't have those eyes. Strength won't kill her. She'll probably be able to find it without my help.

"I'm Medeia." She holds her hand out, and I'm shaking it before I can register that my body betrayed me. I'm not getting involved.

"Jane. I'm here only on Thursday mornings. Other than that, unless you're a night owl, you won't see me." I punch the buttons on my machine. It annoys me that it isn't like the machine Medeia is on. Figuring it out takes away the time I can be making my body ache and exhaust the energy inside. How fucking annoying.

"No, I like the mornings. More productive this way." Her gaze falls back on Anna, and I tell myself that this bitch may be crazy, but dammit if I don't like being near the crazy. Suddenly, the anxious feeling tingling throughout my body stills. *All right, Ramona.*

"I usually do forty minutes. You're welcome to join me at the local coffee shop after this if you want." I don't have to be at the motel today. I hired a girl who needed the job to get away from her overbearing boyfriend. Michelle can handle the morning shift. I pop my earbuds in to listen to my favorite rock music.

"Coffee sounds delicious." She smiles, and it looks awkward on her face, but I suddenly find my heart lurching in her direction. I've made a friend, and I think it's going to get me into trouble again.

# Sneak Peek at Dear Anna

I f you've enjoyed Jane's story, turn the page to read the first chapter of Medeia's tale in *Dear Anna,* available now.

# Medeia's Journal

D<sup>ear</sup> Anna,
       I was the perfect wife.
    You were his whore.
    You plotted against me with the devil, himself.
    Will God let you repent for your sin?
    I WON'T.

# One

"Are you okay, miss?"

"Huh?" I turn my attention to the old man standing three feet from me. The smell of rain mixing with asphalt rises and clogs my lungs. My shirt clings to my body from the assault of raindrops. I push my wet hair back with the hand that's not holding a shopping bag.

"Are you okay, miss?" the stranger repeats. "We saw that you were standing here and we, my wife and I —" he points back toward his van where a worried woman sits staring out the window at me— "wanted to check on you." His smile is a gentle reminder of a time back when strangers didn't just pass by without a kind word.

"Yes. Sorry, I thought I saw someone I know." Embarrassment constricts my chest.

He follows the direction of my eyes. "That couple in there?" He enquires, as he is involved now in solving my dilemma.

I wish he'd leave. "No, they've already walked away." I turn my head again to find my vehicle. "Thank you, though."

"Sure thing, honey. Take it easy." He bids me farewell as he walks back to join his wife in their minivan. The rain exposes his body's hunchback form.

"You, too." I rush to my Mercedes, senses now returning. I feel the coldness of the weather stain my skin, but it's not what penetrates my bones and makes my blood retreat into frozen icicles.

I stare back at the restaurant, pushing my wiper blades to their limit to clear the scene. There before me is my worst fear. Even with my vision blurred by the weather, I still see my husband of ten years dining with a woman who looks like more than just a business associate as he smooths a stray hair away from her face.

My eyes betray me as I watch him kiss the lady on the lips after they place their order with the waitress. There's familiarity in the curve of her face and the way she holds herself—the angle of her chin and the dip at the end of it. I've seen her before. She flicks her hair away, revealing her profile.

Anna.

I'm great with names. They stick with me instantaneously upon meeting a person. Anna is the secretary whose voice floods my ears whenever I call John's office. She's the perky blonde behind the desk whenever I drop something off for him when he is in a business meeting. Now she is the one leaning across the table in rapt attention as John, *my* husband, regales her with a story.

*You got to keep a man interested, Medeia, or he'll stray.*

My mother's mantra comes flooding back in my memory, and I wish I could call her up and tell her all about this. She would know how to fix the damage, but she's dead — gone not even a year now. I'm left to deal with the ease of John's hand in Anna's telling me this isn't the first time they've held onto each other, alone.

Their fingers aren't hesitant to be conjoined. Instead, they flock to each other, taking comfort in the familiarity they find hiding in the nooks of each finger. My eyes stay glued to them as they begin to enjoy their meals, close to the window. It's as if God is on my side and wants them to be observed by me. I take note of how they don't even care, how John, in particular, doesn't care. My husband is not concerned with the fact that he is on display in a restaurant window with a woman who is not his wife. Let the people stare. I search for any trace of a guilty conscience, maybe just a glimpse of him looking over his shoulder to survey the restaurant inhabitants, but I look on in vain. What would he say if I told him someone saw him? Would he lie or fess up? If I were anyone else looking in, I would easily assume they were another couple—not a married man and his whore.

I came to the shopping center this afternoon to buy some things for his birthday. Talk about irony. John consumes this day. I had no idea when a familiar sports jacket caught my peripheral vision, that I would find this scene.

They don't see me because they're too busy laughing and staring at each other like fresh new lovers with no problems. They took no notice of the paralyzed figure in the middle of the parking lot, staring after them. He never looked for my car to make sure the coast was clear. That's even more terrifying than the act itself — the blatant disregard.

Inside I am frozen, but at the surface, my skin begins to warm from the heat of my emotions. My throat is suffocating me as it tightens with the force of infidelity being lodged there and refusing to move. My jaw rigidly locks in a solid clench of anger. The adrenaline shifts the icicles in my veins to move. He texted me this morning that he couldn't meet me for lunch because he had to work through it to catch up.

He chose her over me. After what I did for him, this is my payment? He doesn't even try to hide his whore from the world, but he is sure not to flaunt his wife in it.

And what am I to make of his mistress? No doubt that she is young. My thirty-six-year-old body can still compete, though. I'm an attractive woman, just as she is. Except we are opposites, clear as day. I don't have to look hard to find what my husband sees in her over me. Her shiny blonde hair falls in curls around her porcelain face. My flat brown straight hair envelopes my olive skin tone. You can tell she is a bubbly person from the way she is bouncing as she talks to him. I have never been one to bounce. Bubbly is for the secretaries, which is what Anna is. John's secretary.

She giggles and touches his arm. What could be so funny? My husband is not a comedic guy. He doesn't have a sense of humor. He can stretch out a joke for ten minutes, never reaching the punchline. He's the type of guy who will explain why something is considered funny and ruin the essence of the joke itself. So, what is making Anna laugh? A joke about his wife who doesn't suspect a thing, perhaps?

Medeia Moore — his dedicated wife that does it all for him. I am everything John needs or wants; I make sure of it. I have done everything to keep John's attention through the years. Am I the reason that they are giving themselves over to fits of laughter?

I bow my head, peering at my outfit. The rain has soaked me to the bone, but that's not what makes me look frumpy. Lately, I've been choosing comfort over style when I go out during the day, yoga pants instead of hip-hugging jeans that express the curves beneath. The things that I hide from John when he isn't there. I wouldn't dare wear this when he is around. I gaze back at Anna, and she's shimmering in a tight bodice dress that I would consider too risqué for the office, but she wears it with confidence oozing from the scarlet color.

She's the woman that unfortunately ends up making the rest of us intimidated and small-feeling. We could arrive as done-up as possible, and she would still knock us down in a pair of sweatpants and a t-shirt. Her poise allows her to be a knockout in a potato sack bag.

On our wedding day, I encompassed that very feeling. I was the spitting image of a princess, with my hair curled and makeup better than a supermodel. Ten pounds lighter and much more svelte, and on that day, John stood before God, family, and friends and swore to forsake all others. And since that day, I have worked to remain the perfect image of a rich man's wife: perfect manicure, expensive clothing, heels, hair maintained. It's a strict grooming regimen to give me the bonus appearance of money. It's tiresome, and I do let myself go at times when John isn't home, but I have tried to take his comments into action. I am the perfect woman for John, straight from his design. So, why am I watching him smile at a blonde with spaghetti sauce on her chin? This whorish pig threatens the stability I have dedicated my life to maintain. I feel my shelter slipping through my fingers.

I felt like a million dollars on the day that I married him, and today, I feel like a cheap penny dropped on the ground and not worthy enough to be picked back up. That's not fair. I am worth something as well. My pity party gives way to the righteous anger coursing through my body.

My hand lingers on the door handle, ready to confront him, to tell him what an enormous asshole he is. For all that I have done for him in ten years, that he would dare end it like this. For what I sacrificed to save him. I'll throw the spaghetti plate in Anna's face, smear what I imagine is perfect makeup, like her pristine hair. That's what I'll do. I yank the handle toward me and jump back into the rain. I feel the adrenaline pumping through me, causing my teeth to chatter.

I stomp my way to the first line of cars, looking left and right to cross. This will be my moment. I can't believe after what I have sacrificed for John; it hasn't afforded me fidelity. I've turned my whole life over to John's rules. Why? Then it smacks me in the face like a puddle splashing up from a car. John has all of the money. I came into the marriage with nothing, and that's why I never strayed from the straight line that I needed to walk to be the perfect wife. If I go in there now and let myself be known, I'll put myself in a worse position.

I'll be penniless. John has made it legal, thanks to the prenup, that I will never have any of his money to my name if I leave him. He knows it's my weakness, coming from such a poor family. It's what we had constructed our lives to be, a safety net so that I don't end up like my family, and so that we don't put ourselves in a position similar to the one ten years ago. Oh, god. I turn and run back to the car, leaning into the steering wheel to hide my tears from shoppers running back to the shelter of their vehicles. I can't escape my marriage and be better off —he's designed it that way. Terror shocks my system. I need to get out of here.

I pull the car out of the parking lot, no longer wanting to risk being seen by my husband. If he notices me here now, it will be my demise instead of my triumph. I wipe the tears off my face. He can't get away with this. I will find a way out. In the quiet of my car, I promise myself that. It's not time to confront him, not until I've come up with a plan.

I'll be damned if I go back to the shack of my childhood without a fight.

Keep reading here[1].

---

1. http://bit.ly/DearAnnaKB

# Author's Note

Thank you beyond words for reading *Love, Jane*. She became a reader favorite in *Dear Anna* and I knew that I needed to tell her story to answer the question of why Jane was a ride or die kind of girl. I hope you see her in the light that I do now and understand her character better.

This story deals with domestic abuse, a hard topic for a lot of women to express. If you or a loved one are struggling with domestic violence please reach out to the National Domestic Violence Hotline at 1-800-799-7233.

Thank you for purchasing this book and fighting alongside our girl, Jane. I would love to hear your thoughts, so email with them at authorkatieblanchard@yahoo.com. Reviews help authors get exposure, so please leave one when you're done as well.

Thank you again for your support

Katie Blanchard

# About the Author

The book world knows her as the author of *Pressing Flowers* and *Dear Anna,* but you can call her Katie, the child wrangler with little spare time for the yarn stash piled up in her office. She's a multitasker, but she's too busy juggling to tell you if she's any good at it. She loves stories and the places that they can take you, the lessons you can learn between the covers, and the characters you can fall in love with and idolize. That's why you'll find her awoke before the rest of the family, and long after they've gone to sleep, jotting down words and letting characters come to life through her fingertips.

Follow on these sites to find out more about Katie and upcoming releases:

Facebook[1]

Twitter[2]

Instagram[3]

Website[4]

Newsletter[5]

---

1. http://bit.ly/KBlanchardFBPage

2. http://bit.ly/KBlanchardTwitter

3. http://bit.ly/KBlanchardIG

4. https://www.authorkatieblanchard.com

5. http://bit.ly/KBlanchardNewsletter

# Thank Yous

I can't believe I'm sitting at the computer, typing the thank you part to a third book. I feel so blessed to have achieved this goal, but more so to have the following people in my life.

Thank you to my mother, for who this book is dedicated to. You have given me strength in life to believe that nothing is unattainable. Ever dumb idea that I've come to you with, you've shown enthusiasm and support without falter. You told Christa and me when we were younger that *girls stick together,* and with that, you've instilled a motivation to always look out for one another.

To my father, for being the guy in the all-girl household. You encouraged strength, taught us how to do things stereotypically designed for a man, and you believed that we could do anything. It's because of this mindset that Christa and I set out to conquer challenges without fear that we'll fail. There is no failing.

To Brian, my husband and best friend in life, if it weren't for you, there would be no books. You stand by me, patiently and without fail, being my sounding board for plot problems, the keeper of the children when I need to write, and my constant support when I start freaking out. I love you, and I'd always choose you again and again.

To my kids, for never letting me get a moment's peace. Thank you for the excellent multi-tasker you have made me.

Now, stop. Haha. I love you two beyond words, there is no description that I could put together that would convey how much my heart bursts for you two.

To Christa, my sister, you are my favorite reader. (Don't tell the others.) You reread my stories multiple times without complaint. You even do it without asking. I can't fathom how much faith you put into my crazy mind and the things that it creates. You inspire me. You're my best friend and soulmate.

To Ed, the maestro, for being such a huge fan, I thank you. You have touched me with your kind words and dedication to spreading the news about my writing. Thank you. For putting up with Brian, you deserve a spot in the book right here in the thank yous.

To Carrie, for beta reading that first draft and helping me find the errors. You have been a lifesaver. Thank you for your selfless ways and allowing me to be in your life. I'm honored to call you my friend.

To Traci, for editing and always helping me see a better way to tell my story. I'm beyond thankful that I met you and have you in my life to help me on this journey. Thank you, sincerely, for everything you do.

To Teddi, for another killer cover design, thank you. You always kill it with the designs, making the cover choosing one of my favorite parts of the whole process. Thank you for putting up with me.

To Bex, for proofreading these words. I'm sorry for all the grammatical errors I'm sure I've put you through. Thank you for your kindness.

To Kiki and Colleen from The Next Step PR, you two are amazing. Thank you for your assistance and guidance navigating the marketing side of the book world. Not only are you two amazing at what you do, you have to be the kindest souls I've met. Thank you for your hard work and love. I can't sing your praises enough.

To my ARC readers and the wonderful bloggers sharing this tale, you are so important, and I'm grateful that you gave *Love, Jane* and *Dear Anna* the time of day. That means the world to me. The hard work and dedication that you put in, I see you.

To all my friends for their support.

To the Bibliophiles for their love on social media.

To the person sitting there reading this still... THANK YOU!

CPSIA information can be obtained
at www.ICGtesting.com
Printed in the USA
LVHW011533121119
637105LV00004B/358/P

9 781733 664097